DRAGONS LOST

Suffolk Libraries

AMAZ			7/16
FAN			

DRAGONS LOST

REQUIEM FOR DRAGONS, BOOK I

Daniel Arenson

Copyright © 2015 by Daniel Arenson

All rights reserved.

This novel is a work of fiction. Names, characters, places and incidents are either the product of the author's imagination, or, if real, used fictitiously.

No part of this book may be reproduced or transmitted in any form or by an electronic or mechanical means, including photocopying, recording or by any information storage and retrieval system, without the express written permission of the author.

CADE

Cade was cradling his sister in his arms when the firedrakes arrived, screeching and blowing fire across the sky, to burn out the baby's magic.

He stood within the bakery where he lived and worked with his adoptive parents—and now with the newborn in his arms. Jars of yeast rattled on the shelves. Sacks of flour thumped down, and one opened to spill its white innards across the stone floor. The window shutters clattered, and between them Cade glimpsed the beasts: streaks of scales, streams of fire, claws that shone in the sunlight. Their cries rolled across the village, louder than thunder, so loud Cade would have covered his ears were he not holding his sister.

In his arms, little Eliana wailed, only a few days old. Her parents—the kindly couple who had adopted Cade eighteen years ago, when he himself had been but a newborn—paled and tugged nervously at their aprons.

"They know," whispered Tisha, her lips stiff. She held a rolling pin in her hand as a weapon. "Somehow they always know when they're born."

Her husband, a paunchy and balding man named Derin, turned as pale as the spilled flour. Despite his nervousness, he patted his wife's arm and mumbled, "Eliana will be fine. She'll cry a bit, but she'll live. We lived through it as babes. And we're fine."

A thin woman with graying hair, Tisha nodded and lowered her head. "I know. It's just that . . . after so long, to see our miracle hurt . . ."

The firedrakes' screeches rose louder outside. When Cade glanced out the window, he saw a dozen or more land in the village square. Between the shutters, Cade could only glimpse bits of them—scales, claws, horns, cruel fangs slick with saliva. Whenever a babe was born in the village, somehow they knew. Somehow they always arrived.

For the purification, Cade thought and shuddered.

He had seen purifications before; the screams still haunted his nightmares. With tears, with poison, with branding, the magic was driven out of babes, leaving scars and haunting pain, leaving the child pure. All newborns across the Commonwealth, this empire that sprawled across the lands north of the sea, underwent purification for the glory of the Spirit.

All but me, Cade thought. He had never gone through the ceremony. When he'd been a babe, his parents—he still didn't know who they were—had smuggled him away, had placed him here in the bakery. Since then Cade had lived with hidden magic, a secret that would have every firedrake in the Commonwealth hunt him if they knew.

"Bring out the child!" rose a shout outside. "Bring out the newborn for purification."

Eliana cried harder in Cade's arms.

Tisha, her mother, lowered her head. Tears streamed down her lined cheeks. For over twenty years, Tisha and her husband— these kindly bakers who had taken Cade in—had tried to conceive. For eighteen of those years, Cade had been like a son to them, an adopted boy to a woman with a barren womb. Finally this year, a miracle had happened. Finally this year, Tisha had given birth to a precious babe, a great gift to their home.

Now this babe would scream in agony.

"It's time," Cade said softly, rocking the crying Eliana. "Let's get this over with. It'll only last a few moments."

A few moments of torment, he thought but would not vocalize his fear. *A few moments of poison and fire and screams to fill our nightmares.*

"Bring out the babe!" the cry rose again outside. It was a woman's voice, high and fair yet colder and crueler than steel. The voice of a paladin, a holy knight of the Cured Temple. "Bring out the babe, or my firedrakes will burn this backwater to the ground!"

Cade gave the baby in his arms one last look. Eliana was not his true sister—he didn't know if he had real siblings—but she even looked like him. The baby had the same shock of messy, light brown hair, the same hazel eyes. Rage flared in Cade, overpowering his fear. Suddenly he wanted to put the baby down, charge outside, and summon his magic—the forbidden magic he carried, which all others had lost—and burn the paladins, burn the firedrakes, burn down the entire damned Cured Temple that ruled the Commonwealth.

And why shouldn't I? he thought. *I was never cured, never purified. I'm strong. I'm powerful. I'm—*

Derin placed a hand on Cade's shoulder. The rotund baker stood shorter than Cade, but he stared up at his adopted son with solemn gravity. "Come on, boy. Let's get it over and done with." He turned back toward his wife. "Tisha, stay here. Wait for us. We'll be back with Eliana soon."

The graying woman nodded and wiped her tears away. She stepped forward, gave her daughter a kiss, then turned toward the wall and clenched her fists.

"Now come on, Cade," Derin said. "Let's go."

Cade clenched his jaw, the anger still blazing through him, but nodded. Holding the baby with one arm, he opened the bakery's door. Derin walked behind him. The two stepped outside into the village square . . . into a theater of flame and steel.

Fifty houses formed the village of Favilla, if one could call them "houses"; they were barely more than huts built from pale clay, their roofs domed, their windows round. Men said that many years ago houses would be built three stories tall, wide and roomy, cool in the summers and warm in the winters. But the Cured Temple preached austerity, preached that humble living and suffering brought one closer to the Spirit. And so Favilla remained a model of humility—its huts small, its gardens barren of flowers, its public square devoid of grass. A place of white walls and brown soil. A place of holiness.

Normally the village square was empty. Today a dozen firedrakes stood here, towering over the homes, each larger than the mightiest oaks from the northern forests. They were dragons but not noble, intelligent dragons like the ones men and woman could become before the Cured Temple. Here were wild beasts, no more intelligent than animals, their human forms and human minds torn from them, leaving them rabid and always hungry. Smoke rose from their nostrils. Saliva dripped from their jaws, and fire sparked between their fangs. Their tails whipped from side to side, their scales clattered, and their wings creaked. Their grumbles rolled across the village like thunder.

Cade stared at them, jaw tight. *The Templers rip out our dragon magic, yet they bring dragons here to enslave us. The Templers speak of a reptilian curse infecting their flock, yet they bring great reptiles to slay us if we resist purification.*

His arms trembled with rage as he held his sister.

But I am not purified.

He could summon the old magic, the magic the Temple sought to eradicate. He could grow wings and scales, breathe fire, rise into the sky as a dragon—not a mindless firedrake, a beast with no human form, but a noble dragon, wise and strong. He could fly away with Eliana in his claws, saving her magic—the way his magic had been saved. He could hide her somewhere—the way his parents had hidden him. He could raise her, make sure she learned to control her magic, make sure she grew up with the power—the power to become a dragon, strong and free, not a weak, magicless human for the Temple to oppress.

The dozen firedrakes stepped closer. Smoke blasted out from their jaws, hitting Cade, searing like an open oven full of roaring flames. The beasts' eyes blazed like cauldrons of molten steel. Globs of their saliva thumped to the ground, sizzling, eating holes into the soil.

They were just waiting for him to escape, Cade knew. If he ran, even if he shifted into a dragon and flew, they would chase him. They would catch him. They would slay him. And they would slay Eliana too, rip this precious babe—a miracle child—into shreds of meat to consume.

I cannot flee, Cade thought, trembling. *I cannot risk them taking Eliana's life . . . even if they will now take her magic.*

Cradling Eliana in his arms, Cade looked up toward the riders on the firedrakes. A paladin sat astride each one of the beasts. Holy warriors of the Spirit, the paladins were sworn to fight for the Cured Temple and enforce its purity. They wore armor of white steel plates, and they carried pale banners emblazoned with the Temple's sigil: a tillvine blossom. The same flower, resembling a calla lily, was engraved onto their breastplates and painted onto their shields. The same flower, fair and pale, would now burn Eliana's skin and rip out her dragon soul.

One of the firedrakes stood out from the others. Most of the beasts had dull, monochromatic scales, but this firedrake sported scales in all the colors of fire: red scales, orange scales, and yellow scales in a hundred shades, all gleaming together as if the beast were woven of flame. Its rider, clad in white steel, dismounted the fiery beast and walked toward Cade.

This paladin was female, which was rare. Though the Temple's supreme leader was always female, her warriors were normally male, hulking men, noble-born and brawny. The woman walking toward Cade, however, was slender and no taller than him. Her armor mimicked the curves of her body, the steel plates white as snow, and a silver tillvine blossom gleamed upon her breastplate. She carried sword and shield, but she wore no helmet. Her face was as pale, cold, and hard as her armor. Her eyes were blue, piercing, cruel, lacking all emotion. Like all paladins and priests, the woman had shaved the left side of her head. The remaining hair was swept to the right side, bleached pure white, flowing down to her shoulder like a snowdrift.

The paladin reached Cade and paused. She stared down at the babe in his arms, then back up at Cade. Her eyes . . . by the stars, her eyes cut through him as sure as spears. He felt the chill emanating from that icy blue gaze.

"Do you know who I am?" she said softly. "I am Lady Mercy Deus. You will kneel before me." She stared around her at the other villagers who stood in the square—meek, humble farmers and tradesmen—and raised her voice to a shout. "You will all kneel!"

Cade gasped. Mercy Deus? His insides seemed to crack and shatter. His heart sank. This was no ordinary paladin. Here before him stood the daughter of the High Priestess. The heiress to the Commonwealth. Aside from High Priestess Beatrix herself, Mercy was the most powerful woman in the world.

And she's here in our village.

Cade glanced at his adoptive father. Derin stared back at him, his eyes hard, his mouth thinned into a line. The balding baker nodded, then turned back toward the paladin and knelt. Across the square, the villagers knelt too and bowed their heads.

While the paladins wore filigreed steel and embroidered, richly woven capes, the villagers wore rough burlap tunics—the only garments allowed to them, humble raiment symbolizing their purity.

Cade stared at Lady Mercy for a second longer. She stared back, and her eyes narrowed. Her lips—small and pink—twisted into the slightest of smiles.

Do you dare defy me? she seemed to ask; he could practically hear her voice speaking in his mind. Her hand, gloved in white leather, strayed toward the golden hilt of her sword. *Do you challenge me to break you?*

Cade wanted to resist. Wanted to shift into a dragon right here and attack her, to burn her pretty face, to claw through her steel armor. She couldn't have been much older than twenty, only a couple of years older than him. Why should she bark orders, strut around like a monarch, while he knelt in the dust?

He glanced down at the babe held in his arms. Eliana gazed back at him, calm now, curious.

Cade exhaled slowly.

For you, Eliana. To keep you alive.

He knelt before Mercy, glaring up at her.

The paladin reached out her gloved hands and plucked the baby from Cade's arms. She might as well have plucked the soul from his chest.

As the firedrakes snarled and leaked smoke, and as the villagers knelt, Mercy raised the baby above her head. She walked around the square, displaying Eliana for all to see.

"A child was born in the Commonwealth!" Mercy cried, her voice pealing across the village. "For every hundred babes born in our land, ninety-nine still carry the old curse. The old disease." Disgust dripped from her voice. "Ninety-nine are still born able to change their forms, to become . . . dragons." Mercy spat into the dirt. "The curse has brought nothing but pain to our people. For thousands of years, our enemies hunted us. For thousands of years, we waged wars with dragonfire. For thousands of years, our land bled and burned. But the Cured Temple saved you! The Cured Temple liberated you from your disease! And the Cured Temple will purify this innocent child, freeing her from the curse of our ancestors. She will be cured!"

"Amen!" chanted the villagers.

"Amen!" cried the remaining paladins upon the firedrakes.

A curse, Cade thought, jaw clenched. *A disease*. He could not believe that. He refused to. Perhaps he was the only one left in the world with magic still inside him. Perhaps he was the only soul in the Commonwealth who could become a dragon. But he refused to believe himself cursed. Those secret nights he spent flying over the sea, free upon the wind, a golden dragon in the moonlight . . . those nights had never felt cursed. They had felt like magic. Like wonder. Like a great blessing from ancient times.

You will never know such freedom, Eliana, he thought, gazing at the babe held aloft in Mercy's hands. *You will never fly with me in secret nights, know the warmth of fire in your belly, the soothing chill of wind beneath your wings.* He lowered his head. *You will be purified . . . you will be broken.*

Again Cade had to curb the urge to leap forward, to grab his sister, to shift into a dragon and fly off. He could never escape, he knew. Not with a dozen firedrakes here, these wild dragons who had once been babes like Eliana, whose human forms had been ripped out instead of their dragon magic. The firedrakes would chase him if he fled. They would kill him and his sister.

Cade clenched his fists, trembling with rage. He wished there were others like him, others who had never been purified, who kept their magic secret. Others who could join him, fight with him against the Cured Temple—against the High Priestess, against these pale paladins, against the firedrakes, against this whole damn world.

But there are no others, Cade thought, eyes burning. *I am alone.*

And so he remained kneeling, the anger a rock in his belly.

Two priestesses dismounted a black firedrake—identical twins clad in white robes, the left sides of their heads shaven, the hair on the right side bleached white. They carried forth a wooden altar and placed it in the center of the square. Each priestess placed a bowl upon the altar—one black bowl, one white—each full of leaves. Then they knelt and bowed their heads.

Cade stared at the bowls, stomach souring.

A black bowl to test them, he thought, remembering the old prayers. *A white bowl to cure them.*

He would feel no less disgust to see two blades on this altar.

"By the grace of the Spirit," cried Mercy, "let the purification begin!"

The paladin stepped toward the altar and placed the baby between the bowls. Cade growled, forcing himself to stay still, as Mercy tied down the baby with straps. Eliana began to weep. Soon, Cade knew, she would scream.

Cade glanced to his side. Derin knelt there, and Cade noticed that the baker too clenched his fists and gritted his teeth.

For twenty years he tried to have a child, Cade thought. *And now . . . now to watch this child hurt . . .*

Cade looked back toward the altar. Mercy lifted the black bowl and held it above her head.

"Here I hold the leaves of ilbane," the paladin announced. "The herb is harmless to all pure people." To demonstrate, Mercy plucked a leaf from the bowl and pressed it against her lips. "It will not harm any pure body, a body clean of the disease." She smiled thinly. "But those with dragon magic, those able to shift into reptiles . . . this ilbane will burn them like the very fire they spew. We shall test the babe!"

Across the square, the other paladins—still seated upon the firedrakes—raised their fists. "Test the babe!" they chanted.

Mercy grabbed a fistful of leaves and held them above the bound baby. As Cade watched, he didn't know what he preferred to happen. If Eliana had the magic—as most people did—the leaves would burn her, a pain greater than fire, greater than shattering bones. If she was pure—as only one in a hundred babies were—she would be marked as a breeder, and once she was of age, she would be forced to become pregnant every year, to pump out child after child in hope of eradicating the magic from future generations. That fate seemed even worse than momentary pain.

    Mercy unfolded Eliana's swaddling clothes. Slowly, the paladin lowered her bundle of leaves . . . and pressed it against the baby's chest.

    Eliana's scream tore across the village.

    Cade's fists shook and his teeth gnashed, but a part of him was thankful. The ilbane burned her. Eliana was cursed with dragon magic. She would be spared a life as a breeder.

    Mercy pulled the ilbane leaves back; they left ugly welts across the baby. Eliana still screamed, the poison spreading across her, reddening her skin, stiffening her muscles.

    "The babe is diseased!" Mercy announced to the village. "She must be cured!"

    Cade glanced over to Derin. His stepfather stared back, eyes dark.

    As bad as testing a child was, curing her was worse. Ilbane, the leaves from the black bowl, burned like fire. But the leaves in the *white* bowl . . . they were like a rusty spoon thrust into a person's chest, cutting and carving out the very soul.

    Mercy reached into the white bowl and pulled out a bundle of new leaves. These leaves were thicker, deep green and aromatic. A single blossom bloomed among them, large as a fist—the same blossom engraved into Mercy's breastplate. A tillvine blossom, sigil of the Cured Temple.

"Tillvine!" Mercy said, presenting the blossom and leaves to the crowd. "The most blessed plant of our order. A plant to cure the disease. A plant to purify this innocent child from the evil lurking within her."

A plant to rip out her magic, Cade thought, tasting bile.

He wondered, as he often did, how he himself had been saved from the tillvine. The paladins knew of every child born in the Commonwealth—they always knew—yet somehow Cade had been spared. His parents had smuggled him away, had placed him here in this village. Derin and Tisha never knew how it had happened, how he had escaped purification.

Cade only knew that if he were discovered, the paladins would not merely rip out his magic. They would return him to the capital. They would hang him from the Temple before a crowd of thousands. And they would let the firedrakes roast him alive as the city cheered.

Mercy moved her eyes across the crowd, villager by villager. When finally her gaze reached Cade, she stared into his eyes, and a crooked smile found her lips—a smile as pleasant as a wolf grinning over a dying deer.

She kept her eyes locked on Cade as she crushed the tillvine blossom in her palm, squeezing drops into the babe's mouth.

At first not much happened. Eliana gurgled and tried to spit the liquid out. Mercy held the baby's mouth open, dripping in more of the tillvine juice. The baby swallowed a few drops and blinked. The villagers were silent. Many lowered their heads, jaws tight, eyes closed.

Mercy stared into Cade's eyes, and her smile widened.

"Watch," the paladin mouthed.

And it began.

Like so many times in the village of Favilla, the light of purification glowed.

At first only a thin haze of light rose around Eliana; it looked like mist in moonlight. Then the glow intensified, burning bright, coiling into strands. Eliana thrashed in her bonds. She screamed. Her face reddened, and she seemed barely able to breathe. The light kept rising from the baby, ripping out of her, blasting from her fingertips, nostrils, mouth, leaking like blood, and rising, always rising to the sky.

Cade leaped to his feet. He took a step forward. He froze, fists clenched, knees shaking.

Mercy winked at him.

Eliana's screams rolled across the village.

The light rose in tendrils, hovering above the babe, taking the form of a dragon. Woven of starlight, the apparition reared in the air, tossed back its head, and cried out in agony. The ghostly keen was full of more pain, more mourning than anything Cade had ever heard.

"The babe is purified!" Mercy shouted. A servant approached, holding a bowl of embers and a brand. Mercy lifted the red-hot metal, its tip shaped as a tillvine blossom, and pressed it against Eliana's shoulder.

Flesh sizzled.

Branded, Eliana gave a final scream . . . and fell silent.

Below the starlit dragon—the magic torn free from the babe—Eliana couldn't even scream.

The baby wasn't breathing.

She was turning crimson, then purple.

"You're killing her!" Cade shouted and raced forward.

The firedrakes leaned in, blasting sparks and streams of smoke. Paladins pointed down their lances. Cade ignored them, bounded across the square, and reached the altar. Above, the astral dragon rose higher into the sky, its cry fading into a mournful whisper, soft as a flute, then gone. As the starlit strands dispersed, Cade grabbed his sister and shook her.

"Eliana!" he cried. "Breathe. Breathe!"

The baby lay still in his arms, and tears streamed down Cade's face. He shook her. Again. Again.

"Eliana, breathe!"

He placed a finger in her mouth. He pressed against her frail chest, again and again.

"Breathe," he begged.

The baby coughed, gasped for air, and screamed.

Cade lowered his head, shaking, tears on his lips. "Thank the stars," he whispered.

His legs shook wildly, and he leaned against the altar, nearly falling to the ground.

Overcome with emotion, he banged his elbow against the black bowl, and its leaves spilled across the altar.

A few of the ilbane leaves—herbs for testing the magic in babes—touched Cade's hand.

Bolts of agony shot through Cade—agony pure white and terrible, the pain worse than a thousand hot ovens, than a thousand rusty blades. He leaped back as if struck by a viper.

The village seemed to freeze.

Cade's stepfather had begun to run after him; he now stood frozen halfway across the square. The firedrakes stared down, the paladins on their backs aiming their lances. Mercy stared at Cade, head tilted, eyes narrowed.

Cade looked at his arm. Red, raw welts rose across it where the ilbane had touched him, where it had sensed the magic within him.

With a movement so swift Cade barely saw it, Mercy leaped forward, grabbed more ilbane, and shoved the leaves against Cade's cheek.

He tossed back his head and howled.

The pain blasted through him, endless lightning, endless fire, blades digging through his organs.

Paladins cried out in rage. Firedrakes screeched. Derin shouted his name.

"A weredragon," Mercy whispered, still holding the leaves against him. "An adult weredragon. Uncured." She raised her voice to a shout. "A weredragon!"

She dropped the ilbane and drew her sword.

Cade glanced at his stepfather, seeing the terror in the old baker's eyes.

I'm sorry, Cade thought. *I'm sorry.*

He summoned his magic.

For the first time in open daylight, Cade shifted.

Scales flowed across him, golden and hard as steel. Mercy's sword clanged against them, doing him no harm. He kept changing. His body grew, doubling, tripling in size, growing larger still. His fingernails lengthened into dagger-like claws. Fangs sprouted from his mouth, and a tail lashed behind him. Wings burst out from his back with a thud.

"Slay him!" Mercy shouted.

Across the square, firedrakes blasted down jets of flame.

Cade—a golden dragon, larger than any hut in the village—beat his wings and took flight.

The firedrakes' pillars of flame crashed down against the village square, singeing his paws. He rose higher, soaring into the sky, and beat his wings madly.

I'm sorry, Father, Mother, he thought, looking behind him at the village. He saw Derin gasping, shielding baby Eliana within his embrace. He saw villagers flee. And he saw Mercy leap onto her firedrake and soar, and soon all the beasts were flying, and their dragonfire streamed toward him.

Cade flew higher, dodging the flames. Tears burned in his eyes. He had never flown in daylight before, never flown in the open for anyone to see.

Today he flew faster than ever, heading north toward the mountains, leaving his village behind. He cried out, a torn howl of fear and pain.

Behind him, Mercy shouted from her saddle, and the dozen firedrakes flew in pursuit.

Daniel Arenson

MERCY

A weredragon.

Mercy shook with rage, leaned forward in the saddle, and sneered.

A living weredragon.

The foul creature flew ahead, streaming across the sky, a golden dragon. But he was no true dragon. Mercy had seen his true form—a pathetic, sniveling little peasant boy. Infected. Cursed. Impure.

"Faster, Pyre!" Mercy shouted, digging her spurs into the firedrake she rode. "Faster, damn you!"

Scales in all the colors of flame covered her firedrake, this true dragon, a dragon whose human form had been yanked out. Mercy had cut off two of the scales, leaving room for her spurs to dig into the soft flesh beneath. Now, as Mercy drove in the steel spikes, the beast howled and beat its wings mightily. Streams of smoke blasted from its nostrils, and its saliva dripped toward the fields below. Eleven other firedrakes flew around Mercy, paladins in white armor atop them. The paladins' hair—the pure white hair that grew from only the right side of their heads—billowed like banners.

"We hunt a weredragon, brothers!" Mercy cried and laughed. "A true, living weredragon!"

She had heard tales of weredragons living in the Commonwealth, still infected—those who had escaped purification as babes. Mercy had hunted several herself, slain them with her own lance. This was a great hunt, a great moment of triumph for her god. She licked her teeth as they flew in pursuit. The golden dragon—this Cade Baker—was fast, streaming across the sky just as fast as her firedrakes. But she had trained her firedrakes for stamina, for long flights across the great distances of the Commonwealth. The weredragon ahead would have only flown at night, in secret, probably never more than a mile or two. He would soon tire.

"And then I will break you, Cade," Mercy whispered, her sneer growing into a grin. She imagined how she'd bring him to the capital, how she'd chain him upon the palace balcony, displaying him to the multitudes. She would break him then. She would shatter his bones with a hammer, and she would whip his flesh, and finally when he begged her for death, she would mount her firedrake and burn him with dragonfire. She would laugh as he screamed.

"You cannot escape us, Cade!" she shouted into the wind. "You cannot escape your death." She dug her spurs into her firedrake again. "Blow your fire, Pyre!"

The great multicolored reptile blasted out a jet of flame. Around Mercy, the eleven other firedrakes shot forth their inferno. The dozen fiery streams blasted forward, crackling and spinning. Cade flew just out of range; the last flickers of fire singed his tail, only spurring him onward. Mercy laughed to hear his yelp of pain.

"You will hurt far more before I'm done with you," she said into the wind, her teeth clenched, her grin so wide it hurt her cheeks.

Along with her rage, her pain drove down into her belly, a metal rod forever inside her. The weredragons—those men and women with the disease so many were born with, the disease her Temple cured—had caused nothing but misery. Thousands of years ago, they had formed a kingdom for their kind, a kingdom that had suffered through endless wars, genocides, and tyrannies. They had given their kingdom a name, a name forbidden now, a name Mercy dared not utter, not even think of. And for that name, millions had died.

Throughout history, the weredragons had attracted the wrath of demons, of griffins, of phoenixes. Throughout history, endless wars had been fought for that magic of reptiles.

Until the Cured Temple.

A hundred years ago, Mercy's great-grandmother, a pious woman, had heard the words of the Spirit, the wise god, creator of all. The priestess had raised the Cured Temple, a small but ancient religion, to dominion. It was a religion to cure all weredragons, to remove the illness that had brought so much death. The first High Priestess had begun to cleanse the land of dragon magic. She had burned all scrolls and books bearing the kingdom's old name, had outlawed uttering that name, and had called her new realm the Commonwealth—a realm for the cured. A realm without weredragons.

For a hundred years, Mercy's elders had worked to make this dream a reality, to finally rid the world of the last weredragon. The Spirit taught that when the last weredragon fell, the ancient King's Column—a relic of marble in the capital—would fall too. The world would be cured. The ancient disease would be cleansed away. The Spirit himself would descend to the earth, ushering in an era of peace and holiness.

The Falling, Mercy thought, sucking in breath. The day the column would fall. The day all adherents of the Cured Temple craved.

Perhaps Cade himself was the last weredragon. Perhaps she, Lady Mercy Deus, would be the one to bring about the Falling.

She spurred her firedrake again, racing across forests and hills. The parti-colored beast blew fire again, and Cade kept flying, but she saw him wobbling in the sky. He was weakening. He would not be able to keep flying for much longer.

Mercy tightened her grip around her lance's shaft.

Yes, she craved the Falling. She craved the holiness that would come from cleansing the world. But even more, she craved revenge.

"The weredragons killed him, killed my—"

Pain bolted through Mercy. No, she would not summon that memory now, the memory of a day of fire, of screams, of loss. A day of a soul torn from her.

"Weredragons are murderers," she whispered, and her eyes stung with tears. "And now I will murder you, Cade. Slowly. Savoring every drop of your blood."

Cade dipped lower in the sky. Smoke streamed from his nostrils in two trails. He was slowing down. The firedrakes, meanwhile, only flew faster at the sight. The great beasts tossed back their heads and screeched, the sounds beautiful—the sounds of ripping flesh and snapping bones.

"Burn him!" Mercy shouted.

The firedrakes blasted out their flames.

The inferno shot toward Cade and washed across him.

The golden dragon screamed.

It was a human scream, the cry of a boy, pained, beautiful. Mercy grinned and licked her lips to hear it. Scales heated, expanded, and cracked across Cade, but still he flew.

"We take him alive!" Mercy shouted. She rose in her stirrups and raised her lance. "Barely alive."

She aimed the lance, prepared to thrust it into Cade's wing to cripple him, then drag him back to the capital in chains.

Before her, Cade turned in the sky.

"What's the damn fool doing?" she growled.

With a roar, the golden dragon came charging toward the dozen firedrakes.

"He's taking us head on!" said Sir Castus, a tall man who flew a firedrake at Mercy's right side.

She stared in disbelief. "Burn him!"

Beneath her, her firedrake thrummed, its scales of many colors clattering, as it blasted out flames. Its eleven comrades blew fire too. The jets coalesced into a single strand, an inferno like a dying sun, a great pillar—wider than a city boulevard—that streamed toward the charging gold dragon.

Instants before Cade could hit the fire, he soared higher, dodging the flames. The gold dragon rose toward the sun, then spun and swooped.

His dragonfire rained down.

Mercy screamed and raised her shield.

Cade's inferno rained upon her.

The dragonfire blazed across her shield, and Mercy screamed. Tongues of fire reached around the metal disk to lick her armor. Her firedrake shrieked, the flames cascading across its scales.

"You'll be the one to burn, Mercy!" the golden dragon roared. An instant later, Cade's claws came slamming down.

Mercy gnashed her teeth as she raised her shield. The dragon claws clattered against it. Mercy swung her sword blindly, trying to hit Cade. He dodged the blade, grabbed her shield in his claws, and yanked it free from her grip.

For an instant, Mercy stared up into the roaring jaws of the golden dragon, and she saw her death.

For that instant, terror, all-consuming, filled her.

Cade plunged down, prepared to snap his jaws around her.

Mercy growled, rose in her stirrups, and thrust up her sword.

The blade drove into Cade's palate, piercing him, and blood showered. The dragon screamed and beat his wings, rising higher in the sky.

"Burn him, Pyre!" Mercy shouted.

Her firedrake reared beneath her and blasted flames upward. The other firedrakes joined in. One of the beasts slammed into Cade, knocking the golden dragon aside. Another firedrake thrust its claws, tearing at Cade's scales.

The golden dragon cried out and plunged down in the sky.

As Cade tumbled down by her, Mercy leaned sideways in her saddle and thrust her lance. The blade cracked one of Cade's scales and drove into the flesh. Blood spurted.

The golden dragon cried out and lost his magic.

Cade plunged down in human form, a boy again.

Mercy grinned.

"Grab him, Pyre!"

The firedrake swooped, claws extended. As Cade fell toward the distant forest, Mercy rode her firedrake down in pursuit, prepared to grab Cade and bloody him a few more times before chaining him up.

The land below—rocky mountains covered in pines—raced up toward them. Pyre's claws stretched out like an owl reaching for a mouse.

The firedrake's claws grazed the tumbling boy.

Before the claws could grab him, Cade became a dragon again.

Mercy screamed. As Cade shifted, he ballooned in size. The golden dragon slammed against Pyre, knocking the firedrake back. Mercy nearly tumbled from the saddle.

Cade's fire blasted skyward, hit Pyre's belly, and exploded in a great fountain. Smoke blinded Mercy. She grabbed the saddle's horn, pulling herself back into position. Flames burned at her boots. She screamed and thrust her lance blindly, and her firedrake swayed, and for a moment Mercy didn't know up from down. The other firedrakes streamed around her.

When Mercy finally righted herself, she stared around, sneering and panting.

"Where is he?" she shouted.

Cade was gone.

Mercy rose in her stirrups, staring from side to side. "Where's the boy?"

The other paladins seemed just as confused. They too stared from side to side, seeking Cade.

The golden dragon was gone.

"He must have fallen," said Sir Castus, streaming across the sky to her right. He pointed his lance down toward the mountains. "Probably dead between the pines."

Mercy growled. No. No! She would not let him die. She would kill him herself in the capital for the multitudes to see, for her mother—the High Priestess herself—to smell the blood.

"Then find him!" she cried. "Down into the forest. Uproot every tree if you must! Bring him to me alive, or bring me his corpse!"

The firedrakes swooped. The wind roared, and the mountainsides rushed up toward them. With a shower of shattering branches, the firedrakes crashed through the pine canopy and landed on the rocky slopes. Mercy leaped from her saddle and gazed around, seeking him. Nothing. No sign of him. She saw only trees, boulders, a rocky stream.

Mercy trembled with rage. How could he have vanished? He had flown right beneath her! Her firedrake had burned him! How had he disappeared in the blink of an eye?

The other paladins dismounted. They gathered around her.

"He's probably just dead on a rock somewhere," said Sir Lancino, a gruff man with a cleft chin. He snorted. "I say we return home. The weredragon won't bother us no—"

Mercy stepped toward the paladin and thrust her sword into his neck.

The man gasped and gurgled. Blood filled his mouth. He twitched, held upright upon her blade.

Mercy leaned in closer, sneering. "We will not rest until the weredragon is found."

The other paladins stared, silent. Mercy tugged the blade free. Sir Lancino gave a last gasp, then fell down dead. Mercy spat on his body.

Good riddance, she thought. The man had been a fool, and she had hated that ridiculous chin of his.

She turned toward the other paladins and raised her dripping blade. "Now fan out and find him! Find the weredragon, or I'll slay you all. Go!"

The paladins nodded. Leaving their firedrakes, they began to race between the trees, seeking Cade.

Mercy marched through the forest, sword raised, the hot blood sticky on her fingers.

Cade had hurt her. He had escaped her. He would scream with the pain of ten thousand tortured men.

CADE

Cade lay on the forest floor, bleeding, head spinning, not sure if he was alive or dead. Smoke and flame rose above him, raining ash. He could see nothing but the inferno.

"Where is he?" rose the shriek. "Find the boy! Find him!"

Mercy's voice—no longer fair but twisted with cruelty, dripping bloodlust and rage.

Cade tried to move. He lifted one arm and grimaced with pain. Welts rose across his skin—burns from his own dragonfire, the blaze he'd blown when still in dragon form. His memory slipped in and out of his mind. He had become human again. He had fallen, crashing through his own fire, hidden within the blaze. He had landed here, bruised and burnt. He was dying. He—

"Find him!" Mercy roared.

Firedrakes swooped above, claws reaching through the dispersing smoke. Paladins moved through the forest, boots thumping.

I have to move.

Cade tried to rise to his feet, but pain flared through him. He bit down on a scream and fell. He rolled.

He found himself tumbling down a mountainside, his body slamming against rocks and roots. He crashed into the trunk of a pine, and needles rained down onto him. The firedrakes streamed above, rising and falling from the forest. Trees shattered.

Up, Cade, he told himself. *On your feet. Up!*

He didn't want to rise. He wanted to lie still, to wait for death to take him, to sink into warm forgetfulness, an end to pain.

Stand up!

He balled his hands into fists. He could not die here. Not while his family needed him. Little Eliana—he had to help her. He had to move.

He rose to his feet. His legs swayed, and he began to run.

The pines shook at his sides, and the shrieks of the firedrakes rose from every direction. He was high in the Dair Ranin mountains, and the air was thin. The slopes were steep, strewn with rocks and thick with pines. The trees thrust out from the mountainsides like green stubble on a giant's stony face. Cade stumbled down the slope toward a fold in the land; the trees were thicker down there, a green cloister, a place of shadows and burrows.

A white firedrake streamed above, and Cade cursed and leaped under a pine tree, hiding beneath its lower boughs. He peered between needles. The beast swept down the slope, flying only several feet above the treetops. A saddle still rose upon its back, but no rider; perhaps the man had died in the battle, and perhaps he was searching the mountains afoot. Cade shuddered to think that this firedrake itself had once been human, the soul burnt away, the reverse of purification. Now the mindless beast screeched madly. It passed over Cade, the air from its wings rattling the pine he hid under, and dipped toward the gorge. The reptile soared again, crying out, flying off to seek Cade upon another peak.

When the beast was gone, Cade emerged from under the pine, began walking back down the slope toward the cover of the lower trees, and saw a paladin climbing toward him.

For an instant, they both froze.

The paladin stared up at him—a tall, gaunt man, half his head shaven, the other half sporting a mane of long white hair. His heavy plate armor was just as white, the breastplate engraved with a tillvine blossom.

The paladin reached for his sword.

Cade grabbed a heavy stone the size of a loaf of bread. He hurled it.

The paladin opened his mouth to cry out. An instant later, the stone slammed into his chest, knocking him down.

Cade ran. He leaped down the slope, charging toward the paladin. The man rolled a few feet down, hit a boulder, and began to rise. Cade reached him. He stepped down on the man's blade, pinning the sword to the ground, lifted the same stone he had tossed, and brought it down hard.

The stone slammed into the paladin's face. Teeth broke loose. Blood spurted.

Cade did not allow the horror to overcome him. He slammed the stone down again and again, grimacing at the blood, at the crumbling face, the shattering skull, the leaking brain.

When the man moved no more, Cade dropped the bloodied rock. His body trembled, but he refused to let the fear overcome him.

I killed a man. I—

He gritted his teeth.

Move!

He ran down the mountainside and finally reached the snaking gully between the slopes. He crashed between the pines, stumbled a hundred yards farther down, and found himself standing in a dried riverbed. To his left and right, mountainsides rose like walls, thick with trees. The forest canopy hid the sky. The riverbed spread ahead, mottled with patches of light; the water was gone now, possibly only flowing in spring when the snow melted. Smooth, mossy stones and a carpet of fallen pine needles covered the riverbed.

Cade spared a moment to examine his wounds. He winced. When falling through the sky, his own dragonfire had burned holes into his burlap tunic. The skin below was red and raw, and welts covered his arm. Already bruises were spreading across his legs, and cuts and scrapes covered him. Mercy's lance had left an ugly cut on his side, tearing through the skin. His head wouldn't stop spinning, and again the overwhelming urge to lie down filled him.

He squared his jaw and forced himself to keep walking, to move down the riverbed. He didn't know where he was going, only that he had to keep moving, to put distance between him and the pursuing firedrakes. He heard the beasts still flying above, and their drool pattered down like rain.

Where do I go? Cade thought.

Where *could* he go? He couldn't hope to ever return to his village, not now. The paladins knew about him. They had seen his magic. Soon the High Priestess herself would know that a "weredragon"—a man who had not been purified, who could still become a dragon—lived in the Commonwealth. The Cured Temple would stop at nothing to find him, to break him, to show the people what happened to those who defied purification.

I'll never see my family again. Cade's eyes stung, but he kept walking. For now he had to survive, to—

A firedrake crashed down through the trees above, its scales silver. Cade cursed and leaped for cover, plunging down between a boulder and a leafy brush. The stone pressed against his one side, the leaves against the other.

The firedrake in the gully screeched, a sound like shattering glass. Its claws uprooted trees. Soil and needles rained down. Crouched low, Cade covered his ears as the firedrake's scream echoed inside the gorge, deafening. Dragonfire blasted out, streaming over Cade's head, bathing him with heat.

It hasn't seen me, he thought, crouched low. *If it saw me, I'd be dead.*

He wanted to shift. By the spirit, he wanted to become a dragon, to charge against the firedrake, to slay it. He dared not.

Too many of the beasts flew above the mountains; only by hiding could he hope to survive.

He pressed himself lower to the ground, trapped between boulder and bush, hidden, daring not even breathe. Wings thudded. Scales clanked. More firedrakes flew down to land in the gorge, snorting and cackling.

For a moment, Cade heard nothing but the beasts. Then a high, clear voice cried out.

"Do you hear me, Cade?" It was Mercy's voice, crying out from a stony crest a few hundred yards away. "I know you're here! I found the man you killed. I know you're in these mountains, hiding like a rat."

Cade remained still, fists tight. He wanted to burst out from hiding, to shift into a dragon, to fly toward her and burn her. He dared not. He had to live. For his family.

"Come out, Cade!" Mercy cried. "I only want to talk. I don't want to hurt you. I only want to cure you. Come to me, and we'll sit down and talk, and nobody else needs to die."

He wanted to believe that. Spirit, he did. This day had become a nightmare of such terror he scarcely believed it was happening. If only he could speak to them, work things out . . .

But no. He knew Mercy was lying. When chasing him in the sky, she had not wanted to talk; there had been death in her eyes. She was here to slay him. Cade remained hidden and silent.

"Very well!" Mercy said. "If you will not talk here in the mountains, come talk to me in your village. I fly back to Favilla, and I give you an hour to meet me there. If you don't turn yourself in, your family will pay the price. I will see you soon, Cade Baker!"

The forest shook as firedrakes took flight, air from their wings blasting the trees, sending down a hail of twigs and needles. Smoke filled the sky, and the creatures' shrieks grew distant, finally fading.

For long moments, Cade remained hidden in the brush. Finally he peeked into the gorge. They were gone.

He leaned his head against the boulder and closed his eyes.

What to do?

Cade sucked in breath, struggling to calm himself.

Stay calm. Stay calm, Cade. Think. Plan.

Mercy and the firedrakes were heading back toward the village. If he did not return to confront them, the paladins were likely to burn down his home. Yet if he did return, they would capture him, imprison him, torture him, kill him.

Stay calm. Think.

He left the cover of the boulder and brush. Struggling for every breath, he climbed up the mountainside, making his way higher. The slope was steep, forcing him to climb on hands and knees, gripping at roots and stones. Pebbles cascaded from under his knees and elbows, and the air thinned as he climbed. The pines tilted, stretching out from the mountainside, trunks almost horizontal.

Crack.

The sound rose behind him—a snapping twig perhaps. Cade spun his head around, staring down the slope.

Nothing.

He narrowed his eyes, scanning the landscape, but saw only the rocky slopes sliding down into the forest. Probably an animal, he told himself, and certainly not a paladin; if the paladins saw him here, they'd be charging toward him, not hiding in the brush. He kept climbing.

Finally he reached a granite peak. He didn't like the idea of rising into the open, free from the cover of the pines, but he decided it was a risk he needed to take. He climbed onto the stony crest and stared down south.

His breath died. His insides trembled.

He could see Favilla in the distance, barely visible from here. The firedrakes—he counted eleven of them—were flying toward the village. The paladins rose atop them, their banners streaming. As Cade watched, the firedrakes swooped toward the village . . . and blew their fire.

"Eliana," Cade whispered, eyes stinging. "Mother. Father."

Terror thudded through him.

Mercy was killing them.

Cade knew what to do. He would fly there. He would fight the paladins and their firedrakes, even if he died in their flames.

He leaped into the air, shifted into a dragon, and began to fly.

A shadow leaped from between the trees ahead, small and slender, and Cade caught a flash of red hair. Suddenly a firedrake, its scales orange and red and yellow, was flying toward him. The beast roared, darted forth, and slammed into Cade with a thud.

Cade bellowed and blasted out dragonfire. Where had this beast come from? The creature—a wild, untamed dragon—dodged his flaming jet. Its claws grabbed him. Its wings beat, shoving him down. The two dragons slammed onto the mountainside, cracking the stone.

"Stay down, you fool!" the firedrake rumbled. "Do you want to die?"

Still in dragon form, Cade blinked. Had . . . had this firedrake just spoken to him? Firedrakes couldn't speak. They were just animals, not weredragons like him with the minds of humans.

"Get off!" he said, struggling and whipping his tail, his back to the mountainside.

The fiery beast refused to release him. Its claws pinned him down. Its eyes blazed like smelters, and smoke blasted out from its jaws.

"Shift back into a human!" the firedrake demanded. Cade was surprised to hear it speak with the voice of a young woman. "Now!"

Cade growled and struggled to free himself. He recognized this firedrake. The other beasts were black or white or metallic, their scales unicolor. But this firedrake had scales in various shades of red, orange, and yellow, giving it the appearance of living flame—Mercy's firedrake. A saddle still topped the beast, but no rider. Had Mercy taken another firedrake down to the village?

"Get off me now!" Cade growled and slammed his paws against the beast's head.

He sucked in air, prepared to blow fire, when the firedrake grabbed his head with its claws and slammed it back against the ground.

Cade felt a scale crack at the back of his head. The pain bolted through him, so powerful it knocked the magic out of him.

His body shrank. His wings, scales, and claws vanished. He lay on the mountainside, a human again, blinking feebly. He could barely see more than haze and stars. Strangely, he thought he glimpsed a young woman staring down at him, her green eyes peering between tangles of red hair, and then he saw nothing but blackness.

* * * * *

When Cade finally awoke, the sun was lower in the sky. He found himself lying on a patch of grass, the branches of pines rustling above him. He blinked, groggy. Where was he? What had happened? Why wasn't he home in bed or—

The memories pounded into him with the might of fists.

The paladins. The village. His family.

He made to leap up, to fly back home, but he couldn't move. When he glanced down, he saw that his limbs were bound to the trees with leather straps. Somebody had bandaged his wounds, then left him tied here.

Fear flooded Cade. The paladins had captured him. His family was in danger. He growled, tugging at the bonds, unable to free himself. He let out a hoarse cry.

"Hush!" rose a voice. "Be silent or they'll hear you. Listen to me!"

He turned his head toward the voice. A young woman sat beside him on a fallen log. She looked to be about his age, maybe a year or two older. He had never seen a stranger person. She wore rags—a tattered burlap sack, a rope around her waist, and stockings full of holes, revealing all her toes. Dirt and soot covered her skin. A mane of wild, orange hair thrust out from her head in all directions. The fiery strands fell across her face, hiding most of it. Cade could see little more than a freckled nose, pale cheeks, and green eyes that peered between the tangled strands like fox eyes from within a burrow.

"Who are you?" Cade said. "Did you tie me here? Release me."

She shook her head, and her tangled hair swayed. "I can't or you'll fly south. You'll fly to the village and confront the paladins and firedrakes, and they'll kill you."

"They're killing everyone there now!" he cried, struggling against his bonds. "I don't know who you are, but you must release me."

She shook her head again.

Cade growled, closed his eyes, and summoned his magic. He began to shift, growing into dragon form. As his body grew, the straps around his wrists and ankles tightened, shoving him back into human form. His magic fizzled away. With a sinking heart, he realized he could not shift while bound.

He opened his eyes and looked at the young woman again. Her green eyes stared back from within her tangled hair.

"Who are you?" he repeated.

"The name's Domi," she said. "That's all you need to know. Your guardian."

"Domi," he said patiently, "please. I know you're trying to protect me, but you have to release me. My family is in danger. I must fly to them."

Her eyes flashed. She leaped up from the fallen log, sailed through the air, and landed right atop him, driving the air out of his chest. Her body pressed against him, her knee drove into his belly, and she snarled down at him. Suddenly she seemed as wild and beastly as a firedrake.

"And you'll die!" she said, teeth bared. "You almost died up there in the sky. Sheer luck—and some help from a friend—saved you up there. And your luck has now run out. You can't save your family by charging into a hive of firedrakes. How would you serve them by dying too?" She grabbed a fistful of his hair and twisted it painfully. "You're staying here where it's safe!"

Cade grunted and twisted his head from side to side, trying to free himself from her grip, to knock her off. As he struggled, he noticed something lying between the trees, and he narrowed his eyes.

A firedrake saddle.

He looked back at his limbs. They were bound with straps taken from that saddle.

"Domi," he whispered, "what happened to that firedrake? The one with orange and red scales?"

Finally she got off him. She took a few steps back, and fear seemed to fill her eyes. "Don't ask me about that. Never ask me." Her eyes dampened, and her lips trembled. "Now stay here! Until I say you can leave."

She turned and marched away, disappearing between the trees.

Cade remained lying on his back, bound to the pines. In the distance, he thought he could hear firedrakes screeching. They could still be attacking his home. He had to fly there. He had to try to save his family.

He gave the straps a few more tugs. They wouldn't budge. Was he truly at Domi's mercy? Would she even return or just leave him here to die of thirst or wild animals? He cursed, tugging the bonds again, desperate to escape.

"Domi!" he shouted but heard no reply. "Domi, damn you!"

He grunted and cursed, then noticed something. He sucked in breath.

A sword was hanging off the discarded saddle.

If he could only reach it, he could cut his bonds loose. Yet it lay three feet beyond his grip. He inhaled deeply, raised his chin, and tried to shift into a dragon again.

The magic began to fill him. Golden scales appeared across his body. Wings began to sprout from his back. The leather straps tightened painfully, digging into his widening limbs. He felt the magic slipping away. Just before he could lose his grip on the magic, he stretched out one of his sprouting wings. It scraped across the forest floor. The claw on its tip touched the sword. He almost had it. He—

He cried out in pain as the bonds dug into him. His magic fizzled away, leaving him human again, panting, his wrists and ankles chafed and bloody.

When he looked back at the saddle, Cade saw that his wing had knocked the sword down to the forest floor. It still lay beyond his reach. He inhaled deeply, summoned his magic again, and began to shift. Halfway through his transformation, just before the bonds could shove him back into human form, he hooked his wing's claw around the sword's crossguard and tugged it close.

He lost his magic again. He stretched out his fingers and grabbed the sword's hilt.

He grinned as he tugged and shook the hilt, drawing the blade from its scabbard. It took some finger acrobatics to position the blade properly, but soon Cade cut one arm free. He laughed, relief spreading across him, and quickly lashed the blade against the other straps, freeing his second arm and both legs.

He rose to his feet, leaped into the air, and shifted. He rose into the sky as a dragon.

He flew over the mountains, not caring if any paladin or firedrake saw. He reached the foothills and beat his wings mightily, streaming across the fields and farms.

Finally he reached the village of Favilla . . . and he cried out in agony.

The paladins and their firedrakes were gone. The village, the only home Cade had ever known, lay in ruin.

"Mother!" Cade cried out hoarsely, flying above the devastation. "Father!"

The flap of his wings raised clouds of soot and ash below. Pebbles raced across the ground. Bones scattered. Tears filled Cade's eyes. The humble clay huts had been crushed, the marks of firedrake claws upon what remained of their walls. The gardens still smoldered. And everywhere—everywhere lay the bodies. He couldn't even recognize the corpses; they were burnt black, charred like logs after a forest fire. Bones thrust out through what remained of the flesh. A few splotches of red was all the blood that remained; the rest was all black, all darkness, all death.

"Mother! Father!" Cade cried out, voice torn in agony.

He flew down and landed outside the ruin of his bakery. The roof had caved in. The walls had been torn down. Cade rummaged through the bricks with his claws, trying to find them, to find Derin and Tisha, the only parents he had ever known.

Finally, under a pile of bricks, he found them.

He lowered his scaly head, tears in his eyes.

Derin and Tisha, the bakers who had adopted him, who had raised him as a son, were dead, burnt to nothing but bones and shreds of blackened skin. Empty eye sockets gazed at him as if asking, *Why weren't you here? Why didn't you help us, Cade?*

Cade looked away, tears stinging.

"Eliana," he whispered.

Still in dragon form, he kept digging, praying the girl still lived, praying he did not find a third corpse. Under more bricks he found her cradle, and his breath caught . . . but the cradle was empty. She was gone.

Cade no longer had the will to hold on to his magic. It fizzled away like the last flames in the ruins. He knelt over the empty cradle, lowered his head, and tasted his tears.

An hour later, he stood outside the village over two graves.

He stared down at the mounds of earth, then stared at his hands—hands covered with the ashes of the dead.

"I'm sorry, Mother and Father," he whispered to the graves. "I'm sorry."

He could speak no more. His chest shook with sobs, and he clenched his fists and lowered his head.

A voice spoke behind him, hesitant, softer than the breeze.

"Oh, Cade . . . I'm sorry."

He spun around, heart leaping, ready to fight. But it was not a paladin behind him. Instead he found himself staring at Domi.

She still wore her rags—a tattered burlap sack tied around her waist with a rope, stockings full of holes, and no shoes. More dust than ever coated her skin, and ashes rained into her mop of tangled red hair. Those green eyes of hers stared at him from between the strands, shining with tears.

"I should have been here," Cade said, voice choked. "I should have fought for them, saved them." Sudden anger rose inside him, and his hands balled into fists. "You kept me away. You bound me as they died! Why?" He shook with his rage.

"To protect you," she said softly. "I could not save the villagers, but I could try to save you."

Fresh tears stung his eyes. "I'd have preferred to die with them."

Her eyes narrowed, and she bared her teeth, a wild animal again. "You cannot die! You're too rare. You're Vir R—" She bit down on her words, and her cheeks paled.

"I'm what?" he said.

She sighed. "You're like me."

She took a few steps back, stared at him solemnly, and shifted.

Wings burst out from her back, red and tipped with white claws. Scales rose across her body in all the colors of fire. A tail sprouted from her back, and she grew taller and finally stared at him as a dragon.

Cade recognized the firedrake from the battle, one of the twelve who had chased him.

Mercy's firedrake.

He reached deep inside him for his magic, but before he could shift, Domi released her dragon form, returning to a human again. She approached him slowly, her bare feet sinking into the soft soil.

"You . . . you're no firedrake," he said.

She shook her head, and her matted red hair swayed. "I'm like you, Cade. I was never purified. But while you chose to live as a human, hiding your dragon form, I chose the opposite life. I live as a dragon, pretending to be a mindless firedrake with no human form to shift into, no human thoughts. I bear paladins on my back, and I live in an underground cell, and I serve the cruel Cured Temple—all for the freedom of flying." A wistfulness filled her eyes. "All for a taste of the sky . . . the sky that was taken from us."

So many emotions filled Cade—grief for his slain parents, worry for his missing sister, rage at the Cured Temple, amazement that others like him still lived—that he could only stand still, overcome, not knowing what to say, how to feel, what to do.

Finally he found the words he needed to speak. They left his lips in a whisper. "Are there others?"

Domi smiled tremulously. "There are. At least four others—four others that I know of. They call us weredragons, creatures cursed, diseased, poor souls that need to be purified. But our true name, our ancient name, is . . ." She dropped her voice to a whisper. "Vir Requis."

Others like him. Spirit, there were others who hadn't been purified, who hadn't been branded. Others who could become dragons. Other Vir Requis.

"Where can I find the others?" he said. "Can you take me to them?"

Domi looked from side to side, and fear filled her eyes. "I can no longer help you. Lady Mercy will be seeking me. She left me to keep scouring the mountains and flew here on a different firedrake, but I'm her favorite mount. She'll want to ride me home, and if I don't return to her, she'll think me lost, think me a recalcitrant beast to hunt down. I must return to her now. And you must leave this place. They'll be hunting you. Already they're back hunting you in the mountains." She pointed toward distant figures on the horizon—firedrakes. "You must travel to the city of Sanctus on the coast. Visit the city library. Speak to the librarian. She will help you." She took a few steps back, glancing around nervously. "I must leave."

"Wait!" Cade said, reaching out to her. "What do I tell this librarian? Why would she help me?"

Domi was hopping from foot to foot, anxious to leave. She chewed her lip, then looked back at him. She stepped closer to Cade and, surprising him, embraced him. Her body was soft, warm, slender, and her embrace was full of such goodness, such compassion, that Cade never wanted it to end.

"Tell the librarian the name of our kingdom." Domi caressed Cade's cheek. "Tell her the forbidden name, the name the paladins would kill anyone who utters. The name that means everything, that is who we were, who we can become again." She pressed her lips against his ear, and she whispered a word—whispered it with such awe, such holiness, that goose bumps rose across Cade. "Requiem."

With that, Domi broke apart from him. She took a few steps back, stared into his eyes, and shifted. She rose into the sky as a dragon—a wild firedrake in disguise—and turned to fly away. She glided toward the northern mountains, toward the true firedrakes and their riders.

Requiem.

The word felt too holy to even repeat aloud. New tears filled Cade's eyes, but these were tears of wonder, of awe.

Requiem.

The word—the way Domi had whispered it, the way it echoed in his ear—spoke of ancient magic, of old halls of marble, of something precious, something lost. Something Cade knew that he carried inside him, that he would always seek, that he would never forget.

Requiem.

He looked back at the two graves. He looked at the burnt village. He needed to leave this place. He needed to find his sister. He needed to seek the library in Sanctus, to learn more about that forgotten place, that forbidden word . . . to learn about Requiem.

He rose into the sky as a dragon. He flew east, and he did not look back once.

GEMINI

Lord Gemini Deus, second born to High Priestess Beatrix, stared into the mirror and liked what he saw.

"Do you see this?" he said, looking over his reflection's shoulder at the naked woman in his bed. "A paladin in all his glory. Feast your eyes, my darling, for you'll never see a sight so beautiful again."

His bedchamber was lavish, coated in gold and jewels. The woman in his bed was beautiful, and she stretched with a yawn, displaying her splendid nakedness in the sunlight. But Gemini returned his eyes to his own reflection; it was fairer by far. He was a tall, slender man of twenty-two years, young enough for youthful beauty, old enough for masculinity. Like all paladins and priests, he shaved the left side of his head, leaving only stubble. Long, luxurious hair cascaded down to his right shoulder, bleached white as snow. His cheekbones were high, his eyes blue and clear, and he wore priceless armor of white steel. He turned to admire all angles.

"I prefer you naked," said the woman in his bed. She patted the mattress. "Remove that armor and return here to my arms."

He spun toward her and frowned. "What for?" He snorted. "I've already planted my seed inside you. I'm done with you. Leave."

Hurt filled her eyes. "But . . . my lord."

"I didn't say you can talk back." He drew his sword and stroked the blade with a handkerchief, polishing the steel. "I'm pureborn. No dragon disease ever filled my blood. It's my duty to give you peasant girls pureborn babes, not tolerate your prattle."

He pointed his blade at the door. "Leave and never return here, and never speak to me again, or next time I'll thrust my sword into you instead of my manhood."

Her eyes dampened, and she fled toward the door, pulling on her tunic. Gemini watched her leave, admiring the rear view. She had a good figure to her, he thought, curved in the just the right places, but there were plenty more women in the Commonwealth, and the last thing Gemini Deus needed was one puttering around his chamber and thinking herself his lover.

Today Gemini would find a greater prize than a woman. Today he would seize a power that would deal his older sister a blow as sure as a gauntleted fist.

"You might be older, dear Mercy, and you might be heiress to the Cured Temple." Gemini smiled thinly, sheathing his blade. "But soon I will be more powerful by far."

He left his bedchamber, stepping out into a corridor. The walls were carved of marble, inlaid with golden leaves and jewels, and murals sprawled across the vaulted ceiling, depicting ancient scenes of myth. Arched windows lined the southern wall, affording views of the city of Nova Vita, capital of the Commonwealth. It was a dreary view, Gemini thought, simply miles of the filthy commoners' huts. The sight disgusted him, and the sunlight burned his eyes.

He snapped his fingers toward a maid who knelt before him, clad in livery. "Girl! Go clean my bedchamber. Change the sheets, empty my chamber pot, and refill my jugs of wine."

The servant bowed. "Yes, my lord."

Hideous thing, Gemini thought as the girl hurried into his chamber. Why couldn't the damn priests hire beautiful help for once? He was second born to the Temple, for Spirit's sake. He shouldn't have to look at scrawny, mealy-faced servants.

"Girl!" he barked. "Wait. Come back."

She hurried back into the hallway and bowed her head. "My lord?"

"After you're done cleaning my chamber, leave this temple. Return to whatever brothel or filthy alleyway you came from." He snickered. "You're done here."

Tears filled her eyes, but Gemini only scoffed as he walked away. The girl was lucky he didn't order her stoned to death; that ratty face of hers was practically heretical.

He walked through the Cured Temple, the center of his family's power, the heart of the Commonwealth. The palace was a great jewel, a masterpiece such as the world had never seen. Mosaics of precious metals and gemstones sprawled across the floors, depicting animals of every kind. Murals of stars, suns, and birds covered the ceiling between strands of gold and silver. Columns lined the hallways, topped with golden capitals, and statues of druids stood between them, their eyes jeweled.

Finally Gemini stepped through a towering white archway, leaving the Temple and emerging into the sunlight. He walked down a wide staircase and stepped onto the Square of the Spirit. It sprawled ahead of the Cured Temple, a vast expanse, larger than most towns. During the High Priestess's speeches, hundreds of thousands of souls gathered here to worship her and the Spirit. Today thirty firedrakes stood in the square, great beasts of scales, wings, and claws. They had once been weredragons, humans born with the disease inside them, the curse that let man become dragon. The Temple had burnt out their humanity; now only the beasts remained.

"Ventris!" Gemini barked. "Here. To me." He patted his thigh. "Come."

It was not a firedrake who rushed forth but an old man, clad in leather and wool. Gemini barked a laugh. The firedrakes' keeper was no better than an animal himself.

"Hurry!" Gemini raised his sword. "To me, old man. Now bow."

Ventris reached him, huffing and panting, and bowed his head. "My lord Gemini! I've been training them, my lord. Training them well. Today they're learning how to—"

"You treat them like dogs." Gemini spat. "Training them? Teaching them tricks more like. To sit, roll over, beg for scraps like pups? Are you a kennel master or a trainer of firedrakes?"

Ventris straightened. Sweat dripped down his forehead. Farther back, the firedrakes hissed, smoke blasting out from their nostrils. Their scales clattered, their wings creaked, and fire sparked between their fangs. Their eyes blazed like molten metal. Each one of these beasts, Gemini knew, could crush the Cured Temple and burn everyone in it. Only the harshest, strictest training kept the drakes submissive, under command, under control.

"My lord," said Ventris, "today we're training for aerial assault. Perhaps if you'd like to watch, I could demonstrate how—"

"Watch?" said Gemini. "Do you think me some boy, some pup come to gape at tricks?" He sneered. "I'm a paladin of the Cured Temple! I am the son of the High Priestess! You dare insult me?"

Ventris blanched. He knelt and bowed his head. "No, my lord! I beg your pardon. Forgive me, please. How may I serve you?"

Gemini stared down at the sniveling man. Pathetic wretch. "Is it true, Ventris, that you're not even noble born?"

The graying man looked up, then quickly down again. "I was born to House Erus, my lord, nobles of the eastern coast, lords of—"

"Lords of chamber pots and sea scum." Gemini snorted. "Ventris, I'll be taking command of the firedrakes. I will be supervising their training from now on." He smiled thinly. "Don't think your little games have eluded me. You may dress like a commoner, and you may hold no honor in the Temple, but I know the power your position holds." He licked his lips. "He who rules the firedrakes . . . rules the Commonwealth."

He raised his eyes and stared at the beasts. He inhaled deeply and licked his lips, already imagining it. When he controlled the firedrakes, he would have more power than any army. He would have more power than his sister, that was certain. Perhaps even more than his mother.

All my life, you looked down at me, Mother, he thought, and his hands curled into fists. *All my life, you spat upon me, sister. All my life, you thought me weak, second born, worthless.* His teeth ground. *But I will have power to make you kneel before me.*

Ventris straightened again. The man was sweating. It was disgusting. "Of course, my lord! I would be glad to serve under you, to help you train the firedrakes, to make sure they obey your every command. I—"

Gemini shook his head. "You're done. We're making changes here today. The Cured Temple is but a game, dear Ventris, no different than a game of counter-squares. And you, my friend, are off the board."

With a thin smile, Gemini thrust his sword.

The blade sank into Ventris's belly, and blood gushed.

Gemini's smile widened as he yanked the blade upward, cutting the man open. As Ventris fell over, spilling his innards, Gemini laughed and stepped back.

"Feast, my friends!" Gemini shouted to the firedrakes. "You have a new lord now, and here is my gift to you! Feast upon your old master!"

The firedrakes screeched, beat their wings, and pounced. Gemini laughed and stepped back. The great reptiles squealed as they tore into the body, ripping it apart, fighting one another for the morsels. One firedrake tugged off a leg and gulped it down. Another grabbed the torso, the juiciest cut, while two others tried to rip the meat free from the glutton's jaws. Three other firedrakes lapped at the bloody cobblestones.

"This will be your last meal for a while," Gemini said softly, gazing at them. "You're going to learn hunger now, friends. You're going to learn true obedience. You're going to learn what a true master is." As they shrieked, the blood tossing them into a frenzy, Gemini turned to stare south. Somewhere beyond that horizon, his sister flew on the hunt. "And you, Mercy, will learn who has the true power in this Temple. You too will learn who your master is."

The smell of death filled his nostrils, and Gemini smiled.

DOMI

Domi flew on the wind, a wild beast with scales the color of fire, and joined her fellow firedrakes above the mountains.

Of course, she wasn't actually a firedrake. Not truly. Firedrakes had no human forms, no human minds. As babes, their human bodies had been burnt in sacramental fire, leaving only a dragon's egg, a hard stone that hatched a rabid reptile, a beast who thought of nothing but blood, flight, and fire, no more intelligent than a hound or horse. Domi had never been burnt, never been cured, never lost her human soul; she was a proud Vir Requis, a child of a forgotten kingdom.

And there is one more among us, she thought, a light of hope rising inside her. *There is Cade.*

She had only ever met four others, and they—like Cade—lived as humans, hiding their dragon forms. But Domi had chosen a different life. She hated her human form. As a girl, she was small, weak, a scuttling little thing with a mane of red hair, spindly legs, and darting eyes. The human her was little more than a mouse. But as a dragon . . .

She inhaled deeply. As a dragon—a firedrake in disguise—she was strong. She was proud. She could fly on the wind, blow fire, taste the sky. Even if she had to bear Mercy upon her back, even if she had to serve the cruel Temple that hunted her kind, Domi preferred this life.

Better to fly as a dragon, hiding in plain sight of the Temple, than live as a cowering human, she had always thought.

Yet when Domi landed on the mountain among the others and saw Mercy's eyes, she suddenly doubted that thought.

Domi had seen Mercy mad before. Daughter of High Priestess Beatrix, heiress to all the Commonwealth, Lady Mercy Deus had been bred for righteous rage. The young woman, clad in white armor, half her head shaven and the other half sporting long white hair, always seemed mad at the world. Yet now . . . now Domi saw new fury in her mistress's eyes, a rage no longer icy but hotter than dragonfire, a rage that twisted Mercy's face and blazed out from her blue eyes. Night was falling, and the paladins had lit torches; the light painted Mercy's face red.

"Where were you, you miserable cull!" Mercy shouted, marching toward Domi.

Still in her dragon form—she almost never revealed her human body—Domi lowered her head, a mark of submission. She lowered her wing, forming a ramp for Mercy to climb.

Yet Mercy did not mount her. The paladin grabbed a torch from one of her men and shoved it forward, slamming the fire onto Domi's tenderspot.

Domi howled with pain.

Each firedrake, when brought into service, had two scales surgically removed, leaving the flesh bare. The paladins called these *tenderspots*—places for them to drive their spurs into the hides of firedrakes. Every few days, when new scales began to grow, the paladins yanked them off again—a ritual of pain that never ended, like having one's fingernails repeatedly pulled off. Mercy had often dug her spurs deep into Domi's tenderspots—a pain Domi tolerated for a chance to fly as a dragon—but the paladin had never burned her. Now Domi's flesh sizzled, and she yowled.

"Where were you, you worthless beast?" Mercy demanded. She grabbed Domi's horns and tugged her head down, banging Domi's scaly chin against the granite mountaintop.

Domi lowered her eyes, daring not show a single sign of aggression. She had seen what had happened to firedrakes who growled at their masters.

"It's just a dumb animal," said Sir Castus. He spat. "Probably got lost."

Domi stared at the burly Castus. A gruff paladin with a scar splitting his face, he was holding a bundle under his arm.

Eliana, Domi realized, sucking in breath. The paladin was holding Cade's sister!

Mercy knelt and leaned closer. With Domi's head pressed against the ground, Mercy was able to stare directly into her eyes.

"Oh, but you're not as dumb as you look, are you?" Mercy whispered. She caressed Domi's snout. "No, there's some sense in you. You're not as mindless as the other beasts."

Sudden panic flared in Domi, and her heart pounded. Had Mercy seen her become a human? Did the paladin know?

I can burn her now, Domi thought, feeling the flames rise in her gullet. *I can burn her dead, burn them all.*

She forced herself to gulp down the fire.

No. If I kill Mercy, her brother will become heir. And if anyone is crueler than Mercy, it's her brother, Lord Gemini Deus. Domi shuddered. *If I kill Mercy, I myself will die. The other firedrakes will make sure of that.*

So Domi only mewled pathetically, begging for forgiveness.

Mercy straightened and kicked. Her steel-dipped boot slammed into Domi's snout, cracking a scale and rattling her teeth. Domi yelped.

"I know you understand me," Mercy said softly. "If you ever cross me again, you pathetic lizard, I will drive my spear so deep into your tenderspot it'll come out the other side. You were a bad beast today. You flew off. You lost your saddle. And when we return home, you will pay."

With a grunt, Mercy grabbed Eliana from Sir Castus and stuffed the baby under her arm. Eliana screamed. Mercy ignored the sound and climbed onto Domi's back.

Domi's saddle was missing; she had used the straps to bind Cade. Mercy rode bareback. The paladin dug her spurs into the tenderspots, and Domi winced; the burnt spot especially ached. She kicked off the mountain, beat her wings, and rose into the sky. Around her, the other firedrakes took flight too. Two no longer bore riders, their paladins dead in the forest.

"Keep scouring the mountains!" Mercy shouted toward the other paladins. "Uproot every tree and turn over every stone. Do not return to the capital until you've found the boy!"

The other paladins nodded upon their firedrakes. The beasts fanned out, traveling across the piney slopes. Already they swooped to uproot trees.

Mercy dug her right spur deeply into Domi. "You turn north, beast. We fly back to Mother. Fly!"

Domi flew.

Leaving the mountains behind, she glided on the wind, leaving the others behind. Whenever she slowed down, Mercy's spurs dug again. The paladin had always been an impatient flyer, but today she spurred Domi onward with extra urgency.

She's not just mad at me, Domi realized. *She's mad about Cade. That he exists. That she lost him.*

As they passed over the village, Domi looked down at the ruins. Night had fallen, but scattered fires still burned below, and Domi's eyes were sharp. Nothing but the shells of huts and scattered skeletons remained. She could no longer see Cade below. Hopefully the boy was traveling east toward Sanctus, toward the library, toward the aid he'd find there. Hopefully he wouldn't be foolish enough to shift into a dragon again.

Don't die, Cade, she thought. *Damn you, don't be an idiot. Stay alive.*

She sighed as they flew onward, traveling across grassy plains and leaving the ruins behind. All her life, Domi had known only four other Vir Requis. For years, they believed there were no others. All her life, Requiem had been just them, a secret carried within five hearts. Now another rose. Now the paladins were on the hunt. Now, Domi thought, everything would change.

Mercy will fetch reinforcement, Domi thought. *She'll scour the land. She'll seek Cade in every town and city.*

Again Domi felt the fire rise inside her. She rolled back her eyes to stare up at Mercy. Riding on her back, the paladin stared ahead with narrowed eyes, the wind streaming her white hair. Eliana lay before her in the saddle; the baby seemed to be sleeping.

I can kill Mercy now, Domi thought. *I can grab her with my jaws and toss her down to her death. I can fly off with Eliana, become a human, vanish into the world, maybe find Cade and run with him forever.*

She looked back ahead, eyes stinging.

No. I cannot. If Mercy were found dead, Domi too would be hunted. Mercy was cruel, but without her Gemini would become heir to the Cured Temple, and then the Commonwealth would truly bleed. Mercy perhaps was heartless, but Gemini had a heart of wildfire, a mad heart that would burn down the empire. Better the tyrant of steel than the tyrant of fire. If Domi cut one head off the hydra, another would grow, and her life—this life she had fought so hard for, a life as a dragon—would forever end. And so Domi flew on, suffering the spurs, suffering the shame.

Dawn was rising when she saw the city of Nova Vita ahead.

As always, whenever she flew home, the sight of the city filled Domi with awe and longing.

Thousands of years ago, Domi knew, the first Vir Requis—wild shapeshifters of the forest—had raised a marble column in this place, founding the kingdom of Requiem. For thousands of years, this holy ground had been the heart of that kingdom, a kingdom for those who can grow wings, blow fire, and take flight as dragons.

Then, a mere hundred years ago—the blink of an eye!—the Cured Temple had risen.

And everything had changed.

The city of Nova Vita, once capital of Requiem, had become a bastion of the Temple.

In the old books in the library, the ones the others kept hidden, Domi had seen illustrations of the old city—its proud towers, its marble columns, its great statues of old heroes, its pale homes with their tiled roofs, its banners displaying the Draco constellation.

All that was gone.

In a mere hundred years, all that had been forgotten.

The old towers had been knocked down, their height seen as heretical, daring to challenge the Spirit above. The old homes, dwellings of marble and lush gardens, had been torn down and replaced with clay huts, their roofs domed—dwellings of pious austerity. The statues had been smashed, the gardens burnt. Even the fabled birch trees which had grown among the homes, symbols of Requiem, had been cut down. All beauty—of sculpture, architecture, even trees—was now sinful, an affront to the beauty of the invisible Spirit.

The city now looked much like the village of Favilla, but a thousand times the size. Rows and rows of clay huts—thousands of them—sprawled across Nova Vita, their domes reflecting the sun. From up here, the city looked almost like the scales of a great pale dragon. Cobbled streets snaked between the homes, and people walked among them. The commoners wore burlap tunics, simple garb to purify the soul. Jewelry, cosmetics, even colored fabrics were outlawed, punishable by stoning. The priests—Domi saw several of them walking down a street—wore white cotton robes, the fabric simple but of finer quality than what commoners wore. Only the paladins, holy warriors of the Spirit, wore steel; Domi could see none of those noble warriors from up here, for they rarely mingled with the other classes.

While the city was a model of humbleness, one building shattered the austerity with the might of a sword shattering a heart.

The Cured Temple rose in the city center, a massive monument reaching up toward the sky. There was only one temple in the Commonwealth, only one center of power for the Cured. It soared here with light and wonder, scratching the clouds, dwarfing all other buildings.

The building was built of white stone, round at the bottom, flaring up into many shards of crystal and glass. Some days it reminded Domi of a crystal fist reaching its fingers toward the sky. Other times it looked to her like a gaudy crown. Today she imagined it as a great crab, stretching many claws toward the sun; indeed it seemed an organic structure, as if it had sprouted from the rock, a natural formation of stone and crystal. Its spikes were of different sizes and shapes, a jungle, but all glittered in the sunlight, and even the smallest would dwarf the mightiest oak in the northern forests. Several firedrakes flew around the monolith, guarding its holiness; they seemed smaller than bees hovering around their nest. Here was a great jewel, a center of light, of holiness, of power.

Here was the bright fist that clutched the memory of Requiem, refusing to release it.

Here, hidden within the Temple, invisible to Domi, rose King's Column.

Her eyes dampened.

King's Column, she thought. *The pillar of our fallen kingdom. The ancient relic of Requiem.*

In the old book—*The Book of Requiem*—it was written that King Aeternum had raised the marble pillar, that it would not fall while Vir Requis lived. Every night, Domi prayed to the stars, the old gods of Requiem, that the column stood forever, even if it was trapped within the Temple.

And every day, the priests and paladins prayed for the Falling—the day they slew the last weredragon, the day the column fell, the day they believed would bring the Spirit himself down to the world, ushering in an era of peace and plenty.

"Down, beast!" Mercy said, digging her spurs deep and twisting them inside Domi's flesh. "Fly to your stable."

Her eyes widened with the pain, but Domi obeyed. She glided down, approaching the splendor of the Temple. The spikes of crystal and glass rose before her, and Domi saw herself reflected in their polished surfaces. Many firedrakes flew around her, paladins upon their backs, guardians of the Temple. As Domi descended farther, she glided by the wide, round base below the spikes. Many narrow windows peered open upon the white stone, and within them, Domi caught glimpses of priests and priestesses walking along pale corridors.

She passed by the last few stories and landed in a courtyard, claws clattering against the white cobblestones. To her right, a great staircase—wide enough for a dozen people to walk abreast—stretched up toward a white archway, leading into the Temple. To her left, a gaping tunnel led beneath the Temple into darkness.

A man stood outside this tunnel, watching Domi with a thin smile on his face.

Domi's heart sank.

Gemini, she thought, belly curdling.

He looked much like Mercy, his older sister. He too wore the white armor of his order. He too shaved the left side of his head, and he too bleached the long hair growing from the right side. His eyes too were blue and cruel. But while Mercy's eyes bore the cruelty of ice, Gemini's malice was a thing of fire, of passion. Mercy was ruthlessly efficient; her younger brother delighted in causing pain.

"Have you given birth while you were away?" he called toward Mercy.

Mercy dismounted and stood in the courtyard, holding Eliana under her arm. "Creating babies is your job, my dear pureborn brother. Mine is to purify the sick ones." She narrowed her eyes. "What are you doing outside the firedrake pits? You are a paladin of the Cured Temple. You are the son of the High Priestess. You should be off hunting upon the back of a firedrake, not lurking outside their lair."

Gemini's eyes flicked toward Domi, and a strange light burned in them. He licked his lips, then looked back toward his sister. "I've developed a taste for tending to the drakes. I dismissed Ventris, the poor caretaker of the beasts. I've taken control of the firedrake pits, dear sister. I'll teach these creatures the proper discipline."

Domi's heart sank deeper. Ventris had been a kind master in the cruel Temple. He often brought the firedrakes fresh meat to eat, clear water to drink, and even played them music on his flute. Whenever Gemini was in the drake pit—and lately the paladin had been visiting more and more often—he would take out all his malice and aggression on the beasts. Many times, Domi had yelped under his rod.

"So the son of the high priestess becomes a glorified stable boy," Mercy said and shook her head sadly.

"Hardly." Gemini approached Domi and placed a hand on her snout. "Firedrakes are far greater than horses. Noble beasts. Mindless, yes. Temperamental. Disobedient. But noble . . . when trained properly."

"This one is certainly not trained properly," Mercy said, looking back at Domi. "The stupid reptile flew off on its own; it was hours before it rejoined the others. Lost its saddle on the way too. Probably chewed it off." She sighed. "Brother, if you insist on becoming their caregiver, at least make yourself useful. Retrain this one. I'll not be flying out again upon a beast so wild."

With that, Mercy turned and marched away, taking baby Eliana with her.

Gemini watched her leave, his smile widening, then looked back at Domi. "Pyre, come!"

He grabbed her horn and tugged. She followed obediently, many times his size, large enough to easily crush him, but she followed. They entered the tunnel and plunged down into darkness. Only a few torches on the wall cast their light. Gemini led the way, tugging her along as she followed, her wings pressed close to her body, her knees bent, and her back scraping along the ceiling.

"Lost your saddle!" Gemini barked as they walked. "Flew off on your own! What kind of lack in discipline was Ventris showing you beasts? I can tell you, Pyre, your good times are over."

The tunnel opened up into a wide chamber, several stories tall, lined with cages. Thirty firedrakes, the personal mounts of the Deus family, lived here in cells so small the beasts didn't even have room to turn around inside them. Domi stared at the animals; they were banging against the bars, hissing, puffing out smoke.

Over a thousand firedrakes lived in the Commonwealth, and most lived out in the open sky, protecting the Temple's forts, monasteries, and borders. Yet here in the city lurked the pets of the High Priestess herself. With no open fields in Nova Vita, theirs was a life of darkness. Domi had often shown recalcitrance to Mercy, hoping to be transferred to the provinces; there she would have open skies and open fields, fresh game to hunt, and no bars around her. Ventris had just begun to recommend that Domi be moved elsewhere, calling her too wild to serve in the city. Now, with Gemini taken over, Domi's hopes to ever leave this pit seeped away.

One of the cellars was empty, its portcullis raised—her chamber. Domi began walking toward it, hoping to curl up and rest, but Gemini tsked his tongue.

"Halt!" he barked. "I'm not done with you, Pyre." He grabbed a whip that hung on the wall. "My sister requested your punishment, and I intend to deal it."

Domi stared at the whip and hissed. A normal whip would not harm her; the lash would crack uselessly against her scales, hurting only when hitting her tenderspots. But this was no ordinary whip. This was a tool Domi had never seen in the pit before, certainly not under Ventris's reign.

A lightning lash, she thought and hissed.

"Yes . . ." Gemini unrolled the whip. "You know what this is, don't you? You're not as mindless as my sister thinks. There is cleverness to you, perhaps more than in any other firedrake. That's why you cause so much trouble, isn't it?"

Domi stared at the whip. The lash ended with a crackling ball of electricity. She did not know what magic or machinery operated the lightning lashes, but she had seen their scars upon firedrakes brought in from the skirmishes against the Horde across the sea.

She lowered her head, showing submission, and began to back away into her cellar.

"No!" Gemini shouted. "To me!"

He lashed his whip.

The tip crackled with energy, blue and searing, then hit her shoulder. Domi yowled. It felt like a bolt of lightning hitting her. She stumbled back, looked down, and saw that the lightning lash had cracked her scale.

"Lost your saddle!" Gemini said, grinning now, and lashed the whip again. "You won't lose any more saddles under my rule."

He lashed her again and again, cracking her scales, and her roar echoed through the chamber. She wanted to bite him, to tear him apart. At her sides, the other firedrakes screeched inside their cellars, banging against the bars. And still his whip flew.

Finally, sweat drenching him, he relented. He hung the whip back on the wall and wiped his brow.

"Now into your cell!" he said. "Go. Good firedrake. Good. I taught you who's master today. Don't you forget this lesson. Show any other sign of aggression toward me, any sign of disobedience, and I will make today feel like a caress."

She backed up into her cell, her legs shaking. Her scales had cracked and blood seeped from between them. Once she was in the cell, Gemini tugged a lever. The portcullis slammed down, nearly hitting Domi, sealing her within.

Gemini gave her a last look, smirked, and turned to leave the cavern. He took the last torch with him, leaving the pit in darkness.

With Gemini and the light gone, Domi lowered her head. All across the cavern, the other firedrakes screeched madly; she saw no buckets of feed, and they must have felt as hungry as she was. She sighed.

"I chose the life of a firedrake," she whispered into the darkness. "But not like this. Not underground. Not with Ventris gone, with Lord Gemini torturing us for his sport."

Some nights, like tonight, Domi just wanted to burn them all.

Some nights, like tonight, she felt that it would be better to escape the Temple, fly free, and roar for freedom even if all the hosts of the Commonwealth hunted her down.

But no. She could not fight, not now. She could not die just as new hope emerged.

"There is another," she whispered to the shadows. "Another Vir Requis. Another soul who knows the name of our kingdom, the holiest word we have, the word that means everything." Tears streamed down her cheeks. "Requiem."

She waited a few moments, and when Gemini did not reappear, she released her dragon magic. She shrank, becoming a human girl again, clad in rags and covered in soot. At least this way she had room to lie down. She scuttled backward on her bottom until her back hit the wall. There she lay down, pulled her knees up to her chin, and closed her eyes.

"Cade," she whispered.

She imagined that he was lying here with her underground, that she was hugging him instead of her knees. She brought to mind the messy, light brown hair that fell across his brow; his large hazel eyes, fear and anger mingling within them; his tense muscles, ready to sprint. She remembered whispering "Requiem" to him, how her lips had touched his ear, how their bodies had pressed together. Even here on the cold floor, she felt warm, and a smile touched her lips. She reached between her legs and felt the heat there, the longing for him, the animal needs she could not curb. She slept and she dreamed of him.

CADE

He was walking through the grasslands, hungry and thirsty and feeling ready to collapse, when the firedrakes streamed above.

"Spirit damn it!" Cade said. "Damn beasts flying everywhere."

He dropped to his belly, hiding himself in the tall grass. The shrieks rose above him. Wings thudded like drums. The voices of paladins rose too; the riders were calling to one another, though lying facedown in the grass, Cade could not make out the words. He dared to peek over his shoulder and cursed again. Between the blades of grass, he glimpsed them—three flying in a triangle, scanning the grasslands.

Cade lay as still as possible. The grass rose two feet tall, and he reached out and tugged some down around him, hiding his body. He had woven more blades of grass across his burlap tunic and into his hair. He hoped that, lying here, he vanished into the landscape. He had been traveling across these grasslands for three days now, daring not fly, not with firedrakes in the sky. The beasts had been scouring the land, flying overhead every hour.

Seeking me, he knew.

He was a weredragon, unpurified. The Temple had but two enemies: the Horde, a motley army of many nations that mustered across the sea, and the weredragons. Like him.

Only . . . that's not our name, he thought, lying on his belly among the grass. *Not our real name. I am Vir Requis.*

A mantis stared down at him from a blade of grass, its eyes green, and Cade thought of Domi's green eyes, of her body pressed against his, of her lips touching his ear. And mostly he thought of that word she had uttered, the word that would not leave him, that gave him strength even now.

Requiem.

To Domi, he had sensed, the word had been rich with memory, with understanding, a word that conjured lost tales, ancient cities, a world of magic. Cade didn't know more than what he had seen in Domi's eyes, but just the memory of those green eyes, bright and full of awe, infused the word with holiness and magic.

"Requiem," he whispered as the shadows of firedrakes flitted across him.

Only this time, unlike the past ten times, the firedrakes did not keep flying onward. Instead they circled above, their shadows darting across Cade again and again. He heard the paladins call to one another.

"There's a trail in the grass!" one shouted. His voice was still so distant Cade could barely make out the words.

Oh Spirit, he thought, fingers tingling.

He glanced above him. The three firedrakes were flying lower—a black dragon, a bronze one, and a gray one. Upon each beast's back rode a paladin. They were spiraling down toward the grasslands—toward him.

Cade grimaced, a cold iciness flooding him.

Claws thumped down into the grass around him, digging into the land. The smell of the firedrakes blasted his nostrils, scented of oil, fire, and raw meat. The beasts' scales clattered around him, and boots thumped into the grass as the paladins dismounted.

"The drakes smell something," said a paladin.

Another voice replied. "There! A lump in the grass. A man."

With shaky fingers, Cade tugged off his grassy tunic, remaining in his underclothes. He shook more grass out of his hair, rose to his feet, and feigned a yawn.

"Hullo, friends!" he called to the paladins, speaking through his yawn, and stretched out his arms. "Was just having a nap in the grass, I was. Old Barleyman from Ashgrove always said I nap too much, he did. Young Nappy, he'd call me, and—"

"Shut your mouth," said one paladin, a towering man—by the Spirit, he must have stood closer to seven feet than six—in white armor. He stepped closer to Cade. "Who are you?"

The two other paladins approached too. The three firedrakes, meanwhile, moved in slow circles around Cade, sniffing and snorting out smoke.

"I told you!" Cade said, affecting a farmer's accent. "Nappy's my name. Well, it's what they call me in Ashgrove when I walk by. I wander a lot. Ain't got me a home, so I sleep in the grass, and the sky's my blanket. I—"

"Show us your brand," the tall paladin demanded.

Wearing only his underpants, Cade turned around and displayed the back of his shoulder to the paladins. Like purified people, he carried a brand shaped as a tillvine blossom, marking him cured of dragon magic. He did not remember getting the mark. The fake brand had been on his shoulder when, as a baby, he had been left at Derin and Tisha's doorstep.

At the thought of his adoptive parents, grief flared through Cade. He saw their charred corpses again in his mind, saw Eliana's empty crib. The only family he had ever known—gone. The pain suddenly stung so badly his eyes dampened, even here with the paladins scrutinizing him.

"What do you think, Sir Actus?" said the tall paladin.

A shorter, wider man leaned close, peering at Cade's brand. "The blossom is too narrow. Crudely done. Might have been performed by a monk with poor tools. Might be a fake." The squat man turned his head. "Sir Stoen, bring the ilbane! We'll test him."

Cade forced himself to grin dumbly, even though his insides roiled and his heart seemed to sink into his pelvis. "What you paladins testing for? Looking for somebody?"

A leathery man with hard eyes, Sir Stoen pulled a bundle of ilbane from his firedrake's saddle and came walking forward with the leaves. The acrid stench and heat blasted Cade.

Oh bloody Spirit's beard . . .

Heart thudding against his ribs, Cade leaped into the air and shifted.

"Weredragon!" the tall paladin shouted.

Cade beat his wings three times, rose only several feet into the air, and spewed down dragonfire.

The flames crashed down into the grass and showered back up. The three paladins screamed and fell back, the flames washing over them. The three firedrakes screeched madly, strings of saliva quivering between their teeth, and leaped toward Cade.

He beat his wings mightily. He soared higher. Two firedrakes slammed into each other below him. The third blasted up dragonfire.

Cade swerved.

The flaming jet crashed against his tail, and he howled.

He kept flying, rising higher. Air roared around him. More dragonfire shrieked, and he swerved again, dodging a second jet. He flew upward in a straight line, soaring higher and higher toward the sun. When he glanced behind him, he saw only one firedrake pursuing; the other two stood on the grass, paladins leaping into their saddles.

Cade flipped over in the sky and swooped.

He roared, plummeting down toward the soaring firedrake. Both dragon and drake blasted out flames. The jets crashed together and exploded in an inferno. Cade kept swooping, passing through the fire, and bellowed.

He lashed his claws. He bit. He tasted blood. The firedrake crashed down below him, and Cade kept swooping.

The two other firedrakes took flight, singed paladins upon them.

Cade rained down all the dragonfire remaining in him.

The paladins burned. They screamed. Their armor heated, blazing red, and their skin peeled off, and their flesh melted. Still their firedrakes soared, burning beasts with mad eyes, blazing men in their saddles.

Cade flew between them, whipping his tail. One firedrake's claws cut deeply into his side, and Cade cried out, and his blood spilled.

He leveled off just before hitting the ground and flew eastward. The grasslands burned, the fire spreading across them. When he looked over his shoulder, he saw only one firedrake pursuing, a corpse in its saddle. The other two beasts lay in the burning grass, wounded or dead.

The creature chasing him was large and coppery, its wings longer than Cade's, its flight faster. It was gaining on Cade.

Spirit damn it, Cade cursed. The firedrake reached out its claws as it flew, grazing Cade's tail.

Cade sucked in breath and released his magic.

He tumbled down into the grass as a man.

The firedrake overshot him and kept charging forward. Before the beast realized what had happened, Cade shifted back into a dragon and roared out his flames.

The jet crashed against the firedrake. The beast screamed, an almost human sound. Cade leaped forth, landed on its back, and clawed madly, ripping out scales, and blood spilled.

The firedrake crashed down dead beneath him, slamming against the earth.

Cade flew a few more feet, then fell to the ground, panting and bleeding. He released his magic. For long moments he knelt in the grass, breathing raggedly. The fires still blazed behind him, and the corpses of the firedrakes and paladins burned.

Again, in only a few days, he had killed.

"I'm just a baker," he whispered. "Spirit, I'm just a baker. And now my family is gone. My village is gone. And the blood of men stains my hands."

But no. He was not just a baker. Not anymore.

"Requiem," he whispered. The word he did not understand. The word that gave him strength, courage. The memory of Domi's eyes. The prayer of his heart.

Requiem.

He kept walking. He kept moving eastward, to the city of Sanctus, to the library, to find help, to find the meaning of the word he whispered over and over.

MERCY

Mercy had to pause outside the gates of the Temple, take a deep breath, and steel herself.

Be calm, Mercy. You can do this. Her breath shuddered, her fingertips tingled, and the baby whimpered in her arms. *You are twenty-four years old, no longer a child.*

And yet, around her mother, Mercy always felt like a child. Even now, a grown woman and paladin, she felt like a foolish toddler whenever Beatrix turned those icy shards she called eyes upon her.

But she must know . . . know about the boy. Know that I failed.

Mercy's eyes burned, and she clenched her jaw. She raised her chin, sucked in air, and climbed the last few steps toward the Temple gates. A marble archway rose here, inlaid with pearls. Guards stood alongside, clad in white steel and gold, holding spears and shields. They bent the knee as Mercy walked between them. She stepped under the pearly archway, entering the heart of the Commonwealth.

The Cured Temple preached austerity, humility, and the nobility of poverty. Across the Commonwealth, the Temple's flock wore burlap, lived in clay huts, and owned no jewelry or fineries. They served the Spirit by living a life of modesty, feeding on simple bread and gruel, sleeping on hard cots, and devoting their souls to humble living.

Here, inside the Temple, Mercy beheld a world of endless splendor.

A polished mosaic covered the floor, a masterwork inlaid with gold, depicting stars and intricate designs. Marble columns rose in rows, engraved with figures of legendary paladins, and their capitals were gilded. Above the columns spread arches in blue, gold, and silver, painted with scenes from the Cured Book, depicting the miracles of the first druids to have healed the disease. The ceiling was perhaps more glorious than all; murals of clouds, stars, and firedrakes sprawled above in pastels, and between them stretched lines of platinum and sapphires. The precious metals and gemstones gleamed in the sunlight falling through tall, narrow windows.

All the treasures of the Commonwealth—its gold, its gems, its splendor—filled this single, holy heart of the empire. Some said that the Spirit himself dwelled not in the sky but within these very walls.

Mercy took another deep breath.

The Spirit and my mother.

When she spotted a servant walking by, Mercy snapped her fingers. The girl rushed toward her and knelt, head bowed.

"Take this baby to my chambers," Mercy said to the servant, handing Eliana over. "Find her a nursemaid and have her cleaned up and fed."

The servant nodded, took the baby, and rushed off. Mercy watched them leave, and a strange emptiness filled her. She had grown accustomed to the warmth of Eliana against her. Without the baby, Mercy felt naked, barren, too cold. She had felt like this before, she remembered. She had felt such loss once, such coldness, such—

No.

Mercy clenched her jaw.

No, that pain had happened in another lifetime, to another woman. Not to a strong, noble paladin.

She snorted. *I stole the babe as a hostage, not to become some surrogate mother.* As soon as she captured Cade, the babe would be useless; she would kill both at that time.

She walked on down the grand hall. Many priests and priestesses were walking back and forth here, and when they saw her—their future High Priestess—they turned toward her, knelt, and lowered their heads. Mercy walked between them. While those around her wore costly robes of white cotton and gold, her armor was still singed with dragonfire and coated with blood and ash.

Good, she thought. *Let them see that I'm a warrior, that I fight through fire and blood for the Spirit.*

She passed through the grand hall, under more archways, and through many other chambers. Each one was more wondrous than the one before. Statues of gold, silver, and marble rose everywhere, depicting ancient druids holding tillvine blossoms. Countless gemstones gleamed upon the ceiling like stars. Precious metals coiled upon the capitals of columns. She kept moving deeper and deeper into the Temple until no more sunlight reached her, and only the lights of lamps guided her way.

Finally, after what seemed like miles, she reached the doors of the inner sanctum—the Holy of Holies.

She had to pause and take another few deep breaths. All the splendor she had passed through—that had been only the skin. The true heart of what the Cured Temple meant, the very backbone of her faith, lay here beyond these oaken doors. And she knew that her mother would be waiting here. Mother was always here these days, lingering, growing older, praying . . . praying for the day they all awaited.

Mercy tightened her lips, opened the door, and entered the holy chamber.

As glittering and detailed as the outer chambers were, this place was simple, austere. While the outer chambers were only a hundred years old, this place was thousands of years old. Marble tiles formed the floor. Plain white bricks formed the round walls. And there, in the center of the chamber, it rose.

King's Column.

It rose hundreds of feet tall, passing through many stories, rising to the very top of the Temple. Mercy had to crane her head back to see its distant capital. It was ancient, but not a scratch marred it. The marble still seemed pure and smooth as if carved and polished yesterday.

Tears stung Mercy's eyes, and she whispered under her breath—whispered the old words of this place.

"As the leaves fall upon our marble tiles, as the breeze rustles the birches beyond our column, as the sun gilds the mountains above our halls—know, young child of the woods, you are home. You are home. Req—"

She bit down on that last form. A forbidden word. A word she dared not utter, not even here.

A figure, all in white, stood before the column. A white robe and hood hid the figure, and a voice rose from within the garment.

"Yes. That was their prayer. The prayer of the weredragons. Yet no more leaves fall here; the trees have been cut down. No more sun gilds the mountains; our walls shield its light. And no more children find their home here, and never more will the old name of this place be uttered."

Mercy nodded and lowered her head. "The name will never be uttered."

The figure turned toward her, revealing the face of a woman. High Priestess Beatrix looked much like her daughter. Her skin was pale, and only the first hints of wrinkles tugged at her mouth and eyes. Her eyes were cold blue shards, calculating, all-seeing. She pulled her hood back, revealing her head—half was shaven, and the other half sported a white braid. A tillvine blossom formed of silver and diamonds gleamed around her neck.

"We have a new prayer now, daughter." Beatrix raised her chin. "When all dragons fall, when all illness is cured, when all evil is cast out, the column will shatter. When the marble falls, the Spirit will descend. With every breath, with every heartbeat, with every hurt I heal, I pray for the Falling."

"I pray for the Falling," Mercy whispered.

Beatrix walked closer to her. Mercy was a tall woman, but Beatrix stood taller. Even in her armor, Mercy felt fragile by the High Priestess, a mere child. Her mother's eyes bored into her, emotionless, shining blue.

"I hear fear in your voice," Beatrix said, "not the devotion the Spirit demands from his followers. Why do you cower before me like a pup?"

Mercy bared her teeth and gripped the hilt of her sword for comfort. "There is a weredragon. A living weredragon."

The thinnest of smiles touched Beatrix's lips. "If there were no weredragons, daughter, King's Column would not be standing before us, and the Spirit would be flowing among us, cleansing the world of all pain. Yes, I know there are living weredragons. But unless you bring me their corpses, what use are your words?"

Mercy found that her jaw was shaking. She forced in air. "I saw one. A real one! A boy. A baker's boy. I . . . I chased him. He slew one of my men. I—"

"And you bring me his corpse?" Beatrix asked calmly.

Mercy lowered her head, eyes stinging. "I need more men. I left nine to seek him in the mountains, but I must fly out with a hundred more." She dared to raise her eyes and meet her mother's gaze. "I will uproot every tree, upturn every boulder, raze every hut to the ground, and I will find him."

Beatrix turned back toward the column. For a long time she did not speak. Finally a whisper left her throat, trembling with rage. "You saw a living weredragon . . . and you let him get away."

"He was flying too quickly, Mother! He was a vicious beast, a—"

"And what are firedrakes?" Beatrix shouted, spinning around. The calmness was gone from her face, and her eyes blazed with mad rage. "What are they if not vicious beasts? What are you if not a vicious beast?" Beatrix struck her, driving all her strength into the blow, nearly knocking Mercy down. "I thought you were a paladin, a trained warrior of the Spirit. And a baker's boy escapes you?" Beatrix barked a mirthless laugh. "And you dare return to me, stinking of the flight, begging me to aid you?"

Mercy wanted to shout back, to argue, to explain, but she only lowered her head. She stared at the floor. "Forgive me, Mother."

"No." Beatrix's voice shook. "You will not do this. You will not beg for forgiveness. It is not me you must beg forgiveness from but the Spirit himself. You will chastise yourself now, daughter. You will purify yourself in my presence."

Mercy sucked in breath. "I am no child!"

"You are nothing but a child!" Beatrix reached into her robes and pulled out a white lightning lash. "You have sinned before the Spirit. You must purify yourself now here, in this chamber, as he and I watch."

Mercy ground her teeth. She had not undergone this ritual for years, not since she'd been a rebellious youth. But she had no choice; Mother was High Priestess, her word as commanding as the Spirit's voice itself.

With stiff fingers, Mercy unstrapped her breastplate and let it clang to the floor. When she took the lash from her mother, its tip blazed into crackling life, sizzling, lightning blue.

Mercy slung it across her back, then grimaced and nearly screamed as the tip cracked against her back, hotter than fire, cutting through her tunic and burning her flesh.

"Again," Beatrix said. "Twenty times for the Spirit. And hail his name with every blow."

As Mercy slung the lash again and again, chastising and purifying herself, she prayed to the Spirit, but she thought of Cade. He had caused this. When she found him, he would be the one who hurt, who screamed. And she would find him. And she would break him. She swore this with every lash—to the Spirit and to herself.

CADE

He flew through the night, a golden dragon lost in clouds and shadows, lost in grief and memories.

The night was dark. Rainclouds hid the moon and stars, and rain pelted Cade's scales. He had not shifted into a dragon since battling the paladins, but he dared fly now, hidden in the storm. The raindrops ran down his scaly cheeks, and the pain clutched his chest. In the clouds around him, he kept seeing it again and again: the village burning, the smoke rising, the ashes of the dead falling like snow. And always they seemed to stare from within his memory: the blackened skulls of his adoptive parents, their jaws open in silent screams.

"You killed them, Mercy," Cade said into the rain. "You murdered them for no reason." His voice shook. "I'm going to find you someday. And I'll make you pay for your crime."

Just as real as the grief was the worry for Eliana. She was the only family Cade had left, and he didn't even know if she was alive or dead. Had he missed her small, frail body under the rubble? Had somebody smuggled her out of the village in time? Had the paladins themselves kidnapped her? Cade was fleeing now—fleeing for safety, for answers—but he swore that he would not rest while Eliana was missing.

"I'll find you, my sister. I swear it. I will never forget you."

Dawn rose ahead. A haze of silver glowed upon the horizon, and soon rays of golden light broke through the clouds, celestial columns. The rain gleamed like dew on cobwebs, and the storm scattered, the warmth of the sun casting off the clouds. And there in the east, Cade saw it—the sea. The sun rose from beyond the water, casting a gleaming trail all in gold and white toward the shore. There on the coast it lay, sending pale towers toward the sky: the port city of Sanctus.

"Answers," Cade whispered.

He shook off the raindrops, glided down, and landed in a field of grass, white stones, and heather a couple of miles away from the city. He released his magic, returning to human form. When he looked down at his body, Cade sighed. He had never been in such rough shape. His burlap tunic hung in tatters, barely covering his body. That body seemed just as tattered: a hundred scrapes, bruises, and welts covered it. He had barely eaten in days, only a handful of wild hares he had hunted in dragon form. He had barely drunk. Already he looked thinner than he'd ever been, and whenever he tried to clean the dirt off his face, he only seemed to smear more across it. If he wandered into the city, he thought, he was likely to be arrested as a drunk vagrant, tossed into some prison cell, and forgotten.

But he had to advance. What choice did he have? A life in the wilderness, hunting in the nights? Sooner or later, the paladins would catch him; he still saw firedrakes scouring the sky every hour or two. He supposed he could leave the Commonwealth entirely, travel south across the sea, and seek a home among the Horde—that gathering of motley tribes that had banded together in the lands of Terra, forming a crude army to fight the Temple. Yet if he traveled there, he'd learn nothing of Requiem, nothing of Eliana. No. He had to continue to the city of Sanctus, the eastern bastion of the Commonwealth.

Seek the library, Domi had said.

At the memory of Domi, Cade felt some of his anxiety fade. She was a wild beast. She served the paladins, a mount to Mercy herself. She had tied him down, preventing him from saving his family; perhaps Domi was as much to blame for their deaths as the paladins. And yet, when Domi had embraced him, had whispered "Requiem" into his ear, there had been no malice to her. She had blessed him with that word, giving him a precious gift, a holy prayer to cling to.

"Requiem," he whispered here in the field. He raised his chin. He would do as Domi had said. He would seek the library. He would find what this word meant.

Belly rumbling and tongue parched, he walked toward the city. As he drew closer, his eyes widened, and some of his hunger and grief faded under the sense of wonder.

"By the Spirit," he whispered.

He had never seen a settlement other than Favilla, his village. He had heard tales of cities, but he'd been unable to imagine any place so vast. He knew that Sanctus, the city before him, wasn't particularly large as far as cities go; it was certainly smaller than great metropolises like Nova Vita, the capital of the Commonwealth in the west. But even Sanctus, this humble seaside town, was larger than any place Cade had ever seen.

Hundreds of domed huts covered the landscape here, sloping down toward the sea. Several monasteries rose among them, their towers pale and thin, proxies of the Cured Temple that rose in Nova Vita in the west. A massive fortress, its four towers rising even taller than the monasteries' steeples, rose upon an outcrop of stone that stretched into the sea. Several firedrakes perched upon the fortress walls, and others circled above the city. Brigantines anchored in the port, tillvine blossoms painted on their sails. Here was the eastern border of the Commonwealth, and the distant Horde warriors were masters of the sea; this was not only a city of holiness but of war.

"There will be many paladins here," Cade said to himself. "Lovely."

His heart began to beat more rapidly. Had word of his escape reached this place already? Did the paladins in Sanctus know to seek him, to bring him back to Mercy? Cade could not simply saunter into this city, or he'd be caught like a fish leaping into a boat. If Mercy had any sense to her, she'd have sent a firedrake to every city within days of Favilla, warning her men to seek him.

Cade bit his lip, considering. There would be no sneaking into this city; high walls surrounded it, and he saw only one gateway. He glimpsed sunlight on armor—guards.

Guards who might be looking for me.

Cade looked around him. To his left, a copse of aspens grew upon a hill. Their leaves whispered in the wind, catching the sunlight, flashing back and forth like thousands of green coins jostled in a purse. Cade bit his lip.

"I must be crazy," he told himself. "But it might just work."

He approached the trees, plucked off a bunch of leaves, and sat on the ground. He spent a while meticulously tearing, biting, shaping. Finally he stuffed the leaves into his pocket, rose to his feet, and walked on.

Before long he reached the walls of Sanctus. The gates rose before him, several times his height. The oaken doors were opened, revealing a cobbled street lined with homes. A handful of guards stood here, wearing chainmail and white robes embroidered with tillvine blossoms.

"Toll's a copper coin," said one guard, a portly man with a scruffy face. He yawned. "Though you don't look like you got a copper on you."

Cade rummaged through his pockets. He had fled his village in a mad dash, leaving behind everything he owned. In his pocket, in addition to the leaves, he found a fallen button he'd been intending to sew back onto his coat, a purple snail's shell he had picked up a week ago, and thankfully a single copper coin. He handed the guard the coin, the last money he had. With another yawn, the guard stuffed the coin into his purse and gestured for Cade to enter the city.

With a sigh of relief, Cade stepped through the gates and onto the cobbled street.

His breath died when a hand grabbed him.

"Wait a moment," growled another guard, this one tall and gaunt. Holding Cade fast, he glared at the shorter, yawning guard. "You heard what the paladins said. They're looking for someone. A boy, they said. Brown hair like this one got." His voice dropped to an ominous whisper. "Uncured, they said."

Cade's heart burst into a gallop, and sweat trickled down his back, but he refused to show his fear.

"Here's my brand," Cade said, pulling down his tunic to reveal his shoulder. "I'm cured. Look, I carry around ilbane and everything." He pulled out the aspen leaves—the ones he had carefully shaped, tearing them into long, serrated forms. "I like to make tea with ilbane. I figure it keeps weredragons away too." He stuffed one of the mock ilbane leaves into his mouth, chewed, and forced himself to grin. "You want some?" He stretched out a muddy handful of the leaves toward the gaunt guard. "They're good to chew."

The guard cursed and shoved his hand. "Get away from me. You stink of sweat and shite, and you're covered in filth." He grumbled. "Go on, get out of my sight. And I warn you, if I hear you causing trouble in my city, I'll have your bones snapped and your corpse hung from the walls. Now go!"

For the first time since fleeing his home, Cade was thankful he hadn't bathed in a while; perhaps his smell, even more than his fake leaves, had saved his life. Leaving the guards, he walked into the city.

As he walked down the boulevard, he wanted to appear nonchalant, just another city dweller. But he couldn't help it. He walked with his head tilted back, mouth agape, eyes wide. By the Spirit, he had never imagined buildings could be this large! True, the domed huts were the same here as back home—modest dwellings for commoners, their windows round, their gardens barren of any flower. But among the huts rose buildings of splendor; they seemed to Cade like palaces.

A monastery rose ahead, its columns soaring, its dome coated with gleaming silver. Gargoyles shaped as dragons perched upon it, and statues of ancient druids guarded its doors. Priests and priestesses walked between the columns, their robes snowy white and trimmed with gold. The sounds of prayer rose from within, old chants praising the Spirit and calling for the Falling. Cade kept walking. Farther down the boulevard, he caught view of the city fortress; it was still distant, all the way by the sea, but even from here it seemed massive. Its towers soared, topped with perching firedrakes, and beyond the craggy walls spread the sea.

Cade shook his head wildly, looking away.

"The library," he muttered. "I must find the library."

For all their beauty, the monasteries and castles of the Temple were full of enemies, men and women who would hunt him for his magic. If he were to believe Domi, in the city library he would find aid.

He sighed.

I wish you were here, Domi, he thought.

The damn weredragon—no, she was called *Vir Requis*, like him—was probably an enemy too, the woman who had bound him, who had borne Mercy to hunt him. Yet by the Spirit, even now, Cade could not stop thinking how her body—slender yet shapely—had pressed against him, how her lips had touched his ear. He thought that even more than soaring steeples or blue seas, Domi's large green eyes, peering from between the tangles of her red hair, were beautiful.

For a second time, Cade had to shake his head wildly, clearing it of thoughts. He kept walking, exploring the city, seeking any building that looked like a library. He was walking down a narrow, cobbled road lined with clay huts when he froze and sucked in air.

A paladin was marching down the street, leading twenty soldiers.

Cade slinked to the edge of the road, his back to the huts. The paladin was an older man, his face lined, and the hair on his right side—which most paladins bleached as a sign of purity—looked naturally white. He wore the white plate armor of his order, while his men—simple soldiers of common blood—wore alabaster tunics over chainmail. As they marched down the street, a firedrake streamed above, its wings blasting air down onto the street.

An urge filled Cade to shift into a dragon, to fly away or fight, to blow fire. But he forced himself to kneel, as all commoners were required to do at the sight of paladins. He bowed his head. The procession walked before him, and Cade held his breath, praying to any god who'd listen for them to keep walking.

But the paladin halted. His soldiers slammed down their boots behind him, standing at attention. The aging holy warrior turned toward Cade.

Oh damn it. Cade swallowed, keeping his head low.

"You," barked the paladin, his voice scratchy. "I know every face in this city. I don't know you. Rise. Who are you?"

Cade rose to his feet. He knew he should keep his eyes lowered, keep showing subservience, but he couldn't help himself. Hatred for the Temple filled him, and he met the paladin's eyes. Those eyes were small, watery, and pale, but the gaze was piercing nonetheless. A white mustache topped the man's lip, the edge stained red, perhaps from wine.

"I'm a foreigner." Cade tried to keep his voice high, to sound even younger than his eighteen years. "From the farmlands. My parents died years ago, and I've come seeking the library. To. .

." He thought for a moment. "To read the holy books. I wish to study more about the Cured Temple and become a priest someday. I want to learn how to pray really hard to the Spirit, to help bring about the Falling."

Some of the intensity faded from the paladin's eyes. The aging man sighed. "It isn't the priests who'll bring about the Falling, son, but noble paladins who slay weredragons." He pointed down the road. "And the library's on the boardwalk, overlooking the sea. You'll find enough holy books there to pray from, if you can even read them."

Cade bowed his head. "Thank you, my lord."

Once the paladin and soldiers had moved down the road, Cade finally allowed himself to breathe. He kept walking down the streets, heading toward the sea, sparing no more glances at any tower or steeple. Finally he found himself upon a cobbled boardwalk that stretched along the coast. The sun shone overhead, and the water gleamed bluer than Mercy's eyes. Beyond the boardwalk spread a narrow beach, and several priests knelt in the sand, hands pressed together, praying to the Spirit. Fishermen stood upon a breakwater, their rods rising like great spider legs.

Cade turned toward the buildings that rose along the boardwalk. He saw a few homes, a humble monastery with a white dome, and several shops selling burlap, tillvine blossom amulets, and small glass bottles said to contain the Spirit's breath. Few people were here—a handful of commoners who hurried from a shop back to the streets, an elderly priest in white cotton, and a few soldiers in chainmail. Cade walked back and forth along the boardwalk, seeking the library, wondering if he was truly in the right place.

He had imagined the library to be a grand building, as grand as the castle or monasteries, a wonder of architecture serving thousands of readers. When he finally found the building, he realized he had passed by it twice, missing it. He paused outside the simple structure and stared, confused. The walls were built of pale, rough clay, rounded and supporting a domed roof. The door was simple wood. This place was barely larger than Cade's hut back home. If not for the piles of books balanced on the windowsills, he'd have never suspected this might be a library. Could this humble little house truly be the Library of Sanctus, the place Domi had spoken of in such awe?

He knocked on the door.

"Go away!" rose a voice from inside.

Cade blinked. He frowned. He knocked again.

"I said," rose the voice again, more irritated than before, "go away! We're closed."

Cade grumbled. He left the door, approached one of the windows, and stood on his tiptoes to stare inside. The chamber was small and stocked with many shelves and piles of books, more books than he'd ever seen in one place before. A figure sat at the back, shrouded in shadows, mountains of books hiding everything but a bit of golden hair.

"Hello!" Cade said. "Can you let me in?"

"No!" came the voice again—a woman's voice. "Now go away or I'll call the paladins. We always close for Saint Olora Day."

Cade returned to the door and knocked again. "Look, lady, I've been walking across the wilderness for days, I paid all the money I had to enter this city, and I've been looking for this library for hours. I'm not going away. So please, let me in."

An annoyed groan rose from inside. Footsteps thumped, and the door was yanked open.

Cade found himself staring at, he presumed, the librarian. She was a young woman, a little older than him—perhaps twenty years old. Her blond hair hung across her shoulder in a braid, and large, round spectacles perched upon her nose, magnifying her blue eyes. She wore tan leggings, a white shirt, and a blue vest with brass buttons; Cade had never seen anyone dressed so strangely. She carried a book in one hand, and she placed her second hand on her hip.

"Who are you, and what do you want?" she said, eyebrows pushed low.

Cade cleared his throat. "I'm looking for the Library of Sanctus."

"And I'm looking for some peace and quiet."

She tried to slam the door shut, but he placed his foot in the way. "I was told to come here. Can you at least let me inside so I—"

She cut him off with a sneeze. It was a sneeze so loud, so powerful, that her spectacles flew right off her nose. Cade had to catch them before they could fall to the floor.

"Give me those!" She grabbed them from him. "You almost broke them."

"*I* almost broke them?" He raised his eyebrows. "You're the one who sneezed."

"And you made me sneeze! I sneeze when I'm nervous." She sniffed, froze, and swallowed a second sneeze. "Oh, look what you've done. I suppose I'll be sneezing all over the place now." She sighed. "Fine. If you're going to keep arguing and blocking the door and making me ill, you might as well come inside." She grabbed his collar and tugged him. "Come on!"

She pulled him into the library and closed the door.

Dust floated in two beams of light that fell through the windows. The beams illuminated dozens of shelves that covered the walls and rose like a labyrinth across the chamber. Thousands of books were here, bound in leather. From what Cade could see, they all seemed to be prayer books of the Cured Temple. Many were copies of *The Book of Auberon*, the most ancient, perhaps the most holy of the Temple's texts; it recounted the first of the Cured, a druid who had healed many weredragons thousands of years ago. Other books were collections of prayers, guidebooks to achieve austerity, and books of sheet music for holy hymns. Tillvine blossoms were etched onto all the spines.

Cade frowned. Was this the right place? Why would Domi send him, a Vir Requis hunted by the Cured Temple, to a house full of books dedicated to eradicating his magic? Had this all been a cruel joke?

The librarian approached a wooden table. She slammed down the heavy book she carried, raising a shower of dust. Then she hopped up to sit on the tabletop, crossed her legs, and shoved her spectacles up her nose. Cade noticed that she had many freckles on that nose.

"Well?" she said, glaring. "Who are you and why are you here? Nobody but priests visit here."

"My name is C—" He cleared his throat. "Caleric. I've come seeking . . . books."

She rolled her eyes. "Really. Well, *Caleric*,"—she spoke that name as if it were the most ridiculous thing she'd ever heard—"if it's books you want, we have them all. All seven of them. In thousands of copies."

Cade looked around him, frowning. "You have only seven books?"

The librarian nodded. "All seven books the Cured Temple approves for public consumption. About a thousand copies of each one." She held out one dusty hand. "Fidelity the Librarian, at your service. As you can tell, my job here is very fulfilling."

Cade wasn't sure if she was mocking him, herself, or the Cured Temple. When he hesitated and didn't shake her hand, she groaned, rolled her eyes, and returned her hand to her side.

"Do you have any books about weredragons?" he asked, hoping to pry more information from her.

She raised her hands to the heavens. "They're all about weredragons! You do know what the Cured Temple is, don't you?

You know, only the religion that rules the entire Commonwealth and every facet of our lives. If you haven't noticed, the core tenants of the Cured Temple pretty much revolve around weredragons—specifically, how to hunt them down and kill them all."

Cade felt sick. He gulped. "Do you . . . do you believe all that? About, you know . . . hunting them?"

"What I believe," Fidelity said, "is that I'm tired, I'm hungry, and you're disturbing me. If you don't want a book, please *leave*." She hopped off the table, grabbed his arm, and began escorting him toward the exit.

"Wait," Cade said. When she tried shoving him out the door, he placed his hand against the wall, holding himself steady. "I was told to tell you something." He gulped. This could be incredibly stupid, he knew. But something about Fidelity's voice, clothes, and rolling eyes told him that she wasn't the strictest of the Cured Temple's adherents. "It's a word. A secret word."

She groaned. "If the word isn't 'goodbye' I don't want to hear it."

He gulped and leaned closer to her. He closed his eyes, and he whispered that word, putting the same awe, the same secret wonder into his voice as Domi had. He knew this word was a gift, not to be uttered lightly. A gift to be cherished, to be given only at the most important of times.

"Requiem."

His whisper lingered in the following silence.

Fidelity said nothing.

When Cade opened his eyes, he found her staring at him, mouth hanging open. Tears filled her blue eyes, magnified and gleaming behind the lenses of her spectacles.

"Who," she whispered, "taught you that word?"

"Her name is Domi. She—"

She grabbed his collar, tugged his face near hers, and sneered. "Did you hurt her? If you touched a hair on her head, I swear that—"

"If anything, she hurt me!" Cade said. "Fidelity, let me go. Domi is fine. She's unhurt. She—Spirit, I don't know who she is, or why she sent me here, but she told me to find you. To say that word to you. She said you can help me." His voice dropped to a whisper again. "She said you can help a Vir Requis."

Fidelity gasped, released him, and took a few steps back. "Show me." Her voice shook. "Just the beginning. Don't slam against the walls or anything. Just . . . show me something."

He nodded, summoned his magic, and began to shift.

Golden scales appeared upon his body. Wings sprouted from his back, and his tail hit the floor. When his body began to grow larger, to press against the bookshelves, he released his magic, returning to human form.

Fidelity stared at him silently, tears on her cheeks. She leaped toward him, and Cade gasped, sure she would attack him, slay him right here for being a weredragon. But instead she locked him in a crushing embrace, and she wept against his shoulder.

"There is another," she whispered, trembling against him, laughing through her tears. "By the stars, there is another." She sniffed, her eyes red and watery. "Come with me."

GEMINI

He grunted as he lay atop the naked woman, thrusting into her. The bed rattled, the headboard banging again and again against the wall. The woman moaned beneath Gemini, eyes shut, sweat beading on her brow. The priests had ordered her here, commanded her to lie with him, to bear his children. She was here for duty, not love. Yet as Gemini thrust into her again and again, she raised her hips, grinding against him.

She's enjoying this, Gemini thought, sweat trickling down his forehead. He snorted. They didn't always enjoy it. It was their holy task to bear his children, the reason they existed, and often as they lay beneath him, they prayed to the Spirit and clutched their tillvine amulets. Yet this one was a wild thing, crying out in pleasure, digging her fingernails down his back. That was good. If the women the priests delivered to his chamber enjoyed the holy bedding, it made for all the more fun.

Gemini kept at it, trying to savor it, to make it last. The woman beneath him was attractive enough—her hair golden, her lips full and pink, her hips well-rounded—yet as he bedded her, Gemini found his mind straying to the firedrakes in the pit far beneath this chamber.

Firedrakes! He sucked in air and closed his eyes. Magnificent creatures, the drakes. He brought to mind their roaring dragonfire, their beating wings, their muscles moving beneath their scaly skin. As he rode the woman beneath him, he pretended that he was riding a firedrake through the sky, a conqueror, a tamer of the beast.

Pyre. Yes, he liked that one, the female with scales of many colors. She was wild. She was intelligent. Rebellious. Just the sort of firedrake Gemini liked to tame. He envisioned himself riding her through the night, seeking out weredragons to slay, blasting fire into the darkness. He cried out, pretending to blast his own dragonfire.

Drenched with sweat, he rolled off the woman. He lay at her side, panting, spent.

She nestled against him, purring. "My paladin." She kissed his cheek. "I will bear you a great son. I swear to you. A great, pure son with no magic inside him, and he will grow to become a great warrior for the Spirit. A hunter of weredragons." She smiled. "Maybe our son will bring about the Falling."

Gemini snorted. "Unlikely. I've fathered over a hundred sons by now. What are the odds it'll be your whelp that slays the last weredragon?"

He saw the pain in her eyes. Why did they always insist on talking? The priests did not send them here for conversation. Gemini had been born without any dragon magic inside him, born already pure; he had never undergone purification with tillvine, had never needed to. Even his mother—High Priestess Beatrix—and his sister—Lady Mercy—had been born ill, had needed priests to burn out their dragon disease with tillvine.

But not me. I was born superior. Born clean.

Being a pureborn destined him—destined all those like him—to a life of breeding. The pureborn women, and there were a few in the city, bore child after child, pregnant throughout their fertile years. A full half of their babes were pureborns, going on to breed their own pure children. A pureborn man's life was a little busier. Every night, the priests sent another woman to his chamber. Sometimes, when Gemini had been taming firedrakes all day and his appetite was great, he demanded two or even three women to bed. Many of his babies now wailed across the capital—half of them pureborn like himself, destined to save the race, to wipe out the magic.

To bring about the Falling, Gemini thought.

He snorted again. He couldn't care less about the Falling. As far as he was concerned, it could happen long after his death. As long as King's Column stood and weredragons lived, the priests would keep sending him women.

Let the Falling never come, he thought.

"Get out," he said to the woman. "Get out and never come back. I never want to hear from you again. You will not ask for money for your child. You will not loiter around the Temple, asking me to be a father. Get out. Return to whatever hole the priests dragged you from." He shoved her. "And for the Spirit's sake, learn not to scream so loudly in bed. My ear still hurts."

When she had left, tears in her eyes, Gemini rose from his bed. He walked across the room, naked and sweaty. It was a large chamber, lavish, the floor tiles carved of marble inlaid with gold and silver, the walls bright with gemstones, the ceiling painted with scenes of crusty old druids. Ignoring these fineries—he couldn't care less about them—Gemini approached the mirror and stared at his reflection.

As always, he liked what he saw. A tall young man. Slender but well built, his cheekbones high, his lips thin. His eyes blue as sapphires, his hair bleached white as milk. He looked like the masculine version of his sister, a young man in his prime.

My children are blessed, he thought, *to inherit such good looks.*

He looked back at the bed, considering sleep, but he felt too hot, too excited after his time with the woman.

Firedrakes. Pyre.

He pulled on some clothes—a pair of breeches and a tunic of white cotton—and left his chamber. He wanted to see her again. His firedrake. The most special one among them. His pet.

"My Pyre," he whispered, walking down the corridors of gold, marble, and gems.

Ever since he'd been a child, born to the High Priestess herself, Gemini had been fascinated with firedrakes. They were creatures of such strength, some grace, such might. They had been born human—regular babes from human wombs—cursed with the dragon magic. But while most babes were cured, these babes . . . they were destined to a greater fate. Gemini had once watched the ceremony, enraptured as the babe had burned in the fire, how the tiny skeleton had fallen apart, revealing a shining egg—an egg to hatch a wild dragon, mindless, no human form to it, a weapon of the Temple.

But Pyre . . . she was not mindless. No. Gemini had been watching her all year, had seen a cleverness in her eyes, an almost human perception. The old caretaker had missed it, had thought Pyre just another beast to spoil with plenty of food, long flights in the open air, and even scratches behind the ear.

"Fool," Gemini spat.

Now you are mine, Pyre.

He stepped outside the Temple. He walked down the tunnel that delved beneath the palace, eager to see her, to ride her. Torches crackled at his sides, and he grabbed one and carried it with him. Bedding the woman had felt good, but nothing in the world felt as primal, as intoxicating, as erotic as riding a firedrake. The tunnel kept sloping downward, sinking deep into the belly of the earth. Finally, in the cold darkness, he reached the chamber where they slept. Many cells lined the walls, barred, revealing views of slumbering firedrakes. Gemini made his way toward the cell at the back—Pyre's cell.

As Gemini approached, he frowned. It seemed to him, in the dim light, that her cell was empty. He could not see her scales or hear her breathing. He marched closer, wondering if somebody had let the firedrake free.

He heard an inhalation of air. Scales clattered. Large green eyes opened and stared at him, and her snout pressed against the bars.

Gemini smiled.

"There you are."

He reached the cell and stood, admiring the firedrake. Such a special beast. Unlike the others whose scales were monochromatic, this firedrake had scales of many colors: reds, oranges, and yellows in all the shades of fire.

He grabbed the lever and tugged the portcullis open.

"Come, Pyre," he said. "To me."

She stepped out from the cell, scales clanking. Thin plumes of smoke rose from her nostrils. He stroked her snout.

"I'm sorry I hurt you," he said. "I had to teach you discipline. I hope I won't have to hurt you again. You're a special firedrake. You're mine. My pet. Come with me now. We will fly."

He led her through the tunnel and outside into the night. The Temple rose behind them, its crystal spikes rising toward the stars. The Square of the Spirit sprawled before them, a vast expanse, large enough for armies to muster on. Beyond spread the thousands of city homes and workshops, humble huts of clay. Gemini had still not outfitted Pyre with a new saddle; he mounted her and sat bareback.

"Fly, friend." He pressed his bare heels—he wore no spurs or even boots this night—into her tenderspots. "Fly with me."

She flew.

They soared high over the square, so high they soared above the Temple. They flew east across the city, and he looked down at the endless streets, this hive of ants. The stars shone above. One of the constellations, Gemini had always thought, looked a little like a firedrake, like Pyre. Flying here under the stars, he felt as if he rode the constellation itself.

They flew until they left the city behind, and then they glided over the wilderness, floating through endless black. Only him, her, the heat of their bodies pressed together, the fire in her maw. When Pyre tilted her scaly head, and he saw her face, it seemed to him that she was smiling, that she was at peace, that she enjoyed this flight as much as he did.

He kept riding her through the darkness, the wind in his hair and nostrils, rising and falling, and it seemed to him better than loving the woman, better than loving a thousand women. He was riding a firedrake, and he was free, bonded with her, a primal animal of the sky.

CADE

He walked between the bookshelves, following Fidelity through the small library. Cade had a million questions he wanted to ask. What was Requiem? Was Fidelity a Vir Requis too, and did she know others? Who was Domi and how had she known to send Cade here? Yet when he began to ask, Fidelity shook her head.

"Wait."

They reached a heavy oaken shelf topped with holy books bound in leather, tillvine blossoms upon their spines. Fidelity chose one book—a small collection of hymns—and tugged it downward. The entire shelf creaked and slid on secret hinges. Cade's eyes widened. The shelf slid three feet, revealing a trapdoor in the floor.

"I've heard that books can be portals to new places." Cade whistled. "I didn't know they meant it literally."

Fidelity gave him a wry smile. "Wonderful. Now come on. Follow me."

She tugged the trapdoor open, revealing a wooden staircase that led into a cellar. She stepped into the shadows and he followed, walking close behind. She grabbed a glass lamp which hung on the wall and stepped off the last step. Cade joined her, and his eyes widened further. He lost his breath.

"Welcome," Fidelity said, "to the true Library of Sanctus."

"*This*," Cade said, "is a library."

The chamber was no larger than the library aboveground—about the size of his humble bakery back home. But its wonder was not contained by its size. Oak shelves lined the walls, the wood lovingly carved and polished. Glass jars glowed on the top shelves, casting golden, white, and yellow lights, their fuel a mystery to Cade. An aromatic haze hung in the air. Many shelves held curiosities: model ships inside bottles, bowls of seashells and crystals, daggers with jeweled hilts, toy soldiers and dragons carved of polished stone, and counter-squares boards with pieces of ebony and silver.

But mostly the shelves held books, and these books were more wonderful than any of those aboveground. Some books were bound in richly worked leather, their spines displaying trees, stars, suns, and animals. Other books sported covers of precious metal inlaid with gems, while some covers were carved of olive wood. Many books lay open upon tables, displaying colorful illustrations of animals, mythological creatures, and grand cities with many towers. Cade glanced at the titles on the spines: *Old Songs of the Forest*, *Artifacts of Wizardry and Power*, *The True Dragons of Salvandos*, and many other titles hinting at wonder and arcane lore.

Here were no holy books. These were books the Cured Temple would burn—and would burn anyone who read them.

"It's wonderful," Cade whispered.

Fidelity nodded and her voice softened; she spoke with the same wistfulness, the same aura of holiness, that Domi had used when speaking the name of a forgotten kingdom. "The most wonderful place in the world. Here do we guard the world's knowledge."

A raspy, jarring sound rose ahead—somebody clearing his throat. An armchair scraped across the floor, creaking around to reveal a man. Cade started; he had thought Fidelity and he were alone.

With his tattered rags and muddy skin, Cade couldn't have made a pretty sight. The man in the armchair looked even worse. His garments were fine enough—sturdy trousers, a burlap shirt, even good leather boots—but his face made Cade take a step back. It looked, he thought, like the face of a barbarian from the depths of the wilderness, more the countenance of an ape than a man.

The brow was heavy, the jaw square and wide, the forehead deeply lined. It was a massive head, large and craggy like a boulder, the skin olive-toned. White stubble grew across this jagged face, almost thick enough to be called a beard, but the man's eyebrows were black as coal, thicker than most men's mustaches, and his hair was long and wild and darker than midnight, falling halfway down his back.

But worst of all were the eyes. Those eyes were sunken, blacker than pits of oil, and haunted like the dark windows of fallen castles. Here were the eyes of pain itself, the eyes of a man who had seen too much to bear, who carried too many memories, who bore bitterness and rage and grief that would crush men of lesser strength. Cade had stared into the eyes of cruelty before—Mercy's blue glare still haunted him—but this man's eyes were even worse. Cade knew that they would haunt him for the rest of his life.

The man cleared his throat again, an ugly sound. He spoke in a raspy voice. "The world's knowledge? Ha! The legends of a *lost* world." He placed a pipe in his mouth, inhaled deeply, then sputtered out smoke with a cough and curse. "A world gone. Forgotten. A world that can never return." He turned to stare at Fidelity. "Who is this, daughter? Why have you brought him here? Is he some boy you fancy? None may see these books. I will have to snap his neck."

Cade gasped—partly at the threat, partly at the realization that this grizzled, gruff man, leathery and foul and cruel, could have fathered the fair Fidelity with her large blue eyes, silky golden hair, and warm embraces.

"Father!" Fidelity said, her eyes lighting up. "Domi sent him. He's . . . oh, stars, he's one of us. A Vir Requis." She turned toward Cade, smiling. "Show him, Caleric!"

"My true name is Cade," he said softly, suddenly feeling awkward with father and daughter both staring at him. "Cade Baker. From a village called Favilla in the west, south of the mountains. I . . ." He gulped under the man's withering glare. "Never mind the geography for now."

Cade looked around him, mindful of the close quarters, and repeated his performance—summoning just enough magic to grow scales and the buds of wings, then returning to human form before he could topple the shelves around him.

For a long moment, Fidelity's father stared at him, eyes hard. He puffed on his pipe.

"So . . . my daughter has found another," he finally said, but no relief or joy filled his voice, only bitterness.

Cade shook his head. "Technically, I'm the one who found Fidelity. I traveled for days across the grasslands to get here, and—"

"I mean my other daughter." The man coughed. "Domi. She's the one who sent you here, isn't she?"

Cade's eyes widened. "Domi is . . ." He turned back toward Fidelity. "Your sister?"

The two looked nothing alike. Fidelity was all prim and proper, what with her spectacles, braided blond hair, and trim vest with its polished brass buttons. Domi had been a wild ragamuffin, her red hair all in tangles, her skinny body clad in rags, her face smeared with dirt.

Fidelity sighed. "Apparently she is, though I sometimes swear she was switched at birth. Domi is a wild little beast, an errant girl who made very, very bad choices in her life." She looked at Cade, tapping her chin. "At least she made one good choice sending you here. Probably didn't know what to make of you." She stepped closer and placed a hand on Cade's shoulder. "We'll help you. Korvin—my father—is perhaps a little gruff, but he's wise. He'll teach you. He'll—"

"—have no part in this," Korvin finished for her. He placed down his pipe, lifted his chair by the armrests, and spun it back around, turning its back to Cade and Fidelity. "We have no room here to shelter you. Leave this place, Cade Baker, and go home."

Cade gasped. "Go home?"

Even Fidelity seemed taken aback. "Father, I—"

"Silence!" Korvin roared, his voice echoing through the chamber. "Leave this place. Leave me. Go!"

Fidelity began walking toward the exit, but Cade stood still, feet planted firmly on the floor. "No."

Korvin leaped to his feet and stomped around the armchair. Cade had thought Korvin's face intimidating before; now it was terrifying. The man's leathery skin reddened, and his eyes blazed with black fire. His teeth ground. Cade felt the blood drain from his face; Korvin towered over him, an entire foot taller. The man's fists clenched, and veins rose along his arms and neck, and he seemed to Cade as beastly as a firedrake.

"Leave," Korvin said again, the words squeezing through his clenched jaw.

Cade knew that Korvin could crush him, could snap his bones within his gnarled fists. But still he would not budge.

"Cade," Fidelity said softly and placed her hand on his shoulder. "Let's go, maybe tomorrow we—"

"No," Cade again. He stood frozen. He refused to break eye contact with Korvin. "I have no home left. The paladins burned it down. The paladins killed my family—all because of my magic. I traveled for days across the wilderness, fighting the Cured Temple, slaying paladins with my dragonfire, all to find this place. To find answers." Though his insides trembled, Cade forced his voice to remain steady, forced himself to stare into Korvin's eyes. "You want me gone? You'll have to answer some questions first." He took a deep breath and thought of Domi's eyes, of her voice in his ear. "What is Requiem?"

The rage seemed to leave Korvin like air from a deflating bellows. The grizzled giant's shoulders stooped, his fists loosened, and he sighed deeply.

"A memory," Korvin said. "That is all. A forbidden memory we must not speak of."

"Yet a memory we preserve," Fidelity said, "while all others have forgotten." She glanced toward Korvin. "Father, can I show him?"

The man grunted. "No use for it. Pointless to fill the boy's head with dreams. Show him if you must." He trudged across the room, knocking Cade back, and approached the stairs. "But I'll hear none of it. I've had enough of damn stories and the damned dreams of fools."

With that, the burly man stomped up the stairs, leaving Fidelity and Cade alone in the cellar.

Finally Cade allowed himself to let down his guard. He shuddered and wiped his brow; his hand came back damp with sweat. "Blimey, Fidelity, has anyone ever told you that your old man is a right nightmare? I mean, I've seen firedrakes I'd prefer spending an afternoon with."

Fidelity lowered her head. "He does not mean to be cruel. He is hurt. Cruelty always springs from pain. He grieves."

"Grieves for what?" Cade stared up the staircase and shuddered again. "He didn't exactly seem mournful to me. More like he wanted to rip out my throat."

"He grieves for you," Fidelity said softly. "For me. For Domi. For any others who might exist. For my fallen mother. For Requiem." A tear streamed down her cheek. "We all grieve for Requiem."

"Fidelity, you and your father . . . you're Vir Requis too, aren't you?"

She nodded and closed her eyes. Before him, she began to shift. Sea-blue scales appeared upon her body, and indigo wings grew from her back. Before she could complete the transformation and knock down the bookshelves, she released the magic, returning to human form.

"My family and I are Vir Requis," she said. "We've only ever met two others. Until you, Cade. You are a great blessing."

His eyes stung. *Other Vir Requis. I'm not alone.*

"A blessing?" He lowered his head. "Your father didn't seem to think so."

"It is *because* he thinks so, *because* your existence is precious, that he rages . . . rages for what could have been, for what we lost. I will show you."

She took his hand and led him around the armchair. The seat faced a shelf where only one book stood, a single volume wrapped in leather; it seemed to Cade almost like a holy relic. Fidelity gingerly lifted the book and laid it on a table. On its leather cover appeared words in silver: *The Book of Requiem*.

"This book contains all the lost knowledge of a world that was," Fidelity said. "It is the heirloom of our people, a single book containing the lore of a nation." She smiled shakily. "For a hundred years, we few—we who carry the magic within us—have been guarding this book, guarding the hope that someday Requiem can return." She touched his arm. "It's all right, Cade. You can read it."

Cade opened the book and began to read . . . and his body began to shake.

His eyes dampened.

Visions of dragons, marble towers, great wars and great golden eras of peace, heroes, villains, dreams, hopes, kings and queens, pillars of fire, and—

His body trembled wildly. The room spun. He slammed the book shut with a shower of dust.

"It can't be," he whispered.

Fidelity watched him, a sad smile on her lips. "The world that was. The kingdom we once were." Her voice dropped to a whisper. "*Requiem.*"

Cade shook his head wildly. He paced the room, clenching and loosening his fists. "But there's only ever been the Cured Temple! Spirit, Fidelity! A world full of Vir Requis, flying free, no priests to purify us? Great cities of marble? Kings and queens stretching back five thousand years? Dragons—countless dragons—flying openly in the sky?" He laughed bitterly. "A fairy tale. Just a story from a book."

Finally some rage filled her eyes, and she grabbed his arms. "Don't you dare." She shook him. "Don't you dare call Requiem a fairy tale. Requiem was real. We stand now in the very land that once bore that name. Here, on this very coast, Requiem's hero Kyrie Eleison fought the tyrant Dies Irae. We are children of starlight, all of us, not this cruel 'Spirit' the Commonwealth worships. The Commonwealth." She snorted. "It's no more than a hundred years old. Its paladins burned all books and scrolls mentioning Requiem, smashed every statue of the old kings and queens, forbade anyone to even speak the name of our old kingdom. And now they try to purify us of our magic, to make King's Column fall. Do you know why it's even called King's Column?" Her fingers dug into Cade's arms, and she stared at him with blazing urgency. "It was King Aeternum himself, the founder of Requiem, who raised that column over four thousand years ago. The stars of the Draco constellation—our true gods— blessed it, and the stars' magic still keeps it standing. King's Column will stand so long as we do. And I vow to never let it fall."

Cade stared at her in silence for a moment, then breathed deeply. "I need to sit down."

He stumbled toward Korvin's armchair and sank into it. He leaned his head back and narrowed his eyes to slits. It felt like the world was crumbling around him. Derin and Tisha, the only parents he'd ever known, were dead. His village lay in ashes. His sister was missing. And now he learned that his entire reality—the Commonwealth and the Cured Temple that ruled it—were but a lie built upon the ruins of an ancient world . . . a world he was tied to by the very magic inside him.

"It's a lot to take in," Fidelity said. She sat on one of the seat's arms and placed a hand on Cade's shoulder.

He looked at her, feeling too weak to even lift his head off the backrest. "What do we do now?"

"What we've always been doing. Seeking others. Collecting our lore. Maintaining the memory of Requiem so that—"

Shouts rose from above, interrupting her.

"Where's the boy?" a man cried.

"Are you hiding the vermin?" shouted a woman.

The cries of a dozen people or more rose above. Cade heard armor chinking and swords drawn.

"They found me," Cade whispered. "The paladins found me."

"Cade!" the woman cried above. "Come to me, Cade!"

Lady Mercy, he knew.

He leaped to his feet, Fidelity cried out and grabbed *The Book of Requiem*, and the wrath and righteousness of the Cured Temple crashed into the library.

KORVIN

The damn boy ruined us!

Mercy, Paladin of the Cured, stormed into the library, and with her came several soldiers in chainmail. Outside the window, Korvin saw more paladins, and firedrakes screeched upon the boardwalk.

"Where's the boy?" Mercy shouted, blue eyes flashing. "He was seen entering this library." She stood nearly a foot shorter than Korvin, but she grabbed his collar and sneered at him. "Are you harboring a weredragon, old man?"

Korvin looked down at her. A young woman, her blue eyes mad with rage. Her lips sneering, revealing sharp white teeth. Half her head shaved. Her hair long and white, her stance proud, the stance of a lioness.

She looks so much like her mother.

It was Beatrix's strength and pride that had first drawn Korvin to her. That had made him love her. That had later made him flee.

You could have been my daughter, Mercy, Korvin thought, looking down at her. *Had I stayed with your mother, I could have been the one to father you. Yet now you are my enemy.*

He grabbed her wrist and, gently but firmly, pushed her hand back. "No weredragon here, my lady," he said gruffly. "This is a holy place. A place for priests, not brutes."

Her eyes flashed. She drew her sword. "Do you know who I am, old man?"

He stared into her eyes. "I know you well, Lady Mercy Deus, daughter of High Priestess Beatrix."

"And yet you do not kneel before me." She turned toward her men. "Search the library! Tear down every shelf! Find the boy."

Korvin dared not remove his eyes from Mercy. All around him, the soldiers rifled among the shelves.

"Lady Mercy!" one soldier cried out. "A trapdoor! Stairs leading below."

Korvin cursed himself. He cursed the boy. He cursed the Cured Temple and everyone in the Commonwealth. Ten thousand times, he had emerged from the cellar, had carefully closed the trapdoor and placed the bookshelf back above it, concealing the secrets within. Then one boy, one fool who'd come with questions, had shaken Korvin enough for him to leave the trapdoor uncovered.

"Search the cellar!" Mercy began. "Find the—"

Shouting hoarsely, Fidelity and Cade came charging out from the cellar, swinging bookshelves.

The slats of wood slammed into the soldier at the trapdoor, knocking him down.

Everything seemed to happen at once.

Mercy swung her sword at Korvin. As the blade flashed, his old soldier's instincts kicked in, the same instincts that had saved his hide so many times in the war against the Horde. He leaped back, grabbed a thick volume of *The Book of Auberon*, and raised it as a shield. Mercy's sword slammed into the book, cleaving it down to its back cover.

The dozen other soldiers stormed toward him, drawing their blades, and the firedrakes screeched outside, and Korvin saw it before him—saw it again, the same vision he had been struggling to forget since the night his wife had died.

Death.

Again, in his mind, the paladins stormed into his home—not this library but a hut far away. Again Beatrix, his spurned lover, was thrusting her sword again and again into Korvin's wife, laughing, laughing as she died, laughing as he roared in agony. Again Korvin was fleeing into the darkness with Fidelity and Domi, his wife's blood on his hands, his old lover's laughter echoing in his ears.

Beatrix had killed a person he loved. Korvin would not let her daughter do the same.

He roared and charged forward.

Mercy tried to raise her sword in time, but Korvin barreled into the paladin before she could. He was twice her age but also twice her size, and he knocked the paladin down. She fell, armor clanging, and cried out in pain. More soldiers thrust swords toward him. Korvin bellowed, shoved a shelf, and knocked a rain of books onto them.

"Fidelity! Boy! Run!" he cried. "Outside!"

The two were still swinging bookshelves like clubs. Korvin charged toward the door, roaring, and ducked under a soldier's swinging sword. He knocked the man down, but two more soldiers replaced him, blocking the door. Mercy leaped to her feet, growling, and raised her blade. More soldiers came racing into the library from outside, clad all in steel, bearing shields and swords.

Stars of Requiem, Korvin thought.

"Fidelity, boy!" he shouted. "Back against the wall!"

Fidelity's eyes widened. She understood. She grabbed Cade and, instead of trying to make her way toward the exit, pulled him toward the back wall.

Soldiers swung their swords at Korvin.

The blades clattered harmlessly against scales.

Trapped in the library within walls of clay, Korvin shifted into a dragon.

It had been many days since he had summoned the ancient magic of Requiem, and he had never summoned it indoors. He wasn't sure he wouldn't crush himself to death. Ignoring the fear, he let the magic keep flowing through him. Dark gray scales rose on his body, the color of charcoal, thick as armor. His horns slammed into the ceiling, and his tail knocked down soldiers. Bookshelves shattered and fell. A swipe of his claws sent Mercy sprawling. And still Korvin grew. His body slammed into more bookshelves, cracking them, crushing books. He grew larger still, pressing against the walls, and roared, letting the magic flow through him.

Soldiers screamed, crushed.

The walls cracked.

The ceiling caved in.

The library shattered around Korvin in a rain of clay and dust. In the cascading rubble, he roared and tossed his head, his cry rising to the sky, tearing across the city. A charcoal dragon, he beat his wings and soared, leaving the ruin. At his right side, more scales flashed: Fidelity rose there, a slender blue dragon. To his left, a new dragon soared; Cade flew there, his scales golden as dawn.

As the three dragons rose from the devastation, leaving the soldiers in the rubble, they found themselves in a sky full of firedrakes.

Ten or more flew above them. Another dozen took flight from the boardwalk. Paladins rode the great reptiles, holding lances and crossbows. On one of the beasts, Korvin saw Gemini Deus, second-born child of High Priestess Beatrix, a slender man with a hard, pale face much like Mercy's. The firedrakes screeched, formed a ring around the three Vir Requis, and blasted forth their fire.

Korvin roared and blew his flames. Fidelity and Cade soared with him, spewing dragonfire. The jets slammed together, and flames exploded above the city, a fireball like a collapsing sun, crashing down onto the ruined library, the huts around it, the boardwalk, even spreading forth to the beach. Townsfolk screamed and ran, the fire clinging to their tunics. Flames burned across Korvin, heating his scales, cracking them, blazing against his wings. He beat those wings, trying to rise higher, but saw only firedrakes. They swooped, claws outstretched. Their fangs gleamed. And Korvin knew he was going to die.

A figure of fire streamed above.

A firedrake with scales in all the colors of flame dived, roared, and crashed into the drakes around it, forming a path of open sky.

Domi—a roaring dragon, mount to Mercy herself, Korvin's own daughter—stared into his eyes.

"Go!" the fiery dragon whispered.

Before the firedrakes could regroup, Korvin soared through the swath of open sky. Fidelity and Cade soared behind him, breaking through the circling firedrakes. Korvin shot toward the clouds, then leveled off and streamed eastward, flying across the beach and over the open sea. Fidelity and Cade flew at his sides, singed, scales cracked and bleeding.

When Korvin looked over his shoulder, he saw Mercy screaming for Domi—she called her "Pyre," not knowing her secret—to bear her on her back. Other paladins climbed onto their own firedrakes. Soon thirty of the beasts regrouped, riders upon them, and flew in pursuit across the water.

Domi gave Korvin one last look.

Go, Father, her eyes said as Mercy climbed into her saddle.

Then the fiery dragon bellowed, no longer seeming a Vir Requis but a wild firedrake with no human soul, bearing Mercy on her back.

Korvin returned his eyes to the east. He saw nothing but water stretch into the horizon. He flew. Fidelity and Cade flew at his sides.

"You're wobbling, boy!" Korvin shouted. "Fly faster."

The young golden dragon growled. "I've never flown for this long before."

"It shows," Korvin cried over the wind. "Learn fast or you'll be feeding those firedrakes!"

The creatures screeched behind, streaming across the sea, Domi flying at their lead. On the firedrakes' backs, paladins raised crossbows and fired. The bolts shot across the sky. The three dragons scattered, dodging the projectiles.

"Surrender to me now, weredragons, if you want to live!" Mercy cried from Domi's back. "Fly onward and die!"

Korvin growled and kept flying, streaming over the water. Cade and Fidelity flew at his sides, wings beating mightily. The coast disappeared behind them. The crossbows fired again, and Korvin yowled as a bolt skimmed across his scales.

"Faster!" he shouted at Cade and his daughter. "Out of range!"

They flapped their wings with all their strength, shooting across the water. The firedrakes screeched behind. The beasts blew fire, and the jets blazed forward, just reaching Korvin's tail. The heat singed him, and he bellowed, spurred onward to extra speed. All land had now vanished, but the firedrakes showed no sign of slowing down.

And my own daughter flies among them, Korvin thought, feeling ill.

When he looked over his shoulder, he saw Domi there. She was staring at him. The sun began to set, gleaming upon her red and yellow scales; she seemed woven of fire, a great mount of flame for Lady Mercy, more phoenix than dragon.

She has always been like fire, Korvin thought. As a child, Fidelity had always been studious, serious, a little bookworm who stayed up late to read, pondered the meanings of histories, and collected every secret book she could on Requiem. Domi had been the opposite. While Fidelity read books about dragons,

Domi *became* a dragon as often as she could—in secret caves, in moonless nights, in empty fields, flying and dreaming of Requiem. Once the girl had even shifted in her sleep, becoming a dragon in her bed, shattering that bed and cracking the walls of their home.

Finally Domi could bear it no more. When she had turned sixteen, she had fled the library, vowing to never be human again. She vowed that if Requiem could not return, she would no longer live like this, keeping her dragon magic secret. Instead she would be a firedrake, her human form forever hidden.

But I never thought she'd serve Mercy herself, Korvin thought, feeling sick. *Mercy—the daughter of my old lover. The woman who hunts us. The woman who rides Domi now to slay me.*

Flying like this over the sea, he did not know who Domi was more loyal to—her family or her cruel mistress.

The sun vanished behind the horizon, and still the dragons flew, and still the firedrakes pursued. The three dragons managed to widen the gap, but only enough to emerge from the range of crossbows and flames, and then they could widen it no further. Ever the firedrakes flew behind them, their fire lighting the night, their screeches rolling across the sea. Korvin's lungs began to ache, his wings to blaze in protest, his tongue to droop. And still the distant firedrakes roared and gave chase.

"Where are we flying to?" Cade said, banking to fly closer to Korvin. "I see nothing but water! We can't fly like this forever."

"Feel free to stop and let the firedrakes catch you," Korvin said with a growl. "Be glad I don't slay you myself. Mercy followed you to the library."

The golden dragon lowered his head as he flew. "I'm sorry, Korvin. I don't know how they found me. I journeyed in secret. Nobody knew I was coming to the library. Nobody other than . . ." Cade's breath died. "Domi. Oh, Spirit, Domi knew!" A growl rose in him, and Cade began to spin in the sky, to fly back toward the firedrakes. "Domi told them! Domi told Mercy, her very own rider! She—"

"Stop your foolishness!" Korvin slammed into Cade with clattering scales, swiped his tail, and forced the young dragon to keep flying east, away from the firedrakes. "You will not speak of my daughter that way. Domi is perhaps wild, but she's loyal to Requiem. She let us escape."

Yet a chill filled Korvin, and the words tasted bitter in his mouth. Was Cade right? Had Domi truly led Mercy here?

No. No! It was impossible. Domi had knocked the firedrakes aside, letting them flee from the library. Domi bore Mercy as a mount, but only for the pleasure of flying, not for hunting her own kind.

She's good at heart, Korvin thought. *Isn't she?*

"We'll worry about how they found you later," Korvin finally said, glaring at Cade. "And if I discover you were clumsy, that you led the firedrakes to my door, I'm likely to burn you myself. For now, keep flying! Fly faster. Fly until we lose them."

Fidelity, who had flown a few dozen feet above them during the confrontation, glided down to fly at Cade's side. "Fly forward, Cade," the blue dragon said softly. "Fly with me."

They flew onward.

They flew for hours.

The moon rose and fell, and the sun emerged over the horizon again, and their wings ached, and their lungs felt ready to collapse. And still the firedrakes followed.

Korvin panted as he flew. More than anything, he wanted rest. How could the firedrakes still fly? How—

Crossbow bolts flew through the dawn. One slammed into his tail.

"Father, faster!" Fidelity cried, flying ahead.

"Speed up, old man!" Cade said.

Korvin grumbled. He was more than twice their age, but he refused to fly slower. He caught up with them, putting more distance between himself and the pursuit, but every flap of his wings shot agony through him. Fidelity and Cade were weary too; he saw the weak puffs of smoke from their nostrils, the glassiness to their eyes. Still the sea stretched on, no sight of land ahead. Still the firedrakes followed.

"Shift into humans," Korvin said. "Both of you."

Cade tilted his scaly head. "And what, swim?"

"You go swim and rid the world of your foolishness! Fidelity can ride on me alone."

Cade blinked. "I don't understand."

"I think I do," Fidelity said. The blue dragon rose a few feet higher, coming to fly directly above Korvin. She lowered herself, letting her belly skim Korvin's back, then released her magic. When Korvin looked over his shoulder, he saw Fidelity back in human form. Her golden braid flew in the wind, her spectacles slid down her nose, and she clutched a copy of *The Book of Requiem* in her arms.

"How do you even shift into a dragon and still keep the book?" Cade said, still flying beside them. "I've never been able to shift with objects before, not without them clattering to the floor."

Fidelity laughed. "The same way you can shift with your clothes. Your clothes have become a part of you, a second skin. Anything that's a part of you shifts with you, dead or alive. Your hair and fingernails shift with you for the same reason." She smiled. "This book is a part of me. Now ride with me!"

The golden dragon nodded, swerved to fly above Korvin, and released his magic. He thumped down onto Korvin's scaly back and nearly slid off; Fidelity had to grab him. Soon the two were seated together, their legs straddling him. The extra weight shot more pain through him, but Korvin forced himself to keep flying, ever mindful of the firedrakes screeching behind him.

"Now sleep," he told them. "Regain your strength. Then Cade will take a turn with us on his back." A crooked grin twisted his snout. "The firedrakes can't fly forever. Taking shifts, we can fly for a very long time."

"Until thirst kills us," Cade said, then yawned and lay down on Korvin's back. Fidelity joined him and closed her eyes.

As the two slept, Korvin forced himself to keep flying. If before the pain had been bad, now—with the extra weight—Korvin wanted to plunge down into the sea and drown.

Ignore pain, he told himself, flapping his aching old wings again and again. *Pain is irrelevant. You will fly through the pain. It cannot stop you.*

He had felt worse pain in his life: in the war against the Horde as the enemy's spears had torn into him; in his youth, loving Beatrix, learning of her madness, fleeing her rage; in his adulthood, meeting Beatrix again, crying out in grief as the High Priestess stabbed Korvin's wife, her revenge for her spurned love.

And yet I've always kept going, Korvin thought. *For my daughters. For the memory of Requiem.*

And so he ignored the pain. Pain could not stop him. Pain existed only in the mind. He kept flying.

After what felt like hours, the firedrakes were still pursuing. Still the paladins' armor glinted in the distance, and still Korvin heard the cries of their mounts.

"Wake up," Korvin finally said. "Cade, your turn. Shift!"

The young man rose upon Korvin's back, leaped into the air, and fell through the sky. Scales rose across him, wings burst out from his back, and he flew back up. Korvin flew above the young dragon, letting Fidelity dismount him and climb onto Cade's scaly back. Finally Korvin released his magic with a groan, landing on the golden dragon too.

He sprawled out, facedown against Cade's scales. He slept.

They flew on.

The firedrakes pursued.

Still the water spread in all directions, no sign of land.

Hours later, when Fidelity flew as a blue dragon, bearing Cade and Korvin in human forms, the firedrakes finally cried out in rage and turned back.

Cade rose to his feet on Fidelity's scaly blue back, shook his fists at the fleeing firedrakes, and laughed.

"Yeah, get lost!" He laughed. "You can't outfly Vir Requis! You—"

He wavered on Fidelity's back and nearly fell down to the sea.

Korvin grabbed him and pulled him back to a sitting position. "Sit down and shut up." He stared into the east, heart sinking. "Our troubles aren't over yet."

Cade laughed. "Mine are. We escaped them. We—"

Shrieks rose from the east, interrupting him. Cade turned toward the sound and his chest deflated. Korvin cursed, leaped off Fidelity's back, and shifted into a dragon. Cade joined him, and the three dragons flew together, flames crackling in their maws.

"What are they?" Cade cried out.

Ten great beasts, even larger than dragons, were flying from the east. They had the bodies of lions, but their heads were the heads of great eagles, and feathered wings sprouted from their backs. Their cries pealed across the ocean. Riders sat on their backs, bare-chested, their skin tanned bronze and their platinum hair streaming like banners, and they bore bows and arrows. They all cried out for battle.

"Griffins," Korvin said grimly, his belly twisting. "Warriors of the Horde."

CADE

The griffins swarmed around them in the sky, a ring of fur and feathers. Cade gulped.

"By the Spirit," he said, whipping his head from side to side. His scales chinked, and his wings blasted the sea below with air.

The griffins were massive beasts, even larger than dragons. Their lion bodies were slick yet muscular, their hides covered in thick tan fur. Their wings spread out, brilliantly white, the outer feathers as long as men. Their beaks, bright yellow, were as large as dragon snouts and looked even sharper than dragon teeth.

On the griffins' backs rode the strangest men and women Cade had ever seen. They were certainly not men of the Commonwealth; back home, people tended to have pale skin in the north and west, olive skin in the east and south. Many, like Cade, had light brown hair and hazel eyes. But these griffin riders had deeply tanned, golden skin, blue eyes that shone like sapphires, and long platinum hair that reminded Cade of strands of sunlight. Their limbs were long, their faces noble. Men rode bare-chested, while women wore small vests strewn with many beads. They all carried spears and bows, and they cried out lilting battle cries. A few nocked arrows and tugged back the bowstrings.

Cade sneered, drew fire into his mouth, and prepared to blow a searing jet.

"Stop that, boy!" Korvin said, and a slap from the gray dragon's tail knocked the fire out of Cade's mouth. Korvin turned toward the griffins. "Warriors of the Horde! We mean you no harm. We do not serve the Commonwealth but flee it."

The griffins flew everywhere, left and right, above and below, encircling the three dragons. One rider seemed to lead the group; he wore a golden amulet shaped as five serpents coiled together, and his griffin wore a steel helmet emblazoned with the same sigil. He looked different than the other riders, probably of a different ethnicity. While the other riders were tall and platinum-haired, this man was shorter and thickset, his skin olive-toned, his eyes green, his hair and beard jet black.

"What are firedrakes from the Commonwealth doing in our waters?" the bearded man cried out. "This is the territory of the Horde. Turn back now, firedrakes! Back! We do not seek war with the Cured Temple."

Cade snorted and rolled his eyes. "Firedrakes? We're not firedrakes. Spirit's beard. We were fleeing the firedrakes!"

To demonstrate, Cade released his magic.

He fell through the sky, a human again.

As griffin riders gasped, Cade summoned his magic again, turned back into a dragon, and flew up to face the bearded griffin rider.

"You're Vir Requis," the man said, wonder in his voice.

Korvin flew up closer, eyes narrowed, smoke rising from his nostrils. "You've seen our kind before."

The man nodded upon his griffin. "I am Belas, a captain of the Horde. Come with me. You will find rest, water, and food . . . and then you will answer my questions."

The bearded captain waved his arm, then turned and began to fly back eastward. The other griffins followed, and the three dragons flew among them. The water turned a light blue and turquoise below; the sea here was shallower, warmer, full of life. After flying for another hour or two, Cade gasped.

"Islands!" he said. "Look, Fidelity. Islands!"

Flying at his side as a blue dragon, Fidelity frowned at him. "Yes, Cade. Just because I wear spectacles in human form doesn't mean my dragons eyes can't see . . ." She narrowed her eyes, staring forward, and puffed smoke out from her nostrils. "What islands?"

Cade groaned. "You really need a pair of giant dragon spectacles too, I think. Islands ahead! Big ones. Well, three big ones and a bunch of little ones, all covered in trees."

Fidelity squinted, then stared at him. "Are you pulling my leg?"

Korvin flew up to them. "He speaks truth. Here before us—and you'll see them soon as we fly closer, Fidelity—are the islands of Old Leonis, the fallen realm of griffins."

Fidelity gasped. "Leonis! I read about Leonis. Thousands of years ago, griffins ruled this land. They fought a war with Requiem, and many died on both sides. I hadn't thought any griffins still lived. My books said that General Cadigus, a cruel Vir Requis who betrayed Requiem, slew them all."

"Well, we're flying among a bunch of them now," Cade said. "You can see them, right?"

She glowered and slapped him with her tail. "I can see them fine, Cade, and I can see you well enough to slap you senseless, so watch your tongue. Obviously some griffins survived, and obviously they serve the Horde now." She sighed wistfully. "I've always wanted to see the Horde."

Korvin grunted. "You wouldn't speak so wistfully of the Horde if you had faced them in war, as I have. The islands of Leonis are now an outpost of the Horde, and their denizens might hold Vir Requis little love. Be on guard."

They flew closer, and soon even Fidelity saw the islands and gasped with wonder. Cliffs of chalk and limestone soared from the water, leading to peaks lush with trees. Countless birds flew over these patches of rainforest, and several griffins circled higher above, riders upon their backs. A flag unfurled on a stone mountaintop on the largest island, displaying five serpents intertwined.

Flying on his griffin, Belas led them to this island, and Cade saw that its crest was flat, and that a great square of land had been carved out from the forest. Something halfway between a town and a military camp rose here. Flying above, Cade saw hundreds of wooden huts, palisades of sharpened logs, and even a brick fortress upon an earthen motte. Thousands of people bustled about, and they seemed to have come from many lands: some had golden skin and platinum hair, others were pale and dressed in cotton, and some people wore white robes over olive skin. Several griffins stood in the field, cawing and feeding from troughs.

The dragons and their griffin companions began to descend, moving closer to the camp. A shimmer of light caught Cade's eye, and he gasped.

"Fidelity, look!" he said. "Can you see them?"

She stared down, squinting. "What? I can only see smudges."

"They're . . . dragons. I think. I'm not sure. They're not like us."

Several long, reptilian creatures were moving about the camp, hovering several feet above the ground. They had no wings, and Cade couldn't figure out how they floated. They were longer than dragons, he saw—probably a good hundred feet along—but narrow. Scales covered them, shimmering as if made from precious metals. They reminded Cade of snakes swimming upon water. Their eyes were like crystal orbs, and beards hung from their chins.

When Cade described them to Fidelity—she could see no more than the shimmer of their scales—she gasped. "Those are salvanae!" she said. "Mythical true dragons from the west! Unlike Vir Requis, they have no human forms."

"Like firedrakes?" Cade asked.

She shook her head, scattering the smoke that rose from her mouth. "No. Firedrakes used to have human forms; they were Vir Requis once . . . before the Temple broke them. Salvanae are very ancient beings, very wise. In the old days, we Vir Requis called them true dragons. But my books said they all died out centuries ago."

"So much for your books," Cade said. "Griffins and sylvanis—"

"Salvanae," she corrected him.

"—and salvanae. In one day." He gave her a crooked grin. "Maybe flying out into the real world will teach you more than any of those dusty old books."

Korvin flew between them and sneered at Cade. "Dusty old books we cherished. Books that we lost because of you. Now silence, boy."

Belas and his griffins dived down to a clearing in the camp—a circle of earth between many huts. The three Vir Requis glided down with them, and they all landed, claws and talons raising clouds of dust. The griffin riders dismounted and their mounts flew off, and the Vir Requis released their magic, returning to human form.

Cade stared around him with wide eyes.

"I'm standing right in the Horde," he whispered in awe.

Countless people moved all around him. Soldiers in bronze breastplates, the metal forged to mimic their muscles, dueled in the dirt, swords clanging. Other men worked at skinning wild boars, slicing up the meat, and tanning the leather. A few blacksmiths worked in the open, hammering on spearheads and swords. Children scampered underfoot, laughing. A burly giant of a man lumbered by, covered in hair, drinking from a tankard and grumbling; Cade barely reached the man's chest. Scales flashed as a salvana coiled by, hovering several feet aboveground. Cade had to leap back to avoid the true dragon knocking him down. The wooden huts rose all around, and archers stood on the stone fortress a few hundred yards away. Farther back, surrounding the camp like walls, the forest swayed, rich with the song of birds, the call of monkeys, and the rustling of leaves.

"I never imagined so many strange people," Cade whispered. "The Horde is massive."

Belas scratched his beard and barked a laugh. "This is only an outpost, son. The true Horde in the south is hundreds of times the size. We are but guardians of the sea, protectors of—"

A shout rose behind them, interrupting him.

"Stars damn it, you maggoty sack of puke! You owe me five conches. Five! I beat you fair and square, and if you don't pay up, I'm going to shove my hand down your throat, grab your bollocks, and tug them out of your mouth."

Cade turned around, and his eyes widened so much he thought they might pop out.

A woman stood a few yards away, clutching the collar of a young, terrified-looking man. She shook him wildly as she shouted. She seemed to be about a dozen years older than Cade, and a couple of inches taller too. She wore brown trousers, tall black boots, and a tan vest. Her yellow hair was short—just long enough to fall over her ears—and damp with sweat. Her brown eyes flashed as she shook the man.

"You cheated, Amity!" said the man in her grip, struggling to shake her off. "Nobody got such luck with dice, and—"

"Pay now," Amity said, "or I'll dump your flea-ridden corpse into the sea. I—"

"Amity!" Belas turned toward her, his face reddening. "Leave him alone."

The tall, golden-haired woman spun toward Belas, still holding the young man's collar. "Belas! Your son here lost a game of dice, and if the damn goat-shagger doesn't pay, I—"

"Did you cheat?" Belas demanded.

Amity's cheeks flushed. She loosened her grip on the young man. "Well, of course I did." She spat. "Everyone cheats at dice, and—"

"Then let him go," Belas said, "and get your arse over here. We got guests."

Amity groaned, shoved the young man away, and gave his backside a swift kick as he fled the scene. She spat again and wiped her hands against her pants.

"I don't care about no guests." She glared at Belas. "And if you talk about my arse again, I'm going to chop off your manhood and wear it around my neck on a chain."

Cade watched all this with wide eyes. He leaned toward Fidelity—the young librarian was blushing—and whispered into her ear, "Blimey, I love the way they talk here. I'd take the Horde over prim priests and paladins any day."

Amity stomped toward them, grumbling under her breath, and swiped back locks of damp hair from her forehead. She stared at Korvin, then at Fidelity, and finally at Cade. She let her gaze linger on him, and a crooked smile touched her lips.

"What's a matter, kid?" she said. "Your jaw's hanging almost down to your bollocks."

Cade gulped and quickly closed his mouth. He tried to feign nonchalance. "I'm not used to seeing . . ." Women as tall and foul-mouthed? Women as dangerously and intoxicatingly gorgeous? Women who made his blood boil? ". . . griffins," he finished lamely.

Belas stepped forward, blessedly interrupting his embarrassment. "Amity," the bearded captain said, "we found the three flying over the sea toward us. Fleeing the firedrakes. Yes, flying. They were dragons when we found them." He lowered his voice. "Vir Requis."

Amity whipped her head toward him, then back to Korvin, Cade, and Fidelity.

"Bollocks," she said and spat, but Cade noticed that her breath had quickened, that her fingers were trembling.

Belas snorted. "If you hadn't been beating the shite out of my boy, you'd have seen them fly in." He turned toward the three. "A little display?"

Korvin, who had remained silent until now, let out a grumble. "We're not performing monkeys. Belas, I thank you for leading us here. Now if you will shelter us, we. . ."

The gruff man's voice died.

Cade's jaw hung loose once more.

Even Fidelity gasped, covered her mouth, and had to rub her spectacles on her shirt and stare again.

Standing before them, Amity shifted into a red dragon.

"So," the dragon said, fire crackling inside her mouth, "you three want to prove to me that I'm not alone in the world?"

"Another Vir Requis," Fidelity whispered, tears in her eyes.

Cade shifted first, a little embarrassed to find himself shorter than Amity even in dragon form. Korvin and Fidelity followed. The dragons stood together in the camp, staring at one another silently.

It was Cade who broke the silence, speaking the only word he could, the only word that mattered.

"Requiem."

Amity grinned toothily and slapped him with her tail. "You got it, kid."

DOMI

Domi had never been more exhausted in her life. As she flew westward across the sea, heading back toward the Commonwealth, she thought she would lose her magic, plunge down into the water, and drown with Mercy on her back.

Perhaps I should fall and take her down with me, she thought.

All around them, firedrakes were flying back home, panting, weary, dipping in the sky and rising only as their paladins spurred them onward. She spotted Lord Gemini, Mercy's younger brother, riding a burly copper firedrake called Felesar. The paladin whipped the firedrake again and again as it huffed.

One firedrake finally fell and crashed into the sea, dead with exhaustion. Another firedrake had to dive, lift the floundering paladin, and bear two men on its back. Domi envied the fallen firedrake. She too wanted to lie under the sea, to let the pain end.

Mercy kept shouting on her back, digging her spurs again and again into Domi's tenderspots. When Domi could not fly faster, the paladin swung her lightning lash, and pain exploded across Domi, urging her onward. The paladin was wrathful, perhaps more than she'd ever been.

"You let them escape, you miserable little beast," Mercy shouted, digging and twisting her spurs in Domi's flesh. "We had the weredragons surrounded at the library, and you let them go."

The whip hit Domi again, crackling with lightning, and she yowled.

Domi closed her eyes as she flew, bringing back the memory. Flying over the library with the other firedrakes, she had been so afraid. She had been sure that Mercy would slay her father, her sister, and Cade. The foolish boy had been spotted. He had left the corpses of paladins on his way to the city. He had spoken to paladins in the city itself, leaving a trail Mercy had easily followed . . . riding Domi all the while.

I had to knock the other firedrakes aside, Domi thought. *I had to. I had to let them escape.*

She wondered if Mercy knew that Domi had done so on purpose, if she suspected that Domi was not simply a clumsy firedrake, a mindless reptile.

"You stupid, sniveling lizard!" Mercy shouted, whipping her again.

Good. Let her think I'm stupid, nothing but a stupid firedrake. May she never learn the truth . . . that I let my own family escape on purpose. That I too am Vir Requis. That I hide a human soul deep under my scales.

Domi lowered her head. What had her father and sister thought? Had they realized that she had tried to protect them, or did they just see her as a traitor, the Vir Requis who served the paladins who hunt her very people?

"Faster!" Mercy cried, digging her spurs again, and Domi flew on.

Domi did not think she could make it to the shore alive, yet finally the firedrakes saw the coast of the Commonwealth again. The towers and steeples of Sanctus rose ahead. With their last breaths, the firedrakes made for the city. They flew over the warships in the port, nearly crashing into their masts, and finally made it past the piers to the boardwalk. Here the firedrakes crashed down onto the cobblestones—not far from the ruined library—and collapsed.

Mercy leaped off the saddle, turned toward the port, and began shouting orders.

"Ships! All warships—ready to sail!"

Sailors ran forth, and Mercy shouted, and rowboats began approaching from the warships. As the boardwalk bustled, Domi and the other firedrakes lay sprawled across the cobblestones, breathing raggedly. Domi was so weary it took all her effort to cling to her dragon magic; she felt close to losing that magic to her exhaustion, returning to human form here in the paladins' sight.

Just cling on a little longer, she told herself. *Just breathe the next few breaths.*

She lay on the searing-hot cobblestones, the sun baking her, watching the preparations. Troops from the city fortress came marching onto the boardwalk; there they entered rowboats and oared toward several warships that anchored in the port. The ships were massive brigantines, large enough to hold hundreds of men each. Mercy chose a group of firedrakes—Domi breathed out in relief when she wasn't chosen—to fly over and land on the ships' decks.

"We will find the weredragons, and we will butcher them!" Mercy was shouting from the boardwalk. "We will skin them alive and make trophies of their skulls!"

As soldiers cheered, rowing toward the brigantines, Domi closed her eyes.

I can't do this anymore, she thought. *I can't keep serving them.*

If she escaped, Domi knew that she would not live long. Wild firedrakes rarely lived for more than a year or two; the Cured Temple mercilessly hunted and butchered any firedrakes who escaped captivity. And Domi did not even want to consider hiding as a human; what kind of life was that, living as a weak girl, crushed under the Temple's heel? A despair began to grow in her. Perhaps she could escape overseas, join the Horde, find a home there—though stories whispered that the Horde was even more ruthless than the Temple, that its warriors drank the blood of children and tortured women for sport. Perhaps there was no home for Domi in the world anymore. Perhaps all she could do was rise as a dragon, blow her fire, and burn as many of these paladins and soldiers as she could before they shot her down.

A hand touched her snout, and a voice spoke softly. "Dearest Pyre . . . you're exhausted."

Domi opened her eyes to see Gemini staring at her. The firedrake he had ridden during the chase, old Felesar, now stood upon the deck of a warship, prepared to sail out east on a new hunt. It looked like Gemini was staying behind this time.

Domi grunted and blasted out a puff of smoke.

"Little Pyre." Gemini stroked her. "I rode Felesar over the sea, but as I rode him, I thought of you. I pretended that I was the one straddling you, digging my spurs into your tenderspots, whipping you onward with my lash. You are the finest of firedrakes." He knelt, stared into her eyes, and planted a kiss upon her snout. "I love you, my Pyre."

Domi gave a little gurgle. She stared at the young man—his high cheekbones, his strange blue eyes, the white hair that grew from the right side of his head. She could not understand this paladin, second born of the High Priestess. Sometimes he beat her, shouted at her, called her worthless, yet at other times he seemed to love her as a man loves a pet—even as a man loves a woman. She was tempted to snap her jaws and rip him apart, confused by his cruelty and tenderness.

"Brother!" Mercy's cry rose nearby. Domi turned to see the heiress marching forward, face suffused with rage. "This miserable beast has outlived her usefulness. I'll be taking Felesar to be my new mount. I want Pyre put down."

Gemini straightened and bared his teeth at his older sister. "Like the Abyss! Pyre is the smartest firedrake we have. I'll put you down instead."

Domi had thought Mercy had looked mad before. Now the paladin's face twisted into a rabid, monstrous mask of rage, her lips peeling back to reveal teeth and gums. She seemed almost inhuman, almost as if she herself were becoming a dragon. With a howl, Mercy swung her arm, backhanding Gemini. The younger paladin yelped.

"You will put her down, Gemini! But not before you hurt her. You will whip her to death, slowly, over days, as I sail to find the weredragons. I expect a coat of her scales when I return. If I learn from the soldiers that you gave Pyre a merciful death, I will have you tortured."

With that, Mercy spun on her heel, marched toward a rowboat, and entered the vessel with a dozen soldiers. They rowed toward a warship, and soon the great brigantines were raising their anchors, many men and firedrakes upon them, and sailing east.

Domi turned her head back toward Gemini. He stared at her, his cheek red and lip bloodied, and sighed. He attached a chain to her collar, turned, and tugged her.

"Come along, you poor beast."

As the ships sailed away, they walked along the boardwalk. He led her down to the beach, and once they stood in the sand, he drew his sword.

Domi stared at him as he contemplated the blade, and she tensed. If he tried to stab her, she would fight back. She could easily slay him. Her heart beat rapidly, and smoke burst out from her nostrils in short blasts.

I can kill him. I can flee. I can—

Gemini heaved a deep sigh. "You understand, don't you?" He stroked her snout. "You know what Mercy wants, and yet you followed me willingly to the beach. I think that if I did try to put you down, you would rather die than disobey me. My sister calls you worthless, and perhaps you are recalcitrant around her. But I've tamed you. With lash and spur, I made you mine." He clenched his fist, sudden rage twisting his face. "And I will not give you up." He sheathed his sword and climbed onto her back. "Fly, Pyre! Let us fly together—if only for one last time."

The sun began to set and the stars to emerge. Domi was exhausted after the long flight over the sea, but she beat her wings and rose into the air. They flew. Gemini did not lash her, and his spurs barely brushed her tenderspots, and he gently directed her along the beach. They flew several miles south, leaving the city behind, before he allowed her to descend. They landed in the sand. The sun vanished behind the horizon as he dismounted, and the stars shone overhead. The black waves whispered, capped with foam.

Gemini dismounted and stood beside her. The sounds of the city had faded, and in the distance, Domi saw the lights of the warships sailing east—sailing to kill Cade, to kill her father and sister.

"I never wanted this, you know," Gemini said softly. "To be the son of the High Priestess. To be the brother of Mercy." He sighed. "Both those women terrify me. They're strong, proud, intelligent, ruthless, and . . ." He sighed. "Neither one thinks much of me. I had a brother once, did you know? Vanished as a babe; my father stole him away. So of course my mother caught the old man. And she killed him." His jaw clenched, and tears shone in his eyes. "That's what they do to men in my family. Kill us. Abandon us. Or just emasculate us. When I was a child, Mother would threaten to lock me in the palace dungeon, to leave me to rot. She'd take me to that dungeon sometimes, show me the tortured prisoners, threaten to leave me there."

Sudden pity filled Domi, and she gurgled softly and nestled him with her snout. She hated Gemini. She hated him with a passion. Yet now she pitied him too, for he seemed pathetic to her.

"You do understand, don't you?" Gemini said. "They treat you the same way. We're both only animals to my mother and sister. Do you think they ever invite me to their councils? Ever discuss the Falling with me, or the military strategy against the Horde, or plan the hunts of the weredragons? No. They stick me in a bedroom, and they send women in, and they stud me. That's all I am to them—a stud, an animal to breed other animals, no better than a firedrake. All because I was born naturally pure."

Domi imagined that most men would envy this life—to live in a palace, bedding one woman after another—but she only grunted and puffed out a little smoke.

"And the one woman I actually loved," Gemini continued, voice torn with pain. "The one woman I ever chose for myself, ever dared to truly love . . . they . . . oh Spirit, they grabbed her, and . . ."

He fell silent and lowered his head, too overcome to speak.

Domi nuzzled him, cooing softly. Gemini—loving a woman? It seemed impossible to Domi. What woman had caused the paladin such pain?

For long moments Gemini seemed unable to speak. He stood silently, clenching his fists. Tears streamed down his cheeks. Finally he raised his head and looked back at Domi.

"And now Mercy wants me to put you down," he said. "You're not like the other firedrakes. It's as if . . . as if you understand me. You've become my only friend, Pyre. My true pet." He stared into her eyes. "You are the only woman that I love now."

Domi narrowed her eyes, and her heart quickened. Did he know? Did he know that deep within her dragon body there lurked the soul of a true woman?

He kissed the tip of her snout. "Let's sleep here tonight. Together on the beach. I have to obey my sister. I have to put you down. If I let you go, she'll know. She always knows." His tears flowed. "But let's spend one more night together."

He curled up in the sand beside her, laid his head against her, and closed his eyes. She draped a wing over him, and he slept, pressed against her. His sleep was restless, and he kicked, mumbling of dungeons, desperate to escape the prison in his mind.

Do it, Domi, she told herself. *Do it now. Kill him. Bury his body in the sand. Then flee.*

She stared down at him, wanting to see the cruel master who had lashed her bloody, who had all but starved her, who had dug his spurs into her mercilessly. She wanted to see the sadistic son of the High Priestess, the hunter of weredragons.

But she saw only a scared, confused boy—a wretched soul to pity.

And Domi cursed that pity within her.

Suddenly she missed her family. She wanted her father to be here, to tell her what to do; he would tell her to kill Gemini, she thought. She wanted her older sister here, to hear Fidelity's wisdom; perhaps the librarian would urge mercy. Domi even wanted to see Cade, that foolish, headstrong boy with his wide hazel eyes and ridiculously messy hair.

But I'm alone, and I must choose.

She knew that Gemini had made his own choice; he had chosen to slay her in the morning, despite his love for her. He had chosen to obey his sister. He had chosen to do what he always did: be a tool for his family, to hate himself for his actions, to be a breeder, a killer, or whatever else they wanted him to be, and Domi knew that the pain would forever fill him.

He's already dead.

Watching him sleep, Domi released her dragon magic.

Her claws retracted. Her scales melted into her body. She resumed human form—a girl wearing rags, her skin covered in sand and dirt, her eyes peering between strands of red hair.

Sensing the loss of the dragon's warm body, Gemini mumbled and his eyes opened to slits. He gazed at her, confused, still half asleep.

"Goodbye, Gemini," Domi whispered. She touched his cheek. "I give you the gift of life, or perhaps its curse."

She turned and began walking south along the dark beach. The waves reached out to kiss her feet, and the stars shone above. She looked over her shoulder once, and she saw Gemini standing in the moonlight, gaping at her, silent. He did not follow, perhaps thinking this all a dream, perhaps simply too shocked to move.

She turned her head back forward, and she walked on, leaving her old life behind.

GEMINI

"Wait."

His voice was only a hoarse whisper, and his legs trembled. The woman kept walking away, vanishing into the darkness. Gemini took three steps forward in the sand, but he was too dizzy to keep walking, too shocked. He fell to his knees, and the waves splashed around him. He reached out to the young woman.

"Wait!"

His voice was louder now, cracked.

She froze, her back still toward him. The moonlight limned her form—the form of a young, slender woman dressed in a ragged sack. For a long moment the only sound came from the whispering waves.

Slowly, the woman turned around to face him.

Gemini struggled to his feet, his fingers still shaking.

Can it be . . . He blinked. *No, it can't be, but . . .*

He took another step toward her. She seemed startled and took three steps backward; for a moment she seemed torn between wanting to flee and wanting to hear him.

"I just want to talk." Gemini held out his open hands. "No weapons. I just want to talk."

Who was she? He had fallen asleep under Pyre's wing, his firedrake who was doomed to die. He could have sworn he had dreamed of the firedrake shrinking, becoming a woman, gazing at him softly, touching his cheek, then rising, walking away.

A dream. A dream, that was all. It had to be.

Gemini took a few more steps toward the woman on the beach, and finally he could see her clearly in the moonlight.

She was a young woman, perhaps a couple of years younger than him. Her body was slender. He thought her skin was pale, but it was hard to tell; grime and sand covered it. She wore a tattered burlap sack and long stockings full of holes. He could barely see her face; matted strands of tangled red hair hung across it. He could make out only a small, freckled nose and very large, very green eyes that peered at him.

Pyre's eyes.

"Who are you?" Gemini whispered.

She glanced behind her, then back at him. She stared into his eyes, and he nearly drowned in two green pools.

"You know who I am," she whispered.

He reached out a hesitant hand and parted the strands of her hair, revealing her face—a pale face, strewn with freckles and coated with sand.

It's her.

"Pyre," he whispered.

She nodded. She parted the tatters of her tunic, revealing cuts on her sides.

Tenderspots. The very places where he had spurred her.

Once more, Gemini could not stand. He fell to his knees before her, shaking. He reached out and grabbed her hand.

"I'm sorry." His eyes dampened. "Oh, Pyre, I'm sorry. I didn't know. I didn't know you . . . what are you? A weredragon?"

She pulled her hand free and took a step back. "I am Domi. That's all. Just Domi. And I must leave now."

She turned and began walking away again.

He leaped up, raced after her, and grabbed her arm.

She spun back toward him, and fire lit her eyes. Scales began to grow across her body, and her fingernails began lengthening into claws.

Gemini gasped and released her.

"Let me go," Domi hissed, halfway into becoming a dragon. "I can slay you now. I can hurt you—the way you hurt me. The way you hurt so many others." Her magic faded, but the rage remained in her eyes. "Grab me again and my claws will dig into you."

Though his insides roiled, Gemini refused to look away. He raised his chin. "You could have killed me in my sleep. Why didn't you? You're a weredragon. My family hunts weredragons. I myself beat you. I lashed you with my whip until your scales cracked. I dug my spurs into you. I tamed you with pain and blood. Why did you spare my life?"

Her chest deflated and her eyes softened. "I don't know. Because . . . I pitied you. Because I saw pain inside you. Because I know you hurt me to drive out that pain inside you. I wanted to kill you on the beach. A voice inside me cried out: Slay him now! Burn him! But . . . then you wept." She lowered her head. "You told me that you loved me, that I'm the only one you love. And you confused me. It scared me."

"It confuses me and scares me too," he whispered. "Whatever lurks inside me—it scares me. That you're really her, really Pyre, speaking to me now—that scares me too. But I meant what I said." He tasted tears on his lips. "I'm sorry. I'm so sorry that I hurt you, and I will never forgive myself for my cruelty, the cruelty my family bred into me, that my faith demands, that—" He shook his head wildly. "No, I won't even make excuses for what I did. The blame is mine. I'm not a good man, Pyre. I mean—Domi. I've always known that, always known that malice lurks inside me, a lust for cruelty, for pain, for hurting others. It scares me so much, and I'm sorry. And I meant the other thing I said too." He could barely see her through his tears. "That I love you. That you're the only woman I love."

She stared at him and shook her head softly. "This is why I pity you. I could never cause you more pain than the pain already inside you."

"Come back with me," he said suddenly. He reached toward her again, remembered how his touch angered her, and withdrew his hands, but he kept staring into her eyes. "Return with me to the capital. To the Temple. I'll look after you there. You don't have to wear rags anymore; I will cloth you in fine cotton. You don't have to walk around covered in sand and mud; I will provide you with baths, soaps, hairbrushes." He glanced at her tangled hair and couldn't help but laugh—a shaky, scared laugh. "I can provide you with food, wine, shelter, everything you need."

She touched the tangles of her hair, tried to pass her fingers through the knots, and could not. She seemed to consider his words, then shook her head. "No. There's no more home for me in the capital. I swore that I would live wild as a dragon, never as a human." She began to shift again.

"Wait!" he said, and she returned to human form. "Where would you go?"

She shrugged. "The mountains. The deserts. Maybe overseas to the Horde."

"Paladins patrol all corners of the Commonwealth for stray firedrakes and weredragons; they would slay you on sight. And the Horde? They would hear your Commonwealth accent; they too would butcher you. They beat and slay women when they're not enslaving them. I can't let you suffer that fate."

Her eyes flashed. "Enslavement? Beatings? I know something of those. Sort of like how you treat your firedrakes."

The words shot pain through him. "I told you I'm sorry. I truly am—deeply. Let me atone for those sins. Please, Domi. Let me atone. I hurt you. I know that. And I will always feel that guilt. Let me help you now—please. Let me make this right. I hurt you, so now let me save you. Let me tend to you. Come home with me, and let me find you work in the Temple, let me find you a better life. Please." His voice dropped to a whisper. "I love you."

As he spoke those words, he knew that he meant them. Staring at her dirty, cut body—a body he himself had hurt—stirred a mixture of pity, guilt, and love inside him. He had craved to tame Pyre the wild firedrake, and more than anything now, he wanted to protect Domi the woman. To embrace her, kiss her tears away, stroke her hair, tell her things would be all right. To shelter her. To be her protector in a cruel world that would hurt and hunt her.

"Please," he said. "I promise you, Domi. I promise to never hurt you again. I promise to look after you, to give you the life of wealth and security you deserve. Come with me."

She lowered her head, and he saw that tears were streaming down her cheeks, drawing pale lines through the dirt. Finally she looked up at him, eyes sparkling.

"I will go with you."

Relief flooded Gemini, and he took two great steps toward her and pulled her into his arms. Her body was stiff, and she did not embrace him back, but he kept holding her, trying to be gentle, to protect her from the world that wanted to hurt her. He kissed the top of her head.

"Oh Pyre," he whispered, holding her close. "I will always love you. I swear. Always. You are mine now. You will be safe, my pet. You are mine."

DOMI

As Domi walked back to the city with Gemini, she kept cursing herself.

Stupid girl! You should have killed him. He's the enemy of your people. At least you should have fled him! Now you return with him, again his slave.

She looked at Gemini who walked by her side along the boardwalk, holding her hand. The tall, slender paladin showed no sign of his earlier cruelty. With his pale armor, snowy hair, and noble features, he almost seemed handsome to Domi, a strong man to protect her, to give her a better life, to—

No! She tightened her jaw. If she let him care for her, if she became some kind of human pet to him, she would do so for Requiem. Whatever she would be to him—servant, slave, even lover—she would use this chance to infiltrate the Temple. To learn more about High Priestess Beatrix and her powers. To learn more than she'd been able to in the firedrake pit. How did the Temple know whenever a child was born? Did the Temple know of any other living Vir Requis? And perhaps most importantly, Domi could learn the fate of her father, her sister, and Cade.

Living with Gemini, I can help Requiem, she thought. And so she kept walking with him across the boardwalk of Sanctus, letting him hold her hand.

They must have made quite a sight—a paladin all in priceless armor, the white plates filigreed with gold and silver, and a scrawny woman in rags and tattered stockings, her hair a tangle of red like wildfire, hiding her face. Luckily the hour was late. Most of the soldiers had sailed off to hunt the Vir Requis, and those who remained in the city had mostly retired to their beds in the fortress. Only a handful of men remained on the boardwalk, watching the sea.

"First things first, we'll have to get you some proper clothes." Gemini glanced at her rags. "Those old tatters are nearly falling off."

"They're comfortable," Domi said.

A hint of harshness filled his voice. "I'm sure they are. But if you're to be seen with me, you must look like a proper daughter of the Temple, not a waif." He sighed, and his voice softened. "I promised to tend to you. Let me tend to you. Please."

She glanced down at her ragged burlap tunic, the rope around her waist, and her tall stockings that seemed formed of more holes than fabric. She sighed and nodded.

He led her off the boardwalk and along a narrow, cobbled street. Shops and homes rose alongside them, simple huts of clay, their roofs domed. A few trees grew from rings of cobblestones, and behind her, Domi still heard the sea whisper. They walked down several blocks of narrow, twisting streets.

"I saw a place here somewhere . . . where . . . ah!" His eyes lit up. "Here."

He led her toward a round clay house, taller than the others. A statue of an ancient druid rose in the garden, hands pressed together. Ilbane—the plant that burned weredragons—grew around the statue's feet, and Domi froze and hissed. Even from here, she could smell the leaves, feel them burn her.

Gemini squeezed her hand and tugged her along. "Come on. We'll walk along the path. The plants won't hurt you."

She followed reluctantly. Walking along the small, pebbly path through the ilbane garden felt like walking along a bridge over lava. Finally they reached the house's door, and Gemini pounded on it with his fist.

"Open up!" he shouted.

No answer came.

"They're probably asleep," Domi said, glancing up at the moon. The hour was late.

He ignored her and pounded on the door again. "Open up, damn you! In the name of the Temple!"

A light turned on in an upstairs window—the glow of an oil lamp. Footsteps shuffled and the door creaked open, revealing a wizened old woman in a white shawl. Gemini shoved the door wider, nearly knocking the woman down, and tugged Domi into the house. Inside, many robes hung on pegs, and reels of fabrics rose everywhere, reminding Domi of cottony caskets of ale.

"My lord!" said the seamstress, kneeling.

Gemini didn't spare her a glance. He patted Domi's hand and smiled at her, his eyes lighting up.

"Choose, Domi," he said. "Choose any fabric you like, and I'll have the seamstress prepare you a fine tunic."

Domi looked around the house. "All the fabrics look the same. They're all white."

He smiled. "I have much to teach you. They're all different. Some are lush and expensive, others thinner and cheap. Some are cotton, others wool, and some silk. Touch them! Caress them. Choose your favorite."

Domi didn't care what fabric she wore; she'd be happy wearing burlap again like a commoner. But she dared not defy Gemini. She walked among the reels of fabric, caressing them. Finally she chose a light, soft fabric—cotton, she thought.

The seamstress smiled at her. "An excellent choice, my child." She pulled out a strip of tape, and Domi stretched out her arms, letting the woman measure her.

"Have the tunic ready by noon tomorrow," Gemini said when the seamstress was done. He slapped a few silver coins onto the table. "Wake up your girls now if you must, but have it ready.

Deliver it to the fortress, and tell the guards it's for Lady Domi. If you're late, I will be very disappointed. You would not like that."

The seamstress nodded. "It will be ready, my lord."

Gemini took Domi's hand again and guided her out of the house.

He led her through the streets and between the dark homes. Scattered lanterns rose along the streets of Sanctus, and a few stray cats, eyes glowing in the night, were the only life they saw. Finally they reached a stretch of land that thrust out into the sea, something halfway between a small peninsula and a massive breakwater. A road here led them toward Fort Sanctus, guardian of the city and watcher of the sea. Its towers rose into the night, bearing the banners of the Cured Temple, tillvine blossoms upon them.

A few years ago, when Domi had still lived in the library with her father and sister, she had read *The Book of Requiem*. The Temple claimed that Sanctus had always been a city of the Commonwealth, serving the Spirit, but Domi knew better. Over a thousand years ago, Fort Sanctus had been but a single tower, a relic of a kingdom named Osanna. The hero Kyrie Eleison, a great Vir Requis, had hidden in the tower from Dies Irae, a tyrant who had hunted the Vir Requis to near extinction. Kyrie had begun his journey here in Fort Sanctus, eventually finding other Vir Requis, binding together, and raising Requiem from ruin.

The hero Kyrie fought the enemies of Requiem here, Domi thought, head lowered. *While I walk hand in hand with a new tyrant.*

They passed by guards in chainmail and white tunics—commoners drafted into the Temple's army—and entered the grand hall of Fort Sanctus. Domi had never been inside the Cured Temple back in the capital, only in the pit beneath it. Flying by the Temple windows, however, she had glimpsed halls of splendor: marble columns inlaid with jewels, ceilings of gold and azure, priceless tapestries, crystal chandeliers, and statues made of precious metals. Here, far on the eastern coast, was a simpler place. The floor was simple stone, the columns unadorned limestone, the vaulted ceiling fading into shadows. Through arrowslits, Domi glimpsed the dark sea, and the sound of the waves rolled through the fortress in a soothing lullaby.

Gemini led her down a corridor and to the bathing chamber. Several bronze baths rose here, and water was simmering in a cauldron over a fire. Brushes, soaps, and towels lay on wooden tables. Gemini roused a servant who lay sleeping in the corner.

"Prepare a bath!" Gemini ordered the man. "Then head to the kitchens, wake the cooks, and order two meals prepared. Have them delivered to my chambers. Go!"

Soon the bath was full of hot, soapy water. Domi stepped forward and stared at the bath, but she did not step in.

"Go on," Gemini said. The harsh tone, which he had used with the servant, was gone now. His voice was soft, almost kind. "You'll feel better once you've bathed."

She stared down at her body; it was covered in sand, grime, sweat, and mud. She had not bathed in . . . by the stars, it must have been years, not since she had left the library to become an undercover firedrake. She was used to her own smell, but Domi imagined that Gemini's nostrils were not as desensitized.

I wonder if Cade thought me filthy and stinky too, Domi thought. That thought disturbed her more than what Gemini might think. Cade had been angry at her; he had yelled and tried to leave her, maybe had even blamed her for the ruin of his village. But Domi had seen kindness in him, and she had thought of Cade often since that day. If she ever saw Cade again—if he escaped Mercy and could return to her someday—Domi wanted to at least greet him without her stench preceding her.

"Turn around," she said to Gemini. "I won't have you watching me undress."

He nodded and turned to face the wall.

Domi peeled off the tatters of burlap that clung to her skin with mud and sweat. When finally off her body, they disintegrated, falling to the floor in shreds. Only the filth, apparently, had held the rags together; she would wear them no more. She climbed into the hot water, leaned back, and couldn't help but sigh.

It felt wonderful.

"You can turn back now," she said, sitting in the bath, the water up to her neck.

Gemini turned back toward her and frowned. "The water's all gray already."

Her head sticking out from the soapy broth, Domi couldn't help but grin. It was the first time she had smiled in ages, and it felt good.

"I was dirty."

She dunked her head underwater and rubbed the dirt out of her hair. When Gemini handed her a brush, she worked for a long time, clearing out the knots. He made her switch to a second bath then, one of clean water, and she gave herself a second scrubbing. Finally, when her fingers were wrinkled, she stepped out from the bath and wrapped herself in a towel.

"Wear this for now," Gemini said, fetching her a tunic from a shelf. "It's mine. It'll be too large for you, but it'll do until the seamstress delivers your proper clothes."

He turned around again, and when he turned back and saw her in the tunic, Gemini let out a long, pleased sigh.

"You're beautiful," he whispered.

Domi tiptoed, barefoot, across the wet floor toward a tall mirror. She examined her reflection, and she barely recognized herself. Her skin, always coated in dirt, was now very pale and strewn with freckles. Her hair, always a mess of tangles, now hung down neatly past her chin, the color of fire. Only her eyes remained the same—large and green and staring curiously.

He led her out of the bathing chamber, up a staircase, and through a doorway. They entered a bedchamber whose windows overlooked the dark sea. A meal waited on a table by the window, steaming and filling Domi's nostrils with delicious scents. Her mouth watered. When she approached the table, she saw a silver platter with a roast duck upon a bed of leeks and spiced mushrooms, diced potatoes fried with onions, bread rolls topped with grains, a stick of butter, and a bowl of grapes, dates, and cherries. White wine filled a jeweled pitcher.

"Oh Spirit," she whispered.

As a firedrake, she had been given nothing but raw meat in rusty old buckets. Those had been her only meals for years. To eat proper human food . . . by the stars of Requiem, it would be divine, perhaps the thing Domi had missed most about being human.

She looked up at Gemini, seeking his approval. A smile split his face, and he patted her flat belly. "Go and fill this thing."

She raced toward the table and began to feast. She scarfed down the food so fast she barely had time to breathe or swallow. Gemini sat across the table from her, eating little, watching her with a small smile on his face. She ignored him. She stuffed pieces of duck into her mouth, chewing vigorously, and chomped on bread and potatoes between bites of meat. She gulped down the wine straight from the pitcher, holding the vessel with both hands. Grease and wine dripped down her chin.

"Careful or you'll need another bath," Gemini said.

She kept eating. Finally—she must have consumed more food than an army—she could not eat another bite. She slouched back in the chair, patting her rounded belly. She thought she'd never be able to walk again, just sit here and digest for days and days. She couldn't help but hiccup, then covered her mouth with embarrassment, feeling her cheeks blush.

"I told you, Domi," Gemini said. "I'll watch over you. I'll always make sure you have fine clothes to wear, hot baths whenever you'd like them, delicious meals and the best wine in the Commonwealth. You're mine now. You're my woman. My love. You will live like a queen."

A queen in a gilded cage, she thought, and guilt filled her. She was eating the food of the enemy. She was living in splendor while her family fled for their lives. She was dining with a paladin while that paladin's sister led an army to hunt Domi's family.

She lowered her head, the guilt suddenly heavier in her belly than the food.

Gemini rose from his seat, walked toward her, and placed a hand on her shoulder. "We'll keep it a secret," he said, voice soft. "Your disease. We'll tell my sister that Pyre, the firedrake, is dead and buried under the sea. We'll tell her that you're my lover, a pure woman. Nobody will know that you're ill with the dragon curse. We won't tell them."

Domi closed her eyes.

Disease.

Yes, he still thought her diseased of course. He still thought the ancient magic of Requiem a curse, not the blessing Domi knew it was.

He's your enemy, Domi, she told herself. *Never forget that. Never forget who you are.*

She pushed away the empty plates and looked around the room. "There's only one bed. Where do I sleep?" She narrowed her eyes. "I'm not sharing a bed with you, Gemini."

"Of course not," he said quickly, but she saw the hint of embarrassment in his eyes; he had hoped she would. "I'll take the floor. I'm sure you wouldn't mind letting me have one of the blankets, at least."

They lay down to sleep—she on the bed, wrapped in a sheet, he on the floor atop a thick blanket. Soon he was breathing deeply, lost in slumber.

She looked down at him.

Kill him, whispered a voice in her head. *Kill him now. Stab him with the knife on the table, then flee out the window. He's your enemy.*

She closed her eyes. She trembled. She could not.

Sleep was slow to find her, for so much confusion and fear filled her—for her family, for her own life, for the memory of Requiem fading from the world. Finally she thought of Cade again, as she often did before sleeping. She brought to mind his kind, honest face, his large hazel eyes, his messy brown hair. She imagined that he was lying in this bed with her, that it was Cade she shared this chamber with, not a cruel paladin. Finally she slept, pretending that she lay on the beach with Cade under a blanket of stars.

Yet her dreams were different. In her slumber, she saw herself as a paladin, clad in white armor, hunting her family, shooting them with arrows, killing them and laughing with Gemini as they died.

FIDELITY

She sat among the trees, staring down at the codex on the table. She caressed the book's cover, trailing her fingers over the silver words worked into the leather: *The Book of Requiem*.

I gave up so much for this book, Fidelity thought, passing her fingers over and over across the leather.

She could have found a better life. She could have sought purification, burned the magic out of her with tillvine, and perhaps found a life in the Cured Temple. She could have taken a husband in the town of Sanctus, found a life as a wife, content and peaceful, with no dreams of old kingdoms and fallen glory. She could have even joined Roen in the forest, her sweet lover whom she had spurned, and spent a life in his strong arms, kissing him every day, sleeping every night in his arms.

But I chose this book, Fidelity thought, staring at it through the thick lenses of her spectacles. *I chose the memory of a dead land, a lore that is all but lost . . . lost but for this single volume before me.*

She looked up from the book, pushing her spectacles up her nose; with her nose being so small, the damn things kept sliding off every moment.

The others stared back at her: Cade, a boy with messy brown hair, eager hazel eyes, and a nervous energy that had him bouncing in his seat; Korvin, her father—gruff, grizzled, and grumbling, an aging soldier with old pain in his eyes; and Amity, the newest member of their group, her short blond hair falling across her ears and forehead, her one eyebrow raised, her lips twisted into a mocking smile that Fidelity suspected hid a deep fear. The trees of the island rose all around them, walls of greenery, and the song of birds, monkeys, and rustling leaves rose all around. The Horde's camp lay some distance down a dirt path; here, in the forest clearing, the Vir Requis spoke alone.

You should be here with us, Roen, Fidelity thought, feeling hollow without him, a deep emptiness, a sadness that her lover had chosen his life of solitude in the forest, forgetting Requiem, forgetting all that Fidelity fought for. *You should be with us, a man of Requiem, fighting for our kingdom.*

Fidelity took a deep breath and finally spoke.

"We had ten copies of *The Book of Requiem* in the library. Only one remains." She caressed the codex. "Here is all that is left of our kingdom, of Requiem, and—"

"I'm left!" Amity leaped to her feet, pounded her fist into her palm, and snarled across the table. "*We* are left. We're more important than some dusty old book." The tall woman huffed. "No star-damn piece of rotten parchment can replace living, breathing warriors." She spat into the dirt. "The pages of a book are good for wiping your arse, not rebuilding a kingdom."

Cade stared up at the older woman from his seat. "You can't read, can you?" He scoffed. "Even I can read, and—"

Amity growled and grabbed the boy's collar, yanking him from his seat. She stood a couple of inches taller than Cade, and she probably had a few pounds on him too. Korvin had to growl, step between the two, and separate them.

"Return to your seats!" the old soldier barked. "Cade, stop taunting the woman. Amity, if the boy bothers you again, let me slap him silent." When both were seated, Korvin looked back at Fidelity, some of the rage leaving his dark eyes. "Daughter, continue."

Fidelity nodded. "Thank you, Father." She cleared her throat and pushed her spectacles back up her nose. She looked at Amity; the older woman sat fuming, fists clenched and eyes shooting daggers. Fidelity met her gaze. "Amity, you are a warrior, and you are brave and strong; I don't doubt that. But we cannot all be warriors. The world needs librarians too. And the world needs books. Requiem needs its book. This volume contains the lore we fight for. In these pages, we can learn the history of our people: how Aeternum, the first King of Requiem, united the wild Vir Requis of the forests and deserts and raised a column of marble, founding our kingdom; how Queen Gloriae, heroine of Requiem, rebuilt the kingdom after the griffins toppled its halls, ushering in a new era of peace and plenty; how King Elethor and Queen Lyana fought invaders from the south, saving Requiem as the phoenixes burned its forests; how King Valien and Queen Kaelyn defeated the tyranny that had seized the throne, returning Requiem to a path of—"

"Boring!" Amity yawned theatrically. "Bloody bollocks, girl, don't recite the whole damn book. Get to the point before we die of old age."

Fidelity nodded. "Very well. The bottom line is: Countless heroes and battles are recounted in *The Book of Requiem*, and without it, our people have no past, no memory, and thus no future. We need more copies. If this single volume is lost, Requiem is lost."

Cade leaped to his feet, light filling his eyes. "So we'll get to copying! I know how to write. Unlike Am—" At a growl from Amity, he gulped. "I can write new copies. Just bring me some parchment, a quill, some ink, and I'll get to work. If Amity wants to help, she can stroke my hair or rub my feet as I write."

Again the golden-haired warrior leaped to her feet. "How about I rip out your tongue, boy? I'll make parchment from your skin and ink from your blood." She leaped back toward him and knocked him off his seat, and Cade yelped and held up his arms to ward off her attack. Korvin and Fidelity had to leap forward and drag the combatants apart.

"Enough!" Korvin thundered. He yanked Cade backward and shoved him into a seat at the other side of the table. "Boy, you sit here, far from Amity, and you shut your mouth."

Finally, when everyone was seated again, Fidelity continued speaking. "I myself have written a copy of *The Book of Requiem*; it was lost in the library. It can take hundreds of hours to copy a book this size—there are over a thousand pages here, all crammed full of tiny letters. And that's just one copy. We need hundreds of copies, distributed all over Requiem." She took a deep, tingling breath. "Before the paladins destroyed our library, we had acquired a small book—a copy of *The Book of the Cured*—from a passing peddler. It was not written with a quill but printed using a new machine. The peddler explained that in his town, an inventor had created many metal letters, which one could arrange onto a hard, flat sheet of iron. One then coats the letters with ink—like stamps—and presses all these stamps down together onto the page. A single page in a book can be created in a second—hundreds of the same pages can be printed at once." Her eyes lit up. "That's what we need. We need this machine. Then we could print hundreds of copies of *The Book of Requiem*."

Cade gasped and his eyes lit up. "Blimey! We could distribute copies all over the Commonwealth. Fly over towns and drop 'em down! Let everyone learn the truth, learn that the Cured are a bunch of liars. Learn that we're not cursed, that we're Vir Requis." His eyes dampened, and he rose from his seat, leaped toward Fidelity, and grabbed her hands. "It's brilliant, Fidelity. Bloody brilliant! So where do we get this machine?"

She sighed. "That's the problem. They only exist in the city of Oldnale."

Cade's chest deflated. "One of the Commonwealth's largest cities. A stronghold of the Temple."

Silence fell upon the assembly. Fidelity heard only the song of birds, the chirp of insects, the howls of monkeys, and the hum of the Horde's camp in the distance.

Finally Cade nodded. "Fine. No problem. We go to Oldnale. We're no firedrakes; we all have human forms. We walk into the city, we buy this printing press, and we take it somewhere safe."

Korvin grumbled. "It won't be that easy. I've seen Oldnale. I served there as a soldier before they shipped me off to fight the Horde across the sea. Hundreds of Temple soldiers guard its walls and gates, inspecting every item that enters and leaves. They search for anything contraband in the Commonwealth: fabrics other than burlap, cosmetics, jewelry, and banned books. They'd find us smuggling out a printing press, sure as a monkey's backside is red."

"Well, this monkey is going to try anyway." Cade pounded his chest and scratched under his arms.

Amity groaned. She paced across the forest clearing, her leather boots snapping twigs and crunching fallen leaves. "This is all ridiculous." She lifted a fig fallen from a nearby tree and hurled it into the branches, scaring away a flock of parrots. "Sneaking around? Smuggling metal letters up our arses? Writing bloody books about rotting old kings?" She hawked noisily and spat. "To the Abyss with that shite. I've been living with the Horde since I was a girl. I'm one of the Horde." She turned toward Korvin and grabbed his arms. "Korvin, we have weapons here. Soldiers. Griffins and archers to ride them. And we're only an outpost—a hundred thousand Horde soldiers train in the mainland in the south. We must incite war!" She snarled. "We'll convince the Horde that it's time to finally invade the Commonwealth, to crush its paladins, to topple the walls of the Temple."

"War?" Fidelity said, aghast. "Invasion? Amity, we don't want a war. We want to spread the word of Requiem."

The older woman scoffed. "You think you're the only one who cares about Requiem? Griffin shite. While you were holed up in your little library, girl, reading your little books, I was training in swordplay, in archery, preparing to fight for Requiem. I found an army, not some book of fairy tales." Amity's eyes flashed. "Fight with me. With the Horde. All of you. I care about Requiem just as much as any of you. Maybe more!" She drew her sword and swung the blade through the air. "I've been training with this blade since I was a girl. It's time to wield it in battle. It's time to reclaim Requiem with fire and blood and—"

"To what end?" Fidelity said, interrupting her. "So your precious Horde can take over the Commonwealth, replacing the Temple with another foreign power? The people of Requiem—people oppressed, their magic stolen away—must be those to reclaim their own kingdom. To wake up. To find the magic within them, to realize that magic is no disease. To turn the purifications away."

Amity's face flushed and sweat dampened her hair. She stomped forward, grabbed Fidelity's arms, and snarled down at her. Fidelity forced herself to glare back at the taller woman, though fear filled her; Amity was older than her, fiercer and stronger, and could probably snap all her bones.

"I realize this," Amity said in a slow, dangerous hiss. "My parents realized this. They saved me from purification, refusing to let the paladins steal my magic. They paid for that defiance against the Temple with their lives." Her fingers dug painfully into Fidelity's arms. "Never dare question my loyalty to Requiem again, girl. Every breath I take, every beat of my heart, every swing of my sword, every flap of my wings—they are for Requiem."

"Then help restore Requiem's memory," Fidelity said. "I can't do this without you, Amity. I'm a librarian. But I need a soldier helping me. We need to work together, books and blades. Will you help me? Will you be my sister?"

The anger seemed to leave Amity. She released Fidelity and took a few steps away, turned to stare at the forest, and said nothing.

Cade stood in the forest clearing, looking at the others one by one. Finally the boy seemed to make a decision. He took a deep breath and stepped toward Fidelity.

"I'll go with you," he said.

Warmth filled Fidelity and she smiled. Perhaps she had judged the boy too harshly. Cade had come into her library, paladins on his tail, and had disrupted her life. Thanks to Cade, she was now in exile, her library destroyed, all her books but one burnt and buried. Since fleeing the devastation, she had thought Cade a menace. Many times, she had come close to hating him. But now, seeing the eagerness in his eyes, the light that shone there for Requiem, her anger at him faded. She took his hand, kissed his cheek, and smiled to see him blush.

"Thank you, Cade." She turned to look at her father and Amity. "Will you join Cade and me? Will—"

A chorus of shouts rose in the distance, interrupting her. Fidelity frowned, spun around, and faced the forest. The sound came from the Horde's camp: screaming men, shrieking griffins, and above them all the roar of firedrakes.

A distant trumpet blared, war drums boomed, and a man cried out, "The Temple attacks! The Temple attacks!"

Fidelity grabbed her book and clutched it to her chest. Her spectacles slid off her nose and fell to the ground. Fear, cold and all-consuming, gripped her like the claws of a firedrake.

CADE

He ran through the brush, emerged into the camp, and gasped.

"Oh Spirit's flea-ridden beard," he whispered.

When arriving on these islands, the northeastern outposts of the Horde, Cade had thought to find safety from the Cured Temple. Now the might of that cruel faith descended upon the islands with warships, howling soldiers, and a flight of firedrakes. Cannons blasted from the brigantines in the water, soldiers raced across the beaches, and the firedrakes swooped toward the camp, blasting out flame.

Warriors of the Horde raced about, firing arrows. More warriors took flight on the backs of griffins and salvanae, soaring toward the firedrakes. Screams rose and blood washed the camp. Already the flames of firedrakes were burning down huts, and the beasts' claws were tearing men apart.

"Cade, fly with me!" Korvin shouted, emerging from the forest. The old soldier shifted, rose into the sky as a gray dragon, and blasted out flame.

Cade sucked in breath, shifted, and rose into the air. An instant later, Fidelity rose at his side, a blue dragon blowing fire, and Amity soared above them, a roaring red dragon.

Requiem flies again, Cade thought, pride welling in him to fight alongside his comrades.

"The weredragons!" rose a voice above—Mercy's voice. "The weredragons are here! Slay them!"

Cade looked up and growled. Mercy flew above upon a new firedrake, a burly copper beast; Domi was nowhere to be seen.

With screeches like shattering glass, the firedrakes and their riders charged across the sky toward the four dragons.

With heat, blood, and pounding fury, the battle exploded around Cade.

The firedrakes spewed down jets of flame, and Cade screamed as the fire washed across his scales. Mercy's armor flashed above. With her firedrake engulfed in smoke, the paladin seemed to be flying alone through the air. She aimed a crossbow. A bolt whizzed and glanced off Cade's scales, and he cried out in pain. He flew toward Mercy, blasting out flames, only for her firedrake to soar and dodge his dragonfire. Before Cade could pursue Mercy and her mount, two other firedrakes—both black as tar—swooped toward him, claws extended.

The beasts crashed into Cade with the clatter of cracking scales.

Cade tumbled from the sky, tail flailing, wings beating uselessly. He slammed against a burning hut, crashed through the roof, and landed inside the smoky remains of the house. The pain yanked the magic out of him. He returned to human form, coughing, bleeding.

The firedrakes swooped from above, and their twin jets of fire streamed down toward him.

Cade screamed, leaped aside, and ran through what remained of the hut's doorway. He emerged into the battlefield, singed and bleeding, burn marks spreading across his burlap tunic. All around him, warriors of the Horde ran through the camp, firing arrows up at the firedrakes. Already swordsmen of the Temple—burly soldiers clad in chainmail—were emerging from among the trees. Griffins, salvanae, firedrakes, and Vir Requis all battled above, and—

The two black firedrakes burst through the burning hut, scattering logs. They raced toward Cade.

With a yelp, Cade shifted back into a dragon and flew toward them. He roared madly, blasting out fire, and crashed into the pair.

Flames and blood engulfed him.

Claws tore at him. Upon the firedrakes' backs, paladins fired crossbows, and bolts slammed into Cade, cracking his scales. He cried out in pain. He almost lost his magic again. He clung desperately to his dragon form, roared, and closed his jaws around one firedrake's neck. He tugged back, tearing out flesh, spitting out blood. As the wounded firedrake fell, spilling its rider from the saddle, the second beast lashed its claws. The blow slammed into Cade's head, knocking him down.

The firedrake's rider shot his crossbow just as Cade, wounded and dizzy, lost his magic again. The quarrel flew to where his dragon neck had been instants ago, hitting the soil instead.

"Boy, stop playing around and fight as a dragon, damn you!" Amity roared, flying above as a red dragon, three firedrakes on her tail.

Cade shifted back into a dragon, leaped toward the firedrake facing him, and slammed his claws into the beast. The animal screeched, stumbled backward, and crashed into a hut. The structure collapsed, and the firedrake's paladin fell from the saddle.

Cade beat his wings, soared twenty feet into the air, and rained down an inferno of dragonfire.

The flames crashed against the firedrake and its rider. Both beast and man screamed as they burned.

With a brief moment for breath, Cade panted and glanced around. His heart sank.

Spirit damn it.

The Horde's forces were falling fast. The corpses of men from motley nations lay charred, red bones rising from blackened flesh, and the sickening sights and stench reminded Cade of the corpses of his parents. A griffin fell from the sky and slammed down beside him; both the animal and its rider were dead. A salvana coiled overhead, a great flying serpent that blasted lightning from its mouth. Its bolts took down one firedrake, but three others descended upon the salvana, bit deep, and tore the ancient true dragon apart. Scales rained. On the ground, a battle was raging too. Hundreds of Temple soldiers kept emerging from their rainforest, thrusting their swords at the Horde, and Cade still heard the cannons blasting from the sea.

Cade beat his wings and rose high. He spewed out fire, holding back a firedrake, and kept ascending. The battle raged in every direction, and the trees burned.

"Fidelity, do you have the book?" Cade shouted. He saw the blue dragon flying nearby, blowing fire down onto enemy soldiers.

She glanced at him and nodded. "Yes!"

"Then let's get the Abyss out of here!" Cade shouted. "Come on!"

"Not without Korvin and Amity!" she cried back. "Where are they?"

Cade whipped his head from side to side, then had to swerve when a firedrake charged toward him, blowing flames. Cade rose higher, blasted out his own dragonfire, and hit the creature. Fidelity added her flames to his. As a human, she was perhaps only a spectacled, bookish young woman, but as a blue dragon, Fidelity roared and blasted out death from her jaws. The firedrake and its rider crashed down, and warriors of the Horde leaped toward the fallen, lashing swords.

"There!" Cade shouted and pointed a claw. "They're attacking the ships!"

When he looked west, he saw the enemy charging up the island, racing up paths cut into the cliffs. In the water, more Templers kept emerging from brigantines and rowing landing craft toward the beaches. Cannons blasted from the ships, shattering the huts the Horde had raised upon the beaches. As Cade watched, one of the Horde's griffins swooped toward a ship, only for a cannonball to blast toward it. The iron projectile tore the griffin apart. Blood, feathers, and gobbets of flesh fell into the sea, rocking the rowboats still heading to the shore.

A gray dragon and a red dragon—Korvin and Amity—flew above the ships, dodging the cannonballs. Korvin blasted down dragonfire, burning one of the warships, while Amity was battling three firedrakes that flew around her. The firedrakes' riders were firing crossbows. Already Amity bled from several cuts, yet still she fought.

Cade snarled and flew across the island, heading toward them. He had not known Korvin for long, but the gruff old soldier was already dear to him, as precious as a father. Cade had known Amity for even less time, and though the woman had spent the past few days taunting and even smacking him more than once, he suddenly loved her too. She was a fellow Vir Requis; therefore she was his sister. Cade roared as he flew toward them, and Fidelity flew at his side, sending forth her dragonfire.

The firedrakes and cannons turned their way.

Fire blasted across the coast..

As he fought, Cade forgot that he even had a human form, forgot his old life, forgot that he had ever been a baker. Here above the sea, he was a dragon of Requiem, a creature of wrath and nobility, of fangs and fire and claws. A firedrake lashed its claws at him; Cade soared, knocked it aside, and burned it down. A cannonball flew right by him, nearly deafening, and he swerved and swooped, burning the ship.

Yet more firedrakes kept arriving. Soon ten or more were flying toward them, and the cannons kept blasting, and they were only four dragons.

"Korvin, we must fly!" Cade shouted to the older, larger dragon who still flew in the distance. "We have to protect the book. Fly west with me! Korvin, fl—"

With blasting fire and roaring rage, Mercy and her firedrake swooped down. The paladin no longer rode the parti-colored Pyre but her beefy, copper beast. A jet of flame crashed into Korvin, and Mercy stood in her stirrups. She held a lance, its tip smeared with green paste; even from the distance, Cade smelled the acrid stench of ilbane. The paladin, all in white, her bleached hair streaming in the wind, tossed her lance.

The shard flew through the air and sank into Korvin's neck.

"No!" Cade shouted.

Korvin opened his jaws to roar, but no sound left him. Green tendrils spread across the dragon's neck—the poison spreading.

The scarred, charcoal dragon lost his magic.

Korvin plunged through the air, a human again, and crashed into the sea.

"Korvin!" Cade shouted, voice torn.

More firedrakes flew toward them. Their flames crashed against Cade, but still he flew forward, passing through the fire, trying to reach Korvin. Crossbow bolts slammed into Cade, and he cried out in agony.

"Father!" Fidelity shouted. "Fa—"

Firedrakes charged toward her, lashing their claws. More flew up toward Cade. Without Korvin, the largest of Requiem's last dragons, the firedrakes flew with renewed vigor, their most dangerous opponent fallen.

"Korvin!" Cade cried, trying to see if the man still lived, if he swam. "Mercy, damn you!"

He saw the paladin through the flame and smoke. Mercy still rode on her firedrake, and she raised a new lance, this one too coated with ilbane. She smiled at Cade, and her blue eyes pierced through the smoke to bore into him. Six firedrakes rose around her, and they all came charging toward Cade and Fidelity.

Cade grimaced, prepared to fight and die.

Red scales flashed. Fire exploded. Amity—larger, faster, and wilder than Cade and Fidelity—came storming forth. She placed herself between the firedrakes and the two smaller dragons.

"Fly, Cade!" Amity shouted. "Fidelity, fly with him! Save your book, go!"

With that, the wild red dragon blasted forth a great jet of flame. She charged forward, spread her wings wide, and slammed into the firedrakes, taking all their fire against her. The flames washed across Amity, enveloped her wings, showering outward.

Cade wanted to stay, wanted to fight with Amity, wanted to find Korvin . . . but he could not let them die in vain. He could not die with them, the lore of Requiem forgotten.

I have to flee. With Fidelity and her book.

He grabbed the blue dragon and tugged her back.

"Fidelity, come! Fly with me!"

Amity was still battling the firedrakes, taking on all seven alone. The red dragon was a horror to behold, burning but still alive, roaring, lashing her claws through the inferno, screaming for Requiem.

Hovering above the battle, Fidelity wept. "My father . . ."

"If he's alive, Amity will find him!" Cade shouted and grabbed her with his claws. "We must save the book. Come on!"

Cannons blasted below. One cannonball shot between the two dragons, chipping scales along Fidelity's leg. She cried out. An arrow flew from below and drove into her foot, and she yowled. Green lines spread across her leg—the poison of ilbane.

Gasping, Fidelity lost her magic and tumbled down, a human again.

Cade swooped, grabbed her in his claws, and flew.

"I'm getting you out of here." He beat his wings, flying west as fast as he could. Fidelity lay slumped in his claws, bleeding. A hundred other arrows flew around them.

Cade flew across the sea, heading westward. Behind him, the cannons still blasted, the firedrakes still screeched, and Amity still roared . . . then fell silent.

Fidelity hung limply in his claws, maybe unconscious, maybe dead. Tears ran down Cade's scaly cheeks. He beat his wings and raced across the water, leaving the islands—and two Vir Requis—behind.

GEMINI

He took only one firedrake to the capital, leaving the rest of his retinue—firedrakes, paladins, and men-at-arms—to await his sister in Sanctus. He did not want them around him. Not now. Not anymore. As he flew over the fields, heading home, only one other person was with him: Domi.

She sat before him in the saddle, silent. Her red hair, finally cleared of knots, flew back in the wind to tickle his neck. Her body pressed against him, slender but warm and soft, clad in the white tunic the seamstress had sewn her. Gone was the raggedy doll Gemini had met on the beach; before him now sat a beautiful woman, skin pale and fresh, eyes large and green, a woman Gemini loved. A woman he vowed to never let go.

Their firedrake beat its wings beneath them, its copper scales clattering. It puffed out smoke and grunted as it flew, nothing but a dumb animal. Gemini realized now why he had always been attracted to Pyre, his old firedrake with scales the color of autumn. As a dragon, Domi had never seemed mindless. Perhaps Gemini had always seen the woman within the beast, had always loved her.

Gemini wrapped his arms around Domi's slender waist. Love . . . yes, he loved Domi. And that scared him, spun his mind. Domi was a weredragon. Diseased. She had never been purified, could become a dragon at will. Gemini's faith, his family, his order of knighthood—all were dedicated to exterminating creatures like Domi. It was too late for her to undergo purification; her sins demanded death. Yet as he held her, as her soft hair caressed him, he did not think her a creature worthy of death. She was diseased, yes. There was no doubt of that. But that didn't make Gemini want to slay her. He craved only to protect her, to cherish her. To be the strong man she needed. To save her.

"I will save you, Domi," he whispered.

She looked over her shoulder at him. "I can't hear you in the wind!"

He stroked her cheek. "I said that we're almost there. Almost at the city." He pointed. "Look ahead! You can see it now."

Nova Vita, capital of the Commonwealth, sprawled ahead across the land. They flew over its thousands of clay homes, its coiling streets, its fortresses and monasteries, and finally toward the great Temple. The building shone in the dawn, its base round like a crystal ball, sending up glass shards and spikes like claws, brilliantly white in the sun. The Square of the Spirit spread before the Temple, cobbled and vast enough for armies to muster on. Gemini directed his firedrake toward the Temple gates, and they landed on the flagstones outside.

Countless times before, Gemini would lead Domi—then a firedrake named Pyre—down a tunnel here, into the dungeon beneath the Temple, the bleak chasm where the firedrakes ate and slept. For the first time, he would now take her into the palace above.

Gemini dismounted the firedrake and stood before the staircase that led up toward the Temple gates.

"Stay near me," he said, helping Domi out of the saddle. He held her waist and placed her down before him. "The palace is a place of beauty and splendor, but danger too. My sister has many ears and eyes in this place, and if she finds out, if . . ." He swallowed. "Never mind that. You know what to do. You're Domi, an orphan I met at Sanctus, hired as my servant."

She nodded, looking up at the gates. "Why can't you tell them the truth?" She looked at him. "That you love me?"

He sighed. "Domi, I was born without the disease. Ilbane never burned me. I could never become a dragon. I never needed tillvine to sear the dragon curse out of me. As a pureborn, my blood naturally clean, I'm what they call a Holy Father."

She nodded. "A stud."

He smiled mirthlessly. "Women will come into my bed. I will sleep with them. I will impregnate them. But I don't love them, Domi. I love you. You mustn't forget that. But as a stud, I'm never to fall in love, never to take a wife, never to dedicate myself to one woman. To do so would be a great heresy; the Spirit himself demanded this life of me. I dared to openly love a woman once, and—" A bolt of pain shot through him, and Gemini pushed the memory aside and held Domi's hands. "We must keep our love secret. Some Holy Fathers—studs, if you will—have been known to take concubines, lovers who tolerated the endless stream of other women into their beds. People will perhaps see through the act, know that you're more than just my servant, but as long as they have a pretext to cling to, they'll cling to it. What they must never know, Domi, is that you are diseased. That you are a weredragon. Then I could no longer protect you. Do you understand?"

She bit her lip and nodded. "They will not know."

He stroked her cheek and tucked an errant strand of her hair behind her ear. "I'll look after you here. I promise. It's a dangerous place, but I'll protect you. You're always safe with me. I love you."

She nodded, silent. She was shivering. Gemini felt his heart melt, and such pity and love and lust for her filled him that his head spun. He held her hand in his.

"Come," he said.

They walked up the stairs together, stepped through the pearly gateway, and entered the halls of splendor.

They walked through the glory of the Cured Temple, the heart of their faith, the dwelling of the Spirit himself. Priests and priestesses in white walked among them, golden jewels hanging around their necks. All around spread the splendor of the Spirit: ceilings of gold and azure, mosaics inlaid with gemstones, columns of precious metals, statues, chalices, and murals in pastels. Here was the greatest cathedral the world had ever known, the heart of a god.

As they walked, Domi gazed with wide eyes, and her grip tightened around Gemini's hand. The precious thing was scared, he thought. She was like a wandering pup lost in a world she'd never known. He moved to walk closer to her, their bodies brushing together.

"I will take you to my chambers," Gemini said. "A far finer place than the old room in Sanctus. I—"

A voice rose behind, interrupting him. "Who do you bring into the sacred hall of the Spirit?"

Gemini turned around and felt the blood drain from his face.

All across the hall, priests and priestesses knelt and bowed their heads.

A hundred yards away, standing between columns of gold and amethysts, stood High Priestess Beatrix.

Domi pulled her hand free from Gemini's grip and knelt, head lowered.

"Mother!" Gemini said. "Since when do you wander the halls? I thought you'd be in the Holy of Holies, kneeling before the Column, praying for the Falling."

Beatrix walked toward him, white robes swaying. A cold, dangerous fire lit her blue eyes. Her thin lips frowned the slightest, tugging wrinkles across her pale skin.

"My service to the Spirit is not your concern, son," she said. Her footfalls clattered across the hall's mosaic as she approached. "Who do you bring here?" Beatrix reached them and stared down at Domi, her frown deepening.

"A serving girl," Gemini said. "And she is none of your concern—"

He yelped as his mother backhanded him.

"Silence your slithering tongue!" Beatrix said. "If you talk back to me again, I'll have that tongue cut off and burnt in the kitchen fires. You don't need a tongue to breed pureborn babes."

Gemini clutched his cheek, glaring at her. "Mother!"

She snorted, stared down at the kneeling Domi, and placed a finger under the girl's chin. She tugged Domi's face up toward her.

"Pretty little servant." Beatrix snickered and looked back toward Gemini. "Did you choose her because she's adept at washing your underpants, or because she has precious green eyes and probably precious teats under her tunic?"

Now rage flared in Gemini, replacing the fear. "Mother, I ask that you do not pry into my affairs. I'm a grown man, and—"

"You are nothing but a child. An errant child who's good for nothing but to breed like a barn animal." She snorted. "Your older sister is a true servant of the Spirit. You don't see her collecting pretty little servants to fulfill her carnal desires. Even now, as we speak, Mercy hunts weredragons in the lands of the Horde. Meanwhile, you bring whores onto holy ground."

"I will not have you call Domi a whore." His voice shook with rage. "I will—"

"Domi, is it?" Beatrix barked a laugh. "Your whore has a name? Do me a favor, boy. If you'll stoop to sneaking a woman in behind the priests' backs, at least impregnate her. Give me another pureborn grandson. If you can't thrust a lance like your sister to rid the world of weredragons, at least thrust your manhood."

With that, the High Priestess spun on her heel and marched way, leaving the hall.

The priests and priestesses across the hall straightened and resumed their business, lowering their heads as they passed by Gemini, pretending not to have heard the altercation.

Gemini stood for a long moment, still and silent. Domi looked up at him, and again he saw it in her eyes—pity.

He grabbed her hand. He tugged her along the hallway, almost roughly. The pain simmered inside him, a humiliation mixed with rage. He took Domi up staircases, climbing story by story, until they reached his quarters. His chest felt tight and he could barely breathe. His eyes stung. Clutching Domi's hand, he led her into his chamber and closed the door behind him.

He leaned against the door, forcing himself to take slow, deep breaths.

The chamber was as opulent as the rest of the Temple, the walls, ceiling, and floor covered in gold and gemstones. A nubile young woman lay in his bed, smiling at him, awaiting him, sent here by the priests.

"Get out of here!" Gemini screamed. "Out!"

The woman fled the room, and Gemini fell onto his bed. He lay on his back, struggling for breath, his fists clenched.

Domi stood in the corner, hugging herself. "Would you like me to leave too?" she whispered.

He sighed. The poor little thing was trembling; he had probably scared her half to death. He shook his head.

"Come sit on the bed," he said.

Domi obeyed, and he pushed himself up and sat beside her. She stared at him, eyes huge green pools. When he opened his mouth to speak, he hesitated, not sure what he wanted to say.

She placed a hand on his knee, and her eyes were soft. "You don't have to say anything." Her voice was barely more than a whisper. "You warned me about this place. But I'm glad to be here with you."

He wanted to kiss her then, to remove the tunic he had bought her, to make love to her here in this place—not the emotionless, functional act he performed with the other women, but a true act of love. But he dared not. Something about Domi was too pure for that, too innocent, too fragile to taint with the carnal acts he had performed a thousand times in this bed.

Instead he simply grabbed a blanket and lay on the floor, leaving her on the bed.

"Goodnight, Domi," he said softly.

For a moment she was silent. Then she climbed off the bed, knelt above him, and kissed his cheek.

"Goodnight, Gemini," she whispered, hopped back onto the bed, and soon sank into sleep.

He lay for a long time on the floor, and sleep did not find him. Again and again, he replayed the scene in his mind: his mother backhanding him, berating him, humiliating him. Again and again, he thought of Domi's eyes, of her kiss. His mind was a storm.

Finally he could bear it no longer. He rose from the floor and gazed at Domi. She slept in the center of the bed, looking very small, but she did not seem peaceful. Even in sleep, her brow was furrowed, and she kicked as if suffering a nightmare.

Perhaps neither one of us will ever find peace, he thought.

Gemini hesitated for a moment, not wanting to scare her, then nodded and climbed into the bed with Domi. She mumbled and stirred but did not wake. He crawled under the covers and lay near her.

"Fire," she mumbled in her sleep and winced. "Spurs . . . hurt."

He moved closer to her and placed his arm around her. In her sleep, she nestled close to him, slung a leg across him, and laid her head against his chest. He stroked her hair until her mumblings stopped and her face smoothed. Soon she was sleeping calmly, and finally Gemini too sank into warm, peaceful slumber, holding her close and never wanting to let go.

CADE

When Fidelity opened her eyes, clutched in Cade's claws, she began to squirm at once.

"We have to go back, Cade." Still in human form, the librarian grabbed his claws, trying to loosen his grip. "Cade, we have to go back!"

Gliding over the sea as a golden dragon, Cade exhaled in relief. "Thank the stars, Fidelity. You're alive. Rest."

She wriggled madly, trying to free herself. Her pack dangled across her back, containing the heavy *Book of Requiem*. "We have to go back! Release me. Let me shift." Tears streamed down Fidelity's cheeks. "Father might still be alive."

Cade kept flying, a golden dragon, holding the young woman like an eagle holding a hare. She tried to shift in his grip—her body began to grow in size, and scales appeared across her—but his grip was strong enough to knock her back into human form.

"I'm sorry, Fidelity." Cade's voice was hoarse as he kept flying westward. "I can't let you go back. If you fly back, Mercy will kill you. I can't lose you too." He lowered his head. "He's dead, Fidelity. I saw the lance pierce him, saw him fall . . ." Grief filled his throat, and he could speak no more.

"I don't care what you saw!" Fidelity screamed in his grip. "Release me, Cade! He might still live, or . . . at least I have to find his body. And Amity! Stars, Cade, what of Amity? How can we just abandon them?"

"Because they'd want us to keep going!" Cade said. His wings beat with more fervor, and they streamed across the water. "Your father died so that we could live, so that we could carry on the word of Requiem. Amity died so that we could escape. And she's dead too, Fidelity. I grieve for her too, but she could not have survived that many firedrakes." His voice was hoarse, his eyes damp. "They gave their lives so that you and I could escape, find the printing press, and spread *The Book of Requiem* across the Commonwealth. So that we could rebuild Requiem. If we fly back to fight Mercy, we're dead, and the book will fall into the sea, and their deaths will have been in vain, and the last memory of Requiem will fade. I know you grieve. I know you hurt. I do too. But we can't let our hearts rule us now. We must fly. For Requiem."

Fidelity hung limply in his grip. "I can't just leave my father."

Cade winced, eye stinging. It hurt to push the words out of his throat. "I had to leave my parents. And my sister."

Fidelity looked up at him, silent and pale. She closed her eyes. "So what do we do?"

"We keep flying." He stared ahead, chest feeling too tight. "We keep fighting. If Korvin and Amity are fallen, we will honor their memory and fight on for them. If they're alive, we must trust that they're fighting their own battle now. Our mission lies in the west, in the city of Oldnale back in the Commonwealth. We will print our books—hundreds of books." He looked down at her. "I'm going to release you now—slowly. Shift before you fall. And I hope you keep flying with me."

Slowly, he opened his claws. She shifted as his grip loosened, becoming a blue dragon beneath him, absorbing her clothes, spectacles, and pack into her dragon form. For a moment, Cade thought she'd fly back to the east to find her father. For a moment, the blue dragon seemed to hesitate, turning back and forth in the sky.

Finally, she flew westward with Cade. She flew silently, eyes damp.

For hours, they said nothing.

Finally, when Fidelity was weary, Cade let her ride on his back as a human. Hours later they switched, and he resumed human form and rode on her.

They flew through night and dawn. Clouds thickened overhead, and faded patches of lightning glowed in the distance, followed by rumbling thunder.

Finally, when evening fell again, they reached the coast of the Commonwealth, of this land once known as Requiem.

On the coast, hundreds of lanterns and campfires burned.

Thousands of soldiers were mustered below, and dozens of firedrakes took flight, blasting up pillars of flame.

"Spirit damn it!" Cade hissed, breaking the silence for the first time in hours. "They're waiting for us. Oh, bloody Abyss!"

He beat his wings and soared higher. Fidelity soared at his side, fire flicking between her teeth. The soldiers below cried out, and firedrakes shot up in pursuit, their riders firing arrows.

Lightning flashed.

The sun vanished beneath the horizon.

Cade and Fidelity shot higher and vanished into storming clouds thick with hail.

They flew through the cloud cover, thunder booming, firedrakes screeching all around. Arrows shot through the storm, quickly vanishing; the paladins were blinded by the clouds, shooting randomly. The only light came from the fire the drakes spewed across the sky. Cade could barely see Fidelity by his side, only flashes of her blue scales. With her bad eyesight, he doubted she could see him at all.

"Fidelity!" he said, keeping his voice just loud enough for her to hear. "Fly with me. I'll keep tapping you with my wing. Be quiet and don't blow fire!"

She looked toward him, blinking furiously, brow furrowed. He knew she couldn't see a thing within the clouds; he himself could see little more than hail, flying arrows, and blasts of fire as the firedrakes sprayed their jets through the storm.

Cade tapped Fidelity with his wing, guiding her onward. They flew, heading west—or at least Cade thought they were heading west. The wind buffeted them, nearly knocking them into a spin. Cade had to keep his wings stiff; the storm kept threatening to pump them so full of air he'd whirl. The firedrakes flew all around, appearing and disappearing among the clouds. Their flaming jets rose like the columns of fiery cathedrals, only to quickly vanish under the rain and wind. Cade flew onward, silent, whizzing around the pillars of dragonfire. He kept tapping Fidelity with his wing, guiding her way.

They flew for what seemed like hours before the cries of the firedrakes finally faded, and the beasts no longer blew their fire. The two dragons flew a few miles more before emerging from the storm.

Cade sighed with relief. He found himself flying over empty plains. He saw nothing but grasslands in the night, a few fields, and a distant barn. Clouds still covered the moon and stars.

"Cade, are they gone?" Fidelity glided on the wind, looking around, blinking. "I can't see a thing."

"They're gone," Cade said. "We're flying over fields. There's a farm below. No more soldiers. No more firedrakes. If the clouds part, the moon will shine bright. Until then I'll guide you."

She looked around nervously. "I really can't see anything, only blackness, as if my eyes were closed." She sighed. "I really do need to get large dragon spectacles."

Cade felt so tired and weak every flap of his wings was a battle. When he looked at Fidelity, he saw her panting, her tongue hanging loose, her eyes glazed.

"Let's land and rest," he said. "Here's a good place."

They dived down, stretched out their claws, and landed in a patch of wild grass. Scattered aspens rose around them, and a stream gurgled nearby.

Both dragons were so weary they released their magic at once. They slumped down into the grass, humans again, and lay on their backs. The clouds parted above, finally revealing the moon and stars.

Cade turned his head to the side. In the moonlight, he could see Fidelity more clearly. She clutched her book to her chest, and her spectacles were back. A tear flowed down her cheek.

Cade didn't know what to say. How could he comfort her? How could he heal the grief inside her?

I can't, he thought. *There's nothing I can do to heal her hurt, to bring her father back. All I can do is be here with her.*

"I'm here with you," he whispered. "I don't know how I can help, but I'm here with you. For whatever you need."

She nodded and rolled over toward him, and Cade found himself embracing her. She pressed her face against his chest, and her tears dampened his tunic. He kissed her forehead and held her in his arms until she slept.

Cade lay awake for a long time. He stroked Fidelity's golden hair—her single braid hung across her shoulder—and watched her sleep. When he had first met Fidelity, she had seemed imperious, rude, and condescending. She had scoffed at him, maybe even hated him; he had tossed her life into a spin. Now, looking at her, she seemed younger, more vulnerable, no longer the haughty librarian but a hurt, fragile girl.

Both our lives were tossed into a maelstrom, Cade thought. *And maybe we're both alone in the world now. Maybe you, Domi, and I are the only Vir Requis left.*

At that moment, holding the sleeping Fidelity in his arms, Cade loved her—his last companion, perhaps the only other soul who understood him, who shared his magic.

"I will always protect you," he whispered. "We'll print your book, Fidelity. We'll keep the memories alive."

KORVIN

His eyes fluttered open, then closed again. All was pain, haze, weariness.

"Wake up, big boy," somebody said, and Korvin felt a hand slap his cheek. "Wake up, or I'm going to knock out your teeth and use them as counter-squares pieces."

Korvin grumbled and forced his eyes open. At first he saw only stars and shadows. Slowly a face came into focus: a young woman, her blond hair just long enough to fall across her ears, her smile crooked, her eyes lit with mischief.

"Amity," he groaned. "Let me sleep."

She snorted. "Wake up! You've slept long enough. Breakfast is served."

He looked around him. He was lying on bare rock, and more rocks rose around him. Ahead he heard the sea, saw faint light, and smelled salt.

A cave, he realized.

He tried to push himself onto his elbows, then fell back down and lay on his back.

"I died," he whispered hoarsely. Speaking hurt.

Amity groaned and rolled her eyes. "If you're dead, I'm the bloody High Priestess, because I brought you back to life. Now sit up! I collected some delicious seaweed to eat."

He closed his eyes, forcing himself to think back. He had died. He remembered dying. Mercy—the daughter of his old lover—had thrust her lance into his neck. He had lost his magic. He had fallen under the sea. He had sunk, drowned, and—

He frowned.

Vague memories rose through the haze, flicking in and out of his mind like a fading dream at dawn. He remembered a red, scaly fish, large as a whale, swimming toward him, grabbing him. No, not a fish—a dragon underwater. He had swum with her. He had swum until he could barely stand it, his lungs aching for air, then burst above the water, gulped air, sank again, and bled, so much blood, and—

"Eat," Amity said, stuffing seaweed into his mouth. "You lost a lot of blood, and you need to regain your strength."

He grumbled but he chewed the clammy meal. It did give him strength—at least, enough strength to finally push himself onto his elbows.

He finally got a better view of his surroundings. He lay in a cave, a small chamber not much larger than his fallen library back in the Commonwealth. Outside he saw golden sand and the blue sea. Amity sat beside him and winked. She still wore her brown trousers, leather boots, and vest, though burn marks now spread across them. Welts rose along her arms, but if she felt the pain, she gave no sign of it.

Korvin brought a hand to his neck and winced.

"Hey, don't touch!" Amity said. "I bandaged it all proper like. You're lucky you were in dragon form when that lance cut into you. Would have killed you right away as a human."

Korvin lowered his hand. He stared at the woman, and he spoke solemnly. "I thank you, Amity. You saved my life. But what of the others? Where's my daughter? Where's Cade?" Fear flooded him, cold and all-consuming. "Are they—"

"They're fine!" Amity patted his knee. "The two bloody runts got away. Well, to be fair, they only got away because I placed myself between them and a typhoon of dragonfire. Saved their little arses, I did. Same as I saved yours. I told you, big boy. I'm a warrior."

Ignoring her protests, Korvin shoved himself to his feet. He wobbled for a moment and had to hold the wall for support. Everything hurt—the wound on his neck and the old scars on his back, the scars from his war against the Horde twenty years ago. His breath rattled in his lungs.

"Where are the paladins? What happened to Mercy? What—"

"You're full of questions today," Amity said. "You should rest. Mercy and the other paladins think us dead and drowned. Most are sailing back to the Commonwealth now, trying to find Spectacles and the kid." She raised her hand, silencing him before he could speak. "Don't worry! I gave the pups a good head start, and they're fast enough to make it home. It's the Horde I'm worried about now." She tightened her jaw and lowered her head. "They're all dead, Korvin. Men. Griffins. Salvanae. All gone." She clenched her fists at her sides, and her eyes reddened. "The people who sheltered me, who trained me . . ." Her voice dropped to a hoarse whisper. ". . . who loved me. Mercy butchered them."

Korvin thought again—as he had thought almost every day since—of High Priestess Beatrix arriving on her firedrake, screaming for blood, shouting for revenge. Again Korvin saw the High Priestess stabbing his wife, smiling, blowing him a bloody kiss—her revenge for him spurning her love. That had been many years ago, back when his daughters had been only children, but the pain still dug through Korvin. Now Amity had lost her family—perhaps not a family of blood, but a family nonetheless.

He stepped toward her. "Amity, I'm sorry. I know your pain is great."

Along with his memories, guilt filled Korvin. He had arrived on these islands, fleeing the Temple. Mercy and the other paladins had followed him.

It's my fault, Korvin realized with a chill. *I led the enemy here.*

Amity raised her eyes. They shone with angry tears. "It'll be war now. War between the Commonwealth and the Horde. War again, like the war twenty years ago, when I was just eleven years old and so afraid." She growled and pounded a fist into her palm. "And this time, the Horde will swarm through the Commonwealth and crush the Cured Temple and kill them all. And I'll fight with them."

Korvin stared at the sea outside. "I need to find my daughter and the boy. I need to help them, to—"

Amity grabbed his arm and sneered. "You need to fight with me! You're a warrior. You were a soldier once; I saw it in the way you fought. I saw the scars on you; those are warrior scars." She tightened her grip on him. "I need you, Korvin. Let Spectacles and the kid print their books; they're not fighters like us. You and I, we're soldiers, and all we know is war. Travel south with me—to the continent of Terra, to the vast armies of the Horde that wait there. Not to an island outpost but to the true heart of our empire. Join me in the Horde's fight against the Temple."

Korvin grunted. "I can't leave Fidelity alone."

Amity's eyes flashed. "Your daughter is a grown woman. How old is she?"

"Twenty-one."

Amity snorted. "I was half that age when my parents died, when I had to survive on my own. You're no librarian, Korvin. Look at you, all grizzled, gruff, and grunting. Don't tell me you were happy living in a library, sorting books for a living. No. You were like a bear in a cage there. But now . . . now you can fly free. With me, Korvin." She touched his cheek, and her eyes filled with compassion. "With me."

He stepped outside the cave and found himself on an islet; it was barely larger than the deck of a ship. True ships were sailing far in the west, hoisting the Temple's banners. They were going to hunt his daughter, to hunt Cade, to hunt the last *Book of Requiem* and destroy the last memories of that fallen kingdom. Korvin gritted his teeth and turned to face the south. He saw nothing but the blue sea, but he knew what lay beyond.

The southern continent of Terra. His old scars blazed with new pain. The land of the Horde. The land where he had fought and nearly died. He lowered his head. The land that could now rise up and topple the Cured Temple.

It would seem, he thought, *that I now must choose which enemy is worse.*

And he knew the answer.

Amity came to stand beside him, and a gust of wind ruffled her hair. She looked at him, silent.

"My daughters are in danger," Korvin finally said. "My eldest is hunted, bearing the last treasure of our people. My younger daughter serves those who hunt us, her life forfeit if her secret is revealed. The enemy threatening my family is the Cured Temple, and you're right, Amity. I'm not a man of books or words. I'm not wise like Fidelity, not wild like Domi, not young and eager like Cade. I'm a soldier. That's all I am. Perhaps that's all both of us are." He stared across the southern water. "I drew the enemy to these islands, and the guilt of the dead will forever fill me. Their blood will forever stain my soul. But a beast is awakening here, a beast that has been slumbering for twenty years." He returned his eyes to Amity. "We will travel south to the Horde. We will tell its king what happened here. And we will raise the Horde's wrath and return to the Commonwealth with an army."

FIDELITY

"So how are we going to pay for this printing press?" Cade asked. "The thing probably costs more than a horse."

Fidelity nodded. "It does. It's a big machine."

Cade pulled out his empty pockets. "If you haven't noticed, we're broke. I haven't got a copper to my name, and neither have you."

They were walking down a dirt road, aspen trees rustling at their sides. While Fidelity had allowed herself to wear finer clothes in her library, out here in the open, she wore a burlap tunic and a rope for a belt—the humble garb all commoners wore. If she wanted to blend in, nothing would serve better. She hid her spectacles in her pocket, and she had undone her braid and let her hair hang freely. She hoped that she now looked like yet another commoner, not a librarian on the run. As for Cade, he had begun to grow a beard in hope of better disguising himself, though the scruff looked woefully sparse.

If anyone's looking for people of our description, Fidelity thought, *hopefully we look different—and normal—enough.*

She hefted the pack that hung across her back. Inside lay their greatest treasure: the leather-bound *Book of Requiem*.

The road stretched on between the trees, leading toward the city of Oldnale; it was still too far to see.

"A long time ago," Fidelity said, "three great houses ruled Requiem. House Aeternum ruled the throne, House Eleison ruled the armies, and House Oldnale ruled the farmlands. The legendary heroine Treale Oldnale fought in the great war against the nephilim, evil half demons from the desert. Back then, there were only farmlands here, no cities, but where Treale was born, a village eventually grew, and—"

"Fidelity, I don't need a history lesson." Cade kicked a rock. "What we need is money. Money to buy a printing press to make copies of all these lovely stories."

She glared at him. "I was just getting to that part! See, according to my book, before the House of Oldnale was destroyed in the old Tiran War, back when the evil Queen Solina led wyverns to burn it, and—ow! Cade, stop elbowing me! Fine, no history lessons. Anyway, during the war, the Vir Requis buried a treasure here. A treasure of old Requiem." Her eyes lit up. "We just have to find it, and we'll have the money we need."

Cade rolled his eyes. "Find buried treasure? Fidelity, this isn't some old pirate story. How are we going to find treasure from centuries ago without a map or anything?"

She smiled softly, a sad smile, a smile that filled her with memories and pain buried as deep as that treasure. "We're going to find the Oldnales' descendants."

She closed her eyes. She didn't want Cade to see them dampen.

Roen, she thought, and her heart gave a twist.

It had been four years. Four years since he had shattered her heart. Four years since that summer of joy, love, tears. She had never forgotten him. She had thought she would never see him again. And now she would wander right back to his door.

Cade frowned. "I thought you said the Oldnale farms were destroyed. Something about an evil queen burning them."

"Not all the Vir Requis of that ancient house died," she said. "Most fell in the war, their halls fallen, their fields burnt. But some moved into the forest, lived wild among the trees like the Vir Requis of old before our columns had risen. And two still live there today."

She veered off the road, heading into the forest.

"Fidelity!" Cade said. "The road's over here. Are you going to, uhm . . . water the soil?"

She shook her head. "Come with me."

He followed, glancing around nervously. The woods were thick here, maples and aspens and oaks growing all around, their leaves rustling. It was still summer, but the forest was chilly, and the canopy hid the sky. Blackbirds flittered between the trees, and hares raced across the forest floor. Twisting tree roots grew everywhere, flowing and coiling together like living tentacles, covered with moss. Eyes peered from burrows beneath them. Fallen logs and boulders lay strewn between the tree trunks, and mushrooms grew a foot tall. Dragonflies and fireflies flew around her, lighting the shadows.

Fidelity lowered her head. She remembered herself here as a youth, only seventeen years old, racing through these woods with him, kissing him under the tree, making love to him upon the grass by the—

"Fidelity," Cade said, "you're blushing. Are you all right?"

She cleared her throat and shot him a glare. "I'm fine." She doffed her pack with the heavy book inside. "Here, carry this. Take a turn and be useful for a change."

As he took the pack, she saw the hurt in his eyes, and Fidelity sighed. She touched his arm.

"I'm sorry, Cade. I don't mean to sound harsh. It's just . . . I haven't been here in a long time. And sometimes memories, well, they can overwhelm you."

He nodded. "I know."

But did he know? What would a boy his age know of love? Fidelity saw how he looked at her sometimes, how his eyes sometimes gazed upon her, then quickly flicked away. She knew that Cade found her desirable—he was a boy of eighteen, after all, and she was a young woman, the only young woman he knew. But love? He would know nothing of the pain inside her.

They walked for a long time in silence. The sun dropped lower in the sky. Fidelity knew these woods well, and she walked with a sure, steady pace.

Finally she saw it ahead: Old Hollow.

The forest floor sloped down here into a declivity, perhaps an old crater or dried out pond. A great oak grew from its center, its roots stretching out like the buttresses of a wooden cathedral, covering the sunken bowl of earth, twisting and rising and sinking back into the soil. The oak's trunk was wide as a home, knobby and mossy, and it soared higher than any other tree in the forest, ending with a great crown of rustling leaves. Lesser trees grew around Old Hollow, maples and birches and elms, bending forward as if bowing to their wise elder.

Leaves shook. A head thrust down from among the oak's branches above.

"'ello!"

The man's body was still hidden among the leaves; only the head was visible, hanging upside down. The tree-dweller grinned, revealing two missing teeth. He had a bushy white beard strewn with leaves, tufted eyebrows, and scraggly long hair. His eyes were bright blue, warm and mischievous, and crows' feet stretched out from them, hinting at many years of laughter.

Fidelity couldn't help but smile. "Hello, Julian."

The man swung down from the branch and landed in the dirt, and his grin widened. He wore fur pelts and a necklace of beads.

"Fidelity!" he said, reaching out his arms. "Give an old man a hug."

She laughed—a laugh of relief, of some comfort after so much death and pain. She ran toward him and embraced him. He was a short man, no taller than she was, but stocky. Under his thick white eyebrows, his eyes gleamed.

"And who's your friend?" he said, turning to look at Cade.

The boy approached, looking a little hesitant at the sight of the wild old forester, and reached out his hand. "My name is Cade. I'm a friend to Fidelity and—"

Julian grabbed Cade's hand and pulled him into a crushing embrace. "So you're a friend of mine, laddie!"

Seeing Cade blanch, Julian released the boy, placed his hands on his hips, and laughed.

"Nice to meet you," Cade only said, brushing moss off his clothes, looking as awkward as a shy pup who bumped into a rambunctious hound.

"Julian, is . . . is Roen here?" Fidelity asked, and she heard the tremble to her voice, and she felt a heat rise inside her.

The bearded old man grew somber, and when he looked at her, his eyes softened. "He's out hunting, lassie. He'll be back by evening. Come inside meanwhile. I've got a pot of mushroom stew cooking."

Cade frowned. "Come inside where? I only see a tree, not a house."

Julian bristled and raised his chin. "This is my house!" He lifted a branch and rapped Cade's shoulder. "And you'd be wise not to look down upon it." He turned back toward the great oak, and his voice became wistful. "This tree here is my castle, my temple, greater than any in the realm. Certainly greater than that garish lump of glass and crystal in the capital." He snorted and looked back at Cade. "Don't tell me you worship the Spirit, boy. If you're a man of the Cured Temple, I won't have you here."

Fidelity stepped forward and placed a hand on Julian's shoulder. "Cade's one of us, Julian. He's Vir Requis."

Julian's eyes widened, and his jaw fell open. "Well, I'll be! A fellow Vir Requis. Can you do this, boy?"

The old man took a few steps back and began to shift. Dry leaves fluttered. Twigs snapped. Wings creaked, scales hardened, and finally Julian stood as an old silver dragon.

Cade nodded. "I can." Among the trees, he too shifted, becoming a golden dragon.

The two dragons stared at each other, then released their magic, returning to human forms. Julian's eyes sparkled with tears.

"I'll be," the old man whispered again. "A new one."

He cleared his throat, blinked furiously, and turned around. He hopped toward the tree, scuttled up the trunk, and vanished among the branches.

Fidelity and Cade followed. They climbed over several branches and found a hole leading into the tree trunk. Fidelity entered first, slid down a little wooden slope, and found herself within Old Hollow. Cade slid down next, bumping into her.

"Sorry," he mumbled.

On the inside, Old Hollow hid a cozy little burrow. The walls were formed of the oak tree, smoothed and polished. Rugs covered the floor, and three stools rose around a table. Strings of beads and feathers hung from the walls, and a curtain of lichen formed the ceiling. A pot of mushrooms bubbled over embers. They sat and ate.

For a long time, Fidelity talked.

She spoke of meeting Cade, of fleeing to the islands, of carrying the last *Book of Requiem*. She spoke of the library falling, of wanting to print hundreds of copies, to distribute the books across the Commonwealth, to let people know their magic was blessed, a magic to cherish and protect, not sear away with tillvine. And she spoke of her father falling into the sea, almost certainly dead, and then her voice choked, and her eyes watered, and she could speak no more. Cade took her hand in his under the table, and she squeezed it for comfort.

As she spoke, Julian listened quietly, growing more and more somber. Finally, when her story was told, he placed down his spoon and spoke carefully.

"We'll dig up the treasure," the old man said. "The coins of Old Requiem will shine again in the sunlight. We'll buy the printing press." He reached across the table to pat Fidelity's arm. "I'm here for you, Fi. You know that. Always."

She nodded, sniffing back tears.

Before she could reply, she heard singing from outside. The voice was deep, the song merry, a song of hunting, of planting, of deep woods and rain and sunlight. Fidelity's heart burst into a gallop.

Roen.

Suddenly Fidelity hesitated. She had dreamed of seeing him again for years, yet now she wanted to hide. Julian saw her turmoil, and his eyes softened.

"Go speak to him," he whispered.

She nodded. Leaving the old man and the boy, she climbed out of the tree, hopped down onto the forest floor, and saw him there.

At first he didn't notice her. He was holding a brace of pheasants across one shoulder, a bow across the other, and an axe hung from his belt. He wore tan trousers and tall boots, and his chest was bare in the summer heat. His hair was still a mess, strewn with leaves, and his beard was thick and brown. He was seven years older than Fidelity; he had already been a man when she had left him, but she had been only seventeen, and the pain had never left her.

Perhaps he's forgotten me, she thought as he hung his hunted birds upon a branch, still singing. *Perhaps he pushed me out of his memory while I clung to his.*

"Hello, Roen," she said softly.

He spun toward her and froze. His face remained still, but she saw the feeling in his eyes, the deep pain that surfaced there. His song died on his lips. And she knew: *He never forgot me. He never stopped thinking of me.*

"Fidelity," he whispered.

She approached him hesitantly, dragonflies and fireflies hovering around her. He dropped his bow, approached her with three great strides, and seemed ready to embrace her, then hesitated. She placed a hand on his chest, and her touch seemed to remove all doubt from him. A grin split his face, and he pulled her into his arms. It was an engulfing embrace, the warm, strong embrace she had missed so much. His arms were wide, his chest damp and hot against her cheek. He pulled her up into the air, nearly crushing her against him, and spun her around. She laughed and he placed her down.

"Fidelity," he said again. "I . . . I didn't think you'd return. I'm . . . oh stars, Fi." Something seemed to break inside him, and his smile faded. "I'm sorry. So many times I wanted to tell you I'm sorry, but—"

She placed a finger on his lips, silencing him. "Let's walk."

He nodded.

They left Old Hollow behind, and they walked for a long time through the woods. Fidelity repeated her story, telling Roen about the past few days—and about the past few years. He listened silently as they walked between the trees, as the setting sun's rays fell upon them, glistening with pollen.

"I often missed you," Fidelity finally said. "In the library, at night, when I'd fall asleep holding a book, I wished I were falling asleep holding you." She lowered her head, feeling her cheeks blush. "I wish you had come with me."

Roen sighed and looked around him at the forest. "What I told you then is still true. I'm no man of the city. All I know is these woods. I'm descended of the Vir Requis of Oldnale, and even then we shied away from cities, choosing a life in countryside and forest." He looked at her, eyes pained. "Every day after you left, I hurt. Sometimes I even started to walk through the woods, seeking the road, wanting to join you, but . . . I always turned back. I could not bring myself to live under the heel of the Cured Temple."

"And I could not bear to live without you," she whispered. "But I had to leave. I had to protect the books. And I failed. Now only one book remains." Suddenly she could not curb her tears. "Now my father is fallen. Now my library lies in ruin, and all I have left is this one book, Roen. All I have left is a story and pain."

"You have me," he said and held her hand. "You've always had me. And my father too. Even if we did not join you in the city, we were always here for you. Thinking about you. Loving you. *I* love you, Fidelity."

He kissed her. At first she did not want it. She did not need that old love; it would be too sweet, too painful to lose his love again. She turned her head aside, and his lips brushed her cheek, but then she could resist it no longer. She turned her head back toward him, and she kissed him, a deep kiss that tasted of her tears, the kiss she had dreamed of so often, had missed with such intensity that sometimes her body had been unable to bear it.

She placed her hands in his hair, and he wrapped his arms around her. He knelt before her and pulled her down, and they lay upon the forest floor. She gasped as his hands reached under her tunic, hard and callused hands, yet gentle as they caressed her body, rising to cup her small breasts, exploring her. She closed her eyes as they undressed, as he kissed her body. They made love as they used to, a wild thing like fire.

I missed you, she thought as their naked bodies moved together. *I love you, Roen.*

The sun was setting as they walked back, and Roen lit a tin lantern. Fireflies glowed around them, adding their light. He did not return directly to Old Hollow, but instead he took her to a towering boulder. A rune shaped as a dragon glowed upon it, peeking through a cloak of moss.

"The Vir Requis raised this stone," Roen said. "Back when Requiem still stood. As House Oldnale fell to ruin, we buried a treasure here—a treasure for us to claim when we rise again." He stared at her solemnly, his eyes gleaming in the soft light. "It's time we rise."

He shifted then, becoming a green dragon, and dug through the soil with his claws. Five feet deep, his claws clattered against an old chest. He pulled it out, placed it down before Fidelity, and cracked open the rusty padlock. He returned to human form and opened the chest.

Fidelity gasped with wonder and passed her hands through the treasure. The golden coins chinked. Each was engraved with a dragon on one side, a birch leaf and the word "Requiem" on the other.

"The ancient treasure of Requiem," she whispered.

Roen nodded. "I hate to lose the coins. They are precious. You don't need to use them all; only a few will be enough to buy your printing press." He smiled thinly. "Of course we'll have to melt the gold into a bar or two. It's not exactly legal to use Requiem currency."

They returned to Old Hollow, bearing the treasure, and slept that night outside the tree under blankets of lichen. Fidelity lay awake for a long time, nestled between Cade and Roen. When she closed her eyes, she kept seeing it again and again: her father falling into the sea, bleeding, and Amity roaring and burning.

Finally she clutched her book to her chest, and she slept and dreamed of old Requiem and skies full of dragons.

KORVIN

The two dragons, gray and red, had been flying across the sea for days before they saw the southern land of the Horde.

"The continent of Terra," Korvin said, gliding over the sea toward that distant coast.

Amity flew at his side, a red dragon wreathed in smoke. She grinned toothily. "A land of vicious killers, terrifying beasts, and ancient monsters of terror. Just the sort of gang we're looking for."

Korvin grunted. "Just the sort of gang that could kill us."

"Or kill High Priestess Beatrix." Amity winked.

He gave another grunt and said no more. Amity didn't know that he'd once loved Beatrix, that he had almost married her. She did not know that Beatrix had then gone mad, risen to the High Priesthood, and slaughtered his wife. Amity didn't need to know such things, Korvin decided. His was a private pain, deep, one he would keep buried within him.

And along with those memories dwelled other old hurts. He had been to these lands before, and the nightmares still filled him.

"The Horde," he grumbled. "Did you know that Requiem itself created it?"

Amity raised an eyebrow. "Requiem—created the Horde? Are you mad?"

He shook his head, scattering smoke. "Requiem was not always a land of righteousness and peace. For a generation, a madman named General Cadigus ruled the kingdom of dragons, and he burned all lands around him. He slaughtered the people of

Tiranor and Osanna. He slew most of the griffins of the islands and most of the salvanae, true dragons of the west."

Amity frowned. "Nations of the Horde."

He nodded. "The original four nations, yes. And others joined them—the peoples of Terra, of the northern icelands, of the distant realms west of Salvandos—all gathered to fight Requiem." He laughed mirthlessly. "They thought they could destroy us. Turns out we destroyed ourselves from within. The Cured Temple rose from among our own people, effacing all memories of Requiem, but the Horde remains."

Amity blasted out fire and roared. "The Commonwealth rose upon the ruins of Requiem. She is a new enemy to the Horde. And we'll rise against this enemy, a great invasion." Her eyes lit up. "Imagine it, Korvin! The vast armies of the Horde, seeking revenge for their burnt outpost on Leonis, landing on the coasts, sweeping across the landscapes of the Commonwealth, charging through the capital and putting Beatrix's head on a spike." She laughed. "I'd like to chop off her head myself."

Korvin looked at the red dragon and sighed. He was once like her—eager for battle, filled with fire and brimstone, ready to fight the world. Losing his wife had changed him. He no longer craved battles or glory.

I just want to see my daughters again. I want to raise them in a world where they can fly free, where they no longer have to hide their secret. I want to see Requiem restored with starlight and magic, not bloodshed and flame.

Yet he flew on, for perhaps Amity was right. For years, he had lingered in the shadows, dreaming, whispering of Requiem. Perhaps Requiem needed Fidelity to whisper of her lore . . . and needed him to be a soldier again.

"We would be wise to approach the Horde in human forms," Korvin said. "If we fly in as two dragons, they'll think us firedrakes of the Temple. They'll kill us before we can speak." He blasted smoke out from his nostrils. "The soldiers of the outposts almost did the same, and they'll be less forgiving here in the mainland."

Amity snorted and spat out fire. "If we wander in as humans, they'll think us random beggars come out of the desert. They'd kill us even quicker." She winked at him. "I know the Horde, big boy. Fly on. Stay near me."

He grumbled. "I know the Horde too. The wounds it gave me still ache most days."

And yet he flew on with her, approaching the distant coast.

The noon sun was blazing when they finally reached the continent of Terra.

Five thousand years ago, the great civilization of Eteer had risen upon this coast, a nation of seafarers, first in the world to discover the secrets of metallurgy and writing in clay tablets. That civilization had fallen millennia ago; today all that remained of Eteer were a few columns rising along the coast, crumbling old walls, and ancient tales. Beyond these ruins, covering the dry plains and fields, sprawled Hakan Teer—northern settlement of the Horde.

While the wondrous palaces of Eteer had fallen, a great new wonder rose here: Eras and Elamar, the great Twin Stallions of the Horde. The two statues rose from the beach, soaring toward the sky, hundreds of feet tall—as tall as the Cured Temple in the north. Carved of limestone, they were shaped as wild horses, rearing and kicking, manes flying proudly. Their hooves were gilded and shining in the sunlight. For hundreds of years, Eras and Elamar had guarded the coast of Terra, the gateway to the southern continent.

Beyond the Twin Stallions, thousands of tents sprawled across the land, their coverings made of burlap, wool, or fur. Flags rose among them, displaying five serpents coiling together, symbolizing the different nations of the Horde. This was no mere camp like in the outposts; here was an entire city. Dirt roads ran between the tents, clogged with people: tall and fair Tirans from the desert, their skin golden, their platinum hair long and smooth; survivors of the old realm of Osanna in the north, shorter but wider, their hair and eyes of many colors; native warriors of Terra, the descendants of the old civilizations that had once risen here, their skin olive-toned, their hair dark, their eyes green. The warriors wore motley suits of armor: chainmail, iron plates, studded leather, even wood. They carried assorted weapons: clubs, spears, scimitars, axes, hammers. Many rode horses and chariots. They were more mob than army, not organized into units and subunits but a single mass, wild and fierce.

    Along with the men, beasts dwelled here too. Hundreds of griffins stood beyond the tents, clad in armor. Salvanae, true dragons from the mythical realms of Salvandos, hovered several feet above the surface, their serpentine bodies coiling and streaming. Their scales glimmered, and their beards hung to the ground.

    As the two dragons approached the coast, dozens of those griffins and salvanae took flight and came flying toward them. Riders rode upon them, armed with bows. Shouts rose from among the tents, and archers rushed forth and nocked arrows.

    "I hope you know what you're doing, Amity!" Korvin shouted.

    The red dragon grinned at him. "Follow my lead."

    As the Horde flew toward them, and as archers fired arrows from the shore, Amity released her magic.

    She fell from the sky, a human again.

    Korvin cursed, released his magic too, and fell down with her.

    The arrows sailed harmlessly above them. The griffins and salvanae paused in midflight, hovered, and cried out in surprise.

Amity and Korvin kept falling, rushing down toward the water. An instant before they could hit the ocean, they shifted back into dragons and soared.

"Horde!" Amity cried out. "Hear me, Horde! I am Amity, one of your number. Do not mistake us for firedrakes! We are dragons of Requiem!"

The archers on the coast lowered their bows. The griffins screeched, and the salvanae bugled out unearthly cries, the sound of silver trumpets.

Dragons of Requiem . . .

In the Commonwealth, speaking the word "Requiem" was a capital offense; Amity would be drawn and quartered for speaking such a word in the light of the Cured Temple. Hearing the name of his fallen kingdom spoken in the open brought tears to Korvin's eyes. He prayed that someday even in the north, in his homeland, the name of Requiem would be spoken freely too.

A hundred griffins accompanied them to the shore. The two dragons landed on the sand and stood between the water and the tent city. The griffins landed all around them, and the salvanae coiled above, hovering in place, their long bodies swaying. Soaring above all rose the Twin Stallions of limestone, great guardians of Terra.

A company of men rode forward on horses. They wore iron breastplates engraved with five serpents, and their hair was long and braided. At their lead rode a tall man with long, platinum hair, golden skin, and an eye patch, and he carried a drawn saber. The other riders raised spears, and their banners billowed in the wind.

Amity returned to her human form and raised her chin. "Guardians of the Horde! We come from the outposts of Leonis. The Cured Temple attacks!" She bared her teeth at the riders. "Lower your weapons and take us to your lord."

Korvin returned to human form and stood, chin raised, jaw clenched. The riders stared down at him, and many more soldiers of the Horde covered the beach, hands resting on their weapons. Every breath rattled in Korvin's throat, and his old wounds blazed. Again he was a young man, only a youth, storming these beaches with thousands of his comrades, warriors of the Spirit, fodder of the Cured Temple. Again he saw the flaming arrows slam into his friends, steal their lives, and the blood flowing, and—

"I am Mehdan of House She'al, Guardian of the Coast," said the one-eyed rider, blessedly interrupting Korvin's memory. "Follow."

The riders spun their horses around and began heading into the camp. With a shaky breath and grunt, Korvin followed, and Amity walked at his side.

They entered the tent city of Hakan Teer.

For three hundred years, the people of the Horde had refused to build permanent dwellings. They claimed that their true home was across the sea, in the Commonwealth; they would build no true houses until they reclaimed that land. Still they lived only in tents, a sign of their exile, wandering the great lands of Terra as they grew and gathered their strength. Hakan Teer was no different. Rows of tents spread out here, countless, a great city. Korvin and Amity passed by many tents of warriors; the men sat outside, sharpening swords, cooking game on campfires, drinking grog, and playing games of dice. But inside many other tents, Korvin saw dwellings for women and children. The wives of warriors gossiped, washed laundry in buckets, or wove garments of beads and wool. Children scuttled everywhere, laughing and playing with wooden swords. Goats, dogs, and cats wandered between the tents, hens pecked in pens, and roosters cawed. Hakan Teer, Korvin thought, was a blend between a military garrison, a refugee city, and an unorganized mass of squatters and roaming beasts.

As he looked around him, he picked out different nationalities. Some here had the golden skin, blue eyes, and platinum hair of Tirans; their desert home, Tiranor, had been destroyed long ago in a war against Requiem. Others looked more like people from the Commonwealth; they were survivors of Old Osanna, a land annexed into the Temple's empire. Some people were shorter, their skin olive-toned, their eyes green, their hair black—survivors of the most ancient of civilizations that had once risen on this coast. All had lost their homes. All dreamed of reforming their nations—on the ashes of the northern Commonwealth.

And they just might win this war, Korvin thought, staring at a courtyard where a thousand men and women were drilling with spears and shields. Sweat glistened on their skin, and they bared their teeth as they spun, leaped, and dueled one another. Korvin watched a wild, dark-haired woman shout as she swung her practice sword, knocking down a hairy warrior twice her size. She spat and cried out in triumph as around her a thousand others swung dulled blades against bruising flesh.

They walked on. The land sloped upward from the sea, dry and strewn with rocks. They passed between lumbering warriors, seven feet tall, who bore barrels upon their backs; around a makeshift fortress of branches and rope, caches of weapons visible within their walls; and under gliding griffins and salvanae whose cries filled the air. The camp smelled of sweat and blood, oil and iron, ale and cooking fires and looming war.

After walking for a mile or more, they reached a sprawling stone wall—the only brick structure Korvin had seen so far in this camp. Several guards stood at a gatehouse, armed with spears and holding round shields. The riders who had met Korvin and Amity at the beach dismounted their horses and spoke to the guards. For a moment, the men exchanged quick, harsh words. They spoke in Low Speech, a patois developed within the Horde a few generations ago, mingling the different tongues of its founding nations. Korvin spoke the language well; he had studied it during his two years of combat in this place.

Finally Mehdan—the one-eyed, pale-haired man who had led them here from the coast—turned back toward Korvin and Amity. He spoke in a low voice.

"You will now see the Abina Kahan, King of the Horde. His excellence has seen your approach from the sea; indeed he foresaw it many days ago, and he desires to speak with you."

Abina, Korvin thought. *Low Speech for 'king.' And this king might just restore the kingdom of Requiem.*

With that, the guards swung the doors open. Mehdan entered, not turning to look back. Korvin glanced at Amity. The young, golden-haired woman gave him a wink and grin, and the two passed through the gateway together.

They found themselves in a lush garden. The land outside was dry and rocky and barren; within these walls, a cobbled path led between cedars and pines, and thousands of cyclamens and cacti grew among rocks. Limestone statues of griffins and men rose from carpets of fallen pine needles. Ahead rose a stone mansion, ivy climbing its walls. Two griffins stood before its portico, guarding the stairway that led to the doors.

Amity whistled appreciatively. "Nice place they got here." She poked Korvin in the ribs. "What say you marry me and buy me a mansion like this?"

He grumbled. "What say you watch your tongue when we're walking to meet a king?"

She stuck her tongue out at him. "Like thith?"

He groaned. "Put that thing away before it snags in a branch."

When they entered the villa, they found themselves in a large, round foyer lined with columns. A mosaic sprawled across the floor, depicting eagles, foxes, hinds, and other animals of

Terra. Ferns grew from stone pots, and murals of suns and stars covered the ceiling. A bronze statue of a nude woman holding a pitcher stood in the corner. A great mural covered one wall, larger than life, depicting a handsome king with a long, thick beard battling sea serpents to save a goddess bound to a rock.

Amity examined the mural and whistled again. "If this is a portrait of the abina, he's a handsome one. Might be I'll marry him instead of you, Korvin."

A door opened, and young serving women in white livery approached, their dark hair hanging across their left shoulders in braids. "The abina will see you now," said one and turned to lead them into a second chamber.

They entered a grand chamber, its pale columns supporting a vaulted ceiling, and saw the abina ahead upon a cushioned throne.

Korvin glanced at Amity. *Still want to marry him?* he asked with raised eyebrow.

While the king in the painting was muscular and tall, a proud warrior with the body of a god, the abina before them was paunchy and balding, long past his warrior years. Golden ringlets were strewn through his graying beard, and many jewels adorned his fingers, neck, and wrists. He wore golden robes and held a chalice. Several guards stood at his sides, iron helmets hiding their faces.

Korvin and Amity both knelt.

The abina cleared his throat and stared down at them. His eyes narrowed shrewdly. "I have seen you fly across the sea, shapeshifters." His voice was deep and rumbling. "My men report troubling news. They speak of my outposts in Leonis attacked." The abina leaned forward in his seat, resting his arms on his thighs, and his face hardened. "What of my son? What of Prince Belas who commanded the northern isles?"

Korvin grimaced. Belas—the man who had greeted him at the islands—was the son of the Horde's king?

Amity straightened and raised her chin. "Your son fought bravely, my lord! I am Amity, a warrior of the Horde. I fought with Belas. He slew many of the enemy, and—"

"Where is my son!" the abina roared, rising to his feet. His voice echoed, and his throne nearly toppled backward.

Amity paled, for an instant lost for words. Korvin stepped forward, placing himself between the abina and Amity.

"Your son fell, my lord," Korvin said, voice grim, staring at the king. "I am sorry. I grieve for your loss. I did not know Belas well, but he—"

"Silence!" thundered Abina Kahan. His fists trembled. His lips peeled back. "Who are you, shapeshifter, to bring me news of my fallen son? Of a prince nobler than any man in the Horde or Commonwealth?" The abina tossed back his head, tore his tunic, and roared to the ceiling. "Alas! He is fallen!"

Korvin and Amity lowered their heads. For a long moment, the King of the Horde roared in anguish, and his hands tore at his beard.

Korvin moved closer to Amity. "Why didn't you tell me Belas was his son?" he whispered.

She was pale, staring forward at the bellowing king. Ignoring Korvin, she took a step closer to Kahan.

"My abina," she said, voice trembling at first but soon gaining confidence. "The cowards of the Commonwealth, paladins and their warriors, murdered your son. Let us seek vengeance! My sword is yours, and I vow to serve you, to fight for you. Let us sail north to the lands of the enemy, and—"

The king pointed a shaky finger toward her. Amity was a tall woman, nearly as tall as Korvin, but Abina Kahan loomed over her like an enraged father over an errant daughter.

"You slew him!" Spittle flew from Kahan's mouth. "You and your fellow shapeshifter. You are weredragons! You led the Cured Temple to the islands. You murdered my son!"

Korvin grunted and stepped forward, placing himself between the king and Amity. He had to struggle to keep his voice steady; it shook with anger. "My king, you grieve now. Perhaps next moon, we can discuss this again. Perhaps then—"

"Murderers!" the abina roared. "Guards, capture them! Chain them up! Toss them into my dungeon!"

Korvin had heard enough. He sucked in his magic and began to shift into a dragon.

Before he could complete his transformation, the guards charged forth, swinging maces. The flanged heads slammed into Korvin, knocking him down. He hit the floor with a grunt, and more maces swung down onto him. The pain knocked his magic away. He writhed, kicking, as punches rained down.

"Let us go, you flea-infested, piss-drinking goat!" Amity was shouting. Guards were slamming wooden staffs against her and closing chains around her ankles and wrists. She too tried to shift; as soon as scales flowed across her, a blow from a staff slammed into her head. She fell, unconscious and bleeding.

"Amity!" Korvin shouted. He whipped his head back toward the abina. "Kahan, listen to me. We're here to help you, to—"

A guard's fist slammed into Korvin's head, knocking it sideways. He saw stars. Before he could take another breath, manacles closed around his wrists and ankles. Korvin blinked and tried to shift but could not; the chains held him in human form. A kick from a guard knocked him to the floor. He lay beside Amity. Her breath was weak, and a trickle of blood flowed down her temple.

I doomed her too, Korvin thought, the guilt nearly crushing him. *She too will die because of me.*

Kahan's boots slammed down by Korvin's head. The abina snorted and spoke to his guards. "Toss them into the dungeon for now, but ready the horses. We head south to the mountains at dawn. We'll feed these murderers to Behemoth there. The old boy is hungry."

Hands grabbed Korvin and Amity, yanking them up. Korvin kicked and shouted as the guards dragged them out of the chamber, down a tunnel, and into an underground cell. The door slammed shut, sealing them in darkness.

GEMINI

Again a woman moaned in his bed. Again Gemini moved atop her, doing his duty to the Spirit, planting his pureborn seed into her womb.

"My lord," the woman moaned, eyes closed, sweat dampening her dark hair.

Once these nights had been things of passion, of lust, of wonder and laughter at his luck to serve as a Holy Father, to bed another woman every night. But they had become tedious to Gemini, mechanical tasks. The woman beneath him was attractive enough, all curves and heat, but Gemini no longer cared for such things. He performed his task quickly, then rolled off her and lay in his bed, covered in sweat, winded.

"My sweet lord Gemini," the woman whispered, cuddling against him. "I'm sleepy." She kissed his chest, nestling up for sleep.

"Get out," he said.

She blinked, hurt in her eyes. "My lord?"

"Get out." His voice was strained. "Leave."

Her eyes filled with pain, then with rage, then finally with cold acceptance. She nodded, slipped her tunic back on, and left the chamber.

Gemini sighed, staring at the doorway she'd gone through, then turned his head toward the other side of his bedchamber. Domi stood there in the corner, head lowered, hands clasped together.

"I'm sorry." Gemini was surprised to find guilt fill him. "I'm sorry you had to see that, Domi. I wish I could find you your own chamber, but I don't trust my mother enough to let you out of my sight. It would not be safe, and . . ." He swallowed. "Oh, to the Abyss." He patted the bed beside him. "Let's get some sleep."

Domi nodded, still daring not meet his eyes. Her cheeks were flushed. Silently, she climbed into his bed and under the blankets. Gemini pulled her into his arms and kissed her cheek.

"I know this isn't the life you wanted," Gemini whispered to her, stroking her hair. "Until I know you're safe here, that my mother holds you no animosity, I must keep you close. I must protect you. I . . ." A yawn interrupted his words. "I'm bloody tired."

Domi yawned too and closed her eyes. Her body relaxed, and she cuddled against him and laid her head upon his chest. He lay holding her, one hand on the small of her back, the other caressing her hair. Gemini hated women sleeping in his bed—he always cast aside those fertile women the priests sent him—but he found comfort with Domi. He did not want to ever break apart from her. He wanted to lie like this forever, their bodies entwined, two joined into one. He slept holding her.

Their life continued.

Dawns rose, and he walked with Domi through the temple gardens, and he fed her lavish meals, and he bought her jewels and even a finch in a golden cage. She spoke little and often stared at her toes, and her hair always fell across her face—a fragile, frightened little finch of his own, his own precious songbird in a cage.

But sometimes he saw joy in her. Sometimes a smile broke through the darkness that always engulfed her—a true smile, full of light, a smile that filled her eyes, that filled his soul. He lived for those smiles. He lived to make her happy.

In the nights, he took Domi into his chamber, and she stood in the corner, waiting patiently as he performed his duty, as he bedded his women. And every night, as Gemini cast those potential mothers out his door, he took Domi into his bed, and he held her throughout the night. He never made love to Domi, never wanted to feel that he defiled her, that she was just another woman to him.

And every night, as she fell asleep in his arms, he kissed the top of her head, and he whispered soft words to her: "I love you, Domi. Always. You will always be mine."

DOMI

Every night, she stood in the corner, watching him make love to other women. Every night, Domi slept in his arms, and she loved him, and she hated herself.

Forgive me, Requiem, she thought every night, tears gathering behind her eyelids.

And then Gemini kissed her head, and he whispered of his love, and Domi couldn't help it. She couldn't help but feel warm, protected, cherished, and these were new feelings for her. She had spent her life in hiding, afraid, hunted, a wild beast, an exile. Now the most powerful man in the Commonwealth held her in his arms, and Domi couldn't help it.

She loved him.

As she lay in Gemini's arms, his hand stroking her hair, she held him close.

I love you for the pain I see inside you, she thought. *I love you for the fear I sense in you, the broken pieces, the man shattered by his family, the man I want to heal.*

"Look, Domi! A cardinal!"

They were walking through the summer gardens outside the Cured Temple. Birches, maples, and pines rustled around them, and a thousand kinds of flowers bloomed. A man-made stream gurgled at their feet, and the grass rustled in the wind.

Domi gasped and smiled. The cardinal fluttered above, bright red, a splash of brilliant color. She smiled.

"I love cardinals."

"Would you like me to get you one as a pet?" Gemini said. "A companion to your finch?"

She shook her head. "No." Sudden sadness filled her, and she lowered her head. "My finch was born in captivity, and it would not survive on its own. It's accustomed to golden bars around it, life in a comfortable cage, a life of endless food, safety, warmth in the winter, shelter from the heat . . . captivity in luxury." She looked up at the cardinal, and a tear trailed down her cheek. "But this cardinal, with its bright red feathers, is a wild bird, a thing of freedom. It was born to fly in the wild, alone. Sometimes it's hungry. Sometimes it's cold. Often it's afraid and the winds buffet it, and sometimes it doesn't know if it can weather the storm. It has no home, no security, and its life is hard. And it would not choose any other life. It would choose a sky of hail, wind, and hawks over safety in a gilded cage."

She looked away, tears in her eyes.

Gemini looked at her silently, and he softly held her hand.

That night the priests sent another woman into his chamber, another womb for him to fill, to pass on his pure blood, blood without the magic of dragons.

Gemini sent her away without ever touching her.

That night, he stood beside Domi at the window, and they gazed together outside at the night. The stars shone brilliantly over the city. Above, Domi could see the Draco constellation, the stars shaped as the dragon. The brightest among them, the dragon's silver eye, seemed to gaze upon her. In *The Book of Requiem*, it was called Issari's Star, named after the great Vir Requis who had saved Requiem from the demons of the Abyss. Domi wondered who would save her from the Abyss inside her, for not all demons were creatures of the underground. Some demons lived within the soul, harder to kill.

"The stars are beautiful," Domi said.

Gemini nodded. "I would often look at them as a child, wondering what they are. The Cured Temple teaches that they're messengers of the Spirit, but I've always wondered. They seem so far away, too far even for the Spirit to reach. I dared to suggest that once to the priests, ask if the Spirit even had dominion over those distant lights." He laughed bitterly. "My mother ordered Brother Malum to beat me for that question. I stopped asking after that, but I never stopped looking at the stars." He turned toward Domi and held her hands. "It's strange, isn't it? How we always want things we can't reach, can't have, things forbidden."

Domi nodded, and when he leaned in to kiss her, she kissed him back, her hands cupping the back of his head.

He took her into his bed that night, and for the first time, he undressed her, hands gentle. And he made love to her—not a rough, mechanical thing like she'd seen him perform with the other women. Gemini loved her with softness and passion, with hesitation and firm desire. He loved her, and Domi hated herself.

I betray Requiem, she thought, tears in her eyes, as she gasped with her pleasure. *But I love him, stars of Requiem. I love him and I hate myself.*

He slept holding her in his arms that night, but Domi could not sleep. She kept thinking about it again and again—the village burnt, Cade crying out in grief, the library fallen, her family hunted, her homeland forgotten. Gemini mumbled in his sleep, and his arms tightened around her, and Domi felt that she couldn't breathe.

She lay awake until dawn, and when the sun rose, she heard the bird's song. She looked outside the window and saw the cardinal there, red and free. It flew off into the morning.

AMITY

Amity stumbled across the desert, the rope running from her wrists to the horse. Sharp stones cut her soles. The sun blazed overhead, and a thousand men cheered and jeered around her. Her head swam. She swayed. She fell, banging her knees against the rocky, cracked earth.

The crowd around her roared with laughter.

The horse before her kept walking, yanking at her ropes, and Amity dragged behind it. A rock tore open the skin on her arm, and blood smeared the earth.

"Up, you maggot!" shouted a guard, a smirking woman with olive skin, blazing green eyes, and a shaved head. "The Behemoth likes his meat live. Up! You're not dying here on my watch."

A whip cracked, slamming against Amity's back. She yelped, ground her teeth, and rose to her feet. She stumbled along, nearly tripping again.

"I'm going to kill you all!" Amity shouted, voice hoarse, throat torn. "I'm going to cut out your guts and feed them to you! I'm going to chop off your fingers and stuff them into your eye sockets! Abina! Abina Kahan! I'm going to shove my hand so deep down your throat I'll crush your bollocks. Let me go!"

Riding the horse that dragged her, the bearded king burst out with laughter. He twisted around in the saddle to stare at her. Golden threads were woven through his beard, and gilt shone upon his scale armor. Many jeweled rings squeezed his fleshy fingers.

"Still a lot of life to that one!" Kahan said to his men. "The Behemoth likes them feisty." He laughed again and drank deeply from his mug of ale.

"Amity, save your strength!" Korvin called out. His voice was just as raspy as hers. His wrists too were bound, a rope running between them to a horse. He too stumbled after the animal. Blood dripped down his knees and elbows from a recent fall, and his white stubble was thickening into a beard. Dust coated his shaggy black hair, making it look just as pale.

"Silence!" shouted a guard of the Horde, a towering man with long platinum hair, a bronze breastplate, and cruel blue eyes. He swung his whip, slamming the throng against Korvin's back.

Korvin tossed back his head and howled, the cry of a wounded animal. Blood dripped down his back. Korvin was a large man, taller and wider than all but the largest warriors, and with his thick black eyebrows, shaggy long hair, and jagged face like a boulder, he made an imposing figure even while tied and whipped, a bound beast likely to break free any moment. Some in the crowd—the men, women, and children of the Horde—stumbled back, faces blanching. But as Korvin limped along, and as his chin dropped down to his chest, they drew near again, laughing and tossing pebbles at the prisoner stumbling after the horse.

So this is our fate, Amity thought as she walked along, her feet bleeding, her throat so dry she thought it would crack. They had flown here to summon an army to fly north to the Commonwealth . . . now they lumbered south with this army, bound and bleeding, to be fed to the beast.

A gust of wind blew dust up from the desert. It invaded Amity's nostrils and eyes, and she coughed and blinked, almost falling again. When her eyes cleared, she gazed around her. The landscape seemed to sway, to fade into haze, only to reappear whenever she blinked. Here was not a desert of golden dunes or fields of sand; it was a rocky, barren, ugly place, the ground cracked and strewn with many rocks ranging from pebbles to boulders the size of houses. The dry land seemed to stretch forever, fading into horizons that swayed with heat waves.

And everywhere Amity saw the Horde. Here were the men, women, and children who normally camped at Hakan Teer upon the coast; they had packed their belongings, folded up their tents, and come to see the two weredragons—Amity and Korvin—fed to the king's pet. Hundreds of soldiers rode horses in a great herd, and a thousand more marched afoot. The sunlight gleamed against their armor. Each man wore different metals, pieces scavenged, stolen, cobbled together around campfires. Some men wore bronze scales, others wore iron chainmail, while some sported breastplates. Other, humbler soldiers wore mere leather armor studded with metal bolts, and one man even wore a great turtle shell as a breastplate. Their hair was long, and many men sported shaggy beards.

Here was no organized, disciplined army like that of the Commonwealth. Here was a collection of races, from the shaggy Osannans who had once called the Eastern Commonwealth their home, to the proud Tirans from the western desert with their long bright hair and blue eyes, to the olive-skinned tribesmen descended from the ancient Terrans whose civilizations now lay beneath this very dust. Their wives, their children, their livestock all traveled with them, a great hubbub of laughter and song. Above them flew a host of griffins and salvanae, their shadows racing over the army below.

We should be invading the Commonwealth, Amity thought, the rage and pain boiling inside her, blazing through her throat, stinging her eyes, curling her fingers. *This host should be sweeping across the lands of fallen Requiem. Not this desert. I should be leading them, not dragging behind them, not—*

She stepped onto a sharp rock, howled, tried to hop on one foot, but ended up falling. Again she dragged against the ground behind the horse. Again stones cut into her arms, and she cried out with pain.

"Stand!"

Again the slave driver lashed her whip, cutting Amity's back. Again the crowd roared, and the king upon his horse laughed. Amity managed to push herself onto her feet, trembling, bleeding, and walked on.

Step after step, she told herself. *Think about nothing but the next step.*

Yet the pain grew with every one of those steps. Her bare soles ached for shoes. Her muscles screamed for rest. The scratches and cuts along her body cried out for healing. Her lips cracked and bled, and her tongue felt like a strip of dry leather. The sun beat down mercilessly, baking her hair, burning her shoulders and neck and face. She couldn't even summon the strength to turn her head and look at Korvin; she could only stare at her feet, putting every last drop of will toward moving each foot another step.

Ignore the pain. Pain is irrelevant. My body will obey. My body will keep walking.

She kept walking.

She walked for miles.

Through the haze of pain and sunlight, the memories rose.

She was a girl again, struggling to keep moving, not to fall, but she did not walk in a desert; she ran in a forest, so afraid. It was twenty years ago, and she was only ten, only a child, yet already she knew all about death. Already she knew all about being hunted. Already she knew the fear of men trying to kill her, of an entire nation dedicated to ending her life, to slaying all her people, to stamping out all traces of her magic and the very name of her lost kingdom.

"Burn the weredragons!" rose a deep howl in her memories. It was a paladin calling, a man all in white steel, a holy warrior of the Spirit. When Amity—just a little girl—glanced upward, she saw the firedrake gliding over the forest canopy, hiding the moon and stars. The beast opened its jaws, blasting out fire, burning the trees.

"Keep running, Amity!" her mother said, tugging her along.

"Come on, Amity, you have to keep moving!" said her father, his face bleeding.

They kept running. Running through the burning forest. Running through grasslands. Running down city streets. Always running, from forest to village, from wilderness to city slums. Fleeing the wrath of the Cured Temple. Keeping their magic hidden. Keeping their secret alive.

Until you killed them.

Amity's breath quickened into a raging pant. Her fingernails dug into her palms. In the desert around her, she saw that memory too.

We only shifted in darkness, only for a brief flight over the sea.

The temptation had been too great. Too long without shifting into a dragon, and they grew restless, hungry for the sky. And so they had shifted. And they had flown.

And we were seen.

The firedrakes had charged from the coast, blasting fire across the water. Ten massive beasts, their scales white, paladins in steel upon nine of them . . . and a young priestess named Beatrix on the tenth.

Amity grimaced, the memory clawing at her innards. Again she saw the firedrakes blasting their fire, digging their claws into her parents. Again she saw the blood rain down to the dark water. Again she saw Beatrix thrusting her lance, impaling her parents, sending them crashing down to the sea . . . down to darkness . . . to never rise again. To sleep in the depths of that watery kingdom and the murky shadows of Amity's memory.

Amity had fallen that night, an arrow in her shoulder; the scar still hurt in the cold. She had sunk under the water. She had swum, sure she would die, swum in the darkness, under the surface, her lungs aching, her soul tearing, the ghosts of her parents tugging at her feet, calling to her: *Join us, join us . . .*

But she had swum on. She had breached the surface, gulped air, swum again . . . until the firedrakes flew away. Until all that remained to her world was the black ocean, the emptiness, the grief. A girl. Only a child. Alone in the water, alone in the world. Perhaps the last of her kind, the last survivor of Requiem.

She had risen from the water at dawn and flown, flown as she wept, flown until she reached the distant islands of Leonis, until she found the Horde. Found a new home.

Found a reason to live.

On Leonis, still only a child, she picked up her first sword, and she made a vow then. She vowed to become a warrior, to grow taller, stronger, meaner. To sear all grief from her heart, nursing instead a will for vengeance, an iron resolve. To someday return to the Commonwealth with an army, and to thrust her sword into Beatrix's heart like the priestess had thrust her lance into her parents.

"Faster!" cried the slave driver, and the whip slammed against Amity's back. She grimaced and kept dragging her feet forward, following the king's horse, step after step across the desert, moving toward the distant mountains . . . and the beast that lurked within.

When she finally saw the mountains ahead, Amity glared through the sweat that dripped into her eyes. The mountains of Gosh Ha'ar. The holiest ground in all the lands of Terra. Here was the place where the ancient god Adon himself, they said, had reached down his hand, forming man and woman from the clay.

Here, in the bowels of these mountains, lived the Behemoth, and he was always hungry.

Amity turned to look at Korvin. He walked at her side, covered in dust and blood, trudging after the horse that tugged him. She returned her gaze to the mountains ahead.

"Gosh Ha'ar!" cried the men and women of the Horde. "Gosh Ha'ar! The Holy Mount! The Beast will feed!"

No, Amity thought, sneering. *No.*

She had survived the firedrakes of the north. She had survived flying alone across the sea. She had survived trudging across this desert. She would not let this creature of the mountains feast upon her flesh for the amusement of the Horde. A grin twisted her cheeks, cracking her lips, and she tasted blood.

I will face the beast in the mountains, and I will tame it. I will return to the Commonwealth, a great queen, leading an army . . . and leading the Behemoth itself.

CADE

The two dragons flew through the moonless night, carrying wooden crates in their claws.

"The damn things are heavier than an elephant's bottom!" Cade said, panting as he struggled to fly. His wings creaked and his breath rattled.

Fidelity flew at his side in the darkness. She too carried a heavy load in her claws. "Cade, stop complaining and guide me! You know I can't see well in the night."

He groaned. "Just follow the sound of my complaining then. I can't keep tapping you with my wing. Both my wings are about to fall off." He groaned. "Blimey, I imagined that a printing press was small, about the size of a beagle."

Fidelity growled at him. "And I thought your brain was larger than a beagle's. Keep quiet. We don't want anyone hearing us."

Cade thought that with his wings creaking, his breath rattling, and his claws scraping against the crates, he could be heard for miles. But he gave his voice a rest—he needed to save his breath anyway—and flew onward.

They had bought the printing press that morning in Oldnale City, paying with the gold Fidelity had found in the forest, the coins melted into bars. As heavy as this load was, Cade was glad to be out of Oldnale. Along the narrow streets, forts and temples rising all around him, he had felt nervous, a mouse trapped in a labyrinth. Every paladin walking by had set Cade's heart racing. It felt good to be back in the open sky, far from any paladin or priest.

But not far from danger, he thought. Firedrakes still patrolled these skies.

Just as that thought entered his mind, he heard the screeches in the distance. He cursed.

"Firedrakes!" he whispered to Fidelity.

She glanced around, blinking, seeking them in the darkness. "Where?"

Cade stared east. He could see their light there. The firedrakes flew carelessly, blasting out random sparks of flame; luckily, in the night, that meant Cade could see them miles away.

"Still far but coming closer." He scanned the land below. "I see a little clearing in the forest, and we're far enough from the city. This is as good a place as any. Let's land."

Fidelity nodded. As the firedrakes shrieked in the distance, the two Vir Requis glided down. They filled their wings with air and, as gently as they could, placed the crates down in the clearing. As soon as Cade landed, he returned to human form, fell onto his back, and groaned.

"Everything hurts." He moaned. "Those crates almost yanked my claws out."

Fidelity returned to human form too. She pushed her spectacles up her nose, then began to work at weaving her hair back into a braid. "I hate wearing my hair down. It gets in the way, and it's not much of a disguise anyway." She looked around her at the dark clearing. "Nice place, but we'll have to move between the trees. We're too exposed out here."

"Said the sailor to his lady," Cade quipped, then bit his tongue at the harsh look Fidelity gave him.

They dragged the crates between the trees and cracked them open. Inside lay the parts of the printing press: boxes of metal letters, wooden slats, sheets of metal, springs, screws, boxes of ink, and levers.

"It's either a printing press or an ancient torture device," Cade said. "Do you remember how to put it together?"

"No," Fidelity confessed. "But let's try anyway."

They lit their tin lanterns, hung them from the branch of a tree, and got to work.

Dawn was rising by the time the printing press stood in the forest, a mechanical beast larger than either of them.

"It's a bloody dragon," Cade said, tapping it. "A dragon of metal."

"And its weapon is more dangerous than dragonfire." Fidelity passed her hand through a box of metal letters the size of dice. They chinked. "It will fight our war with books. Books are the greatest weapon in the world."

Suddenly she yawned, a great yawn that stretched out her limbs. Cade yawned too. They had not slept all night. But they were too eager to begin their work. They opened the first page of *The Book of Requiem* and began to arrange the metallic letters in a sheet, forming the book's first page.

"What now?" Cade said when the template was ready.

"We print." Fidelity lifted a sheet of paper. "We print it a hundred times for a hundred books. Then we go to the next page. And the next."

Cade's eyes widened and he groaned. "There are over a thousand pages in *The Book of Requiem*! Fidelity! How are we going to print so many sheets?"

She frowned. "Would you rather copy them by hand? A hundred times?"

He sighed. "I suppose not. Are a hundred copies of this book even going to be enough, though? The Commonwealth is large, and, well . . . a hundred copies seem so few."

Fidelity sighed too. "I agree. But it's all the paper we have, probably all the paper we could even buy in town. And we might not even have enough ink as it is. But, Cade . . ." Her eyes lit up, and she touched his arm. "Imagine it! Back in the library, we had only a few copies of the book. Now only one is left. A hundred copies, all over the Commonwealth—we'll drop them in taverns, in temples, in bookshops . . . and more people will know. They'll know that our magic is a gift, not a curse. They'll know about Requiem."

Her eyes sparkled, and her hand on his arm shot warmth through him; that arm felt more alive than all the rest of his body. Cade wanted to feel her infectious joy, but instead, he found himself thinking of Old Hollow: how Fidelity had walked into the forest with Roen, returning with her clothes rumpled; how the two had snuck looks and secret glances; how she had left Roen with a kiss on his cheek, a kiss that hinted at underlying passion she barely tried to hide.

Cade turned away from her. Foolish thoughts. He had no reason to be jealous. He did not like Fidelity that way . . . did he?

He glanced at her; she had returned her attention to the printing press, applying ink and loading a sheet of paper. He watched her work for a moment. She had doffed her burlap tunic, and she wore the same outfit she had worn in her library: tan trousers and a blue vest with brass buttons. Her braid fell across her shoulder, and her spectacles kept slipping down her nose. She was beautiful, Cade thought. She was wise and strong and brave, and she stirred feelings in him that confused him, that made his blood heat, that made him fumble and feel so nervous around her.

She loves Roen, he thought. *That wild, bearded woodsman.*

Cade looked away. So what? What did he care? He was here to work with Fidelity, to spread the word of Requiem, not to fall in love. She was too old for him besides—twenty-one already, a full three years older than him. He was just a boy to her, he knew. Just a foolish boy to help her on her quest.

He thought of Domi next. He had been thinking about her a lot. He had only met Domi briefly, but he had never forgotten those green eyes peering between strands of red hair, how her body had pressed against him, how her lips had touched his ear as she whispered, "Requiem."

It's for Domi that I'll save my feelings, Cade thought. *I swear, Domi, we'll meet again.*

"Cade! Stop moping around over there and help me." Fidelity waved him over. "Help me print the first page."

He shook his head free of thoughts. For now, he would banish both sisters from his mind. He would think only about his task. He approached, and they worked together, pressing down their metallic letters onto the paper.

"Did it work?" Cade whispered.

Fidelity bit her lip. "Let's check."

She removed the paper . . . and they groaned.

It was a mess. An utter mess. Just a few random letters printed among blobs of ink. With a clatter, a dozen metal letters came loose from the machine, banged against its surface, then thumped into the grass.

Cade sighed. "Are you sure we shouldn't just use quill and inkpot?"

It took them twenty-three more sheets of paper, a lot of cursing, and a few frustrated kicks to finally print their first perfect page. By then, the sun had set again.

"Beautiful," Fidelity whispered, gazing at it. Her eyes watered. "It's perfect." She grinned at Cade—a huge, goofy grin. "*The Book of Requiem* is coming together!"

Cade wanted to remark how it had taken a full day to prepare a single page, and how they'd have better luck traveling the world and reading the book out loud to people, but when

Fidelity leaped onto him, embraced him, and kissed his cheek, suddenly things didn't seem so bad.

Cade held her and kissed her cheek. "Good job, Spectacles."

When she broke apart from him, still grinning, he couldn't help but miss her touch, and he grieved for the space now between them.

So much for not thinking about girls, Cade. He sighed.

They ate some of the food they had brought with them—grainy bread, tangy cheese, smoked sausages, and small bitter apples—then lay down to sleep. Fidelity had wanted to continue working, but soon they were both yawning so much they simply lay down in the grass, and they slept.

In the morning they worked again.

By the end of this second day, they had printed a full hundred pages.

On the third day, their technique improved, and they printed a full two thousand pages. Their first copy of *The Book of Requiem* was complete.

Fidelity stared at the printed pages—over a thousand of them—tears in her eyes.

"It's beautiful," she whispered.

They worked for a while, binding the book in a leather cover. The final copy was not perfect—it was not beautiful, well bound, or sturdy like the original. The binding was a little crooked, and splotches of ink marred the pages here and there, and the paper was not nearly as robust as the original's parchment pages. It was a little like comparing a clay hut to a marble palace. But it was *The Book of Requiem*, word for word, a copy of all their lore.

"It's a world of magic, wonder, heroes, and dragons," Fidelity said. "A world of villains, monsters, horrors, but hope too. Of bloodshed but love. Of pain but joy too. It's the world of Requiem, of our people, all existing within a single book." She lifted the heavy tome. "And somewhere, others will read this book. Maybe just one person. But that person will read of dragons, and that person will spread the word—whispering of Requiem to a friend, to family, to a neighbor. We will bring Requiem back to life."

MERCY

She stood in her chamber in the Cured Temple, holding her adopted daughter in her arms.

"Your brother has escaped us, sweet Eliana," Mercy whispered to the child. "Cade has fled like a coward. But we'll find him. And we'll kill him. I won't let him taint this world you were born into."

The babe gurgled in her arms, reaching out to her. Her eyes were huge, hazel, curious. Mercy kissed those tiny fingertips.

"I will protect you, Eliana," she said. "The world is full of darkness. The reptilian disease still roams free, even in the blood of your very brother. The Horde musters on the southern coast, a mob of barbarians who would swarm over the civilization we have built in the Commonwealth, who would tear our society apart. King's Column still stands, even as we pray for the Falling, and the Spirit does not yet descend." She held the babe close. "You are so innocent, and the world is so cruel. I will protect you, but I will also teach you strength, my daughter. You will become a paladin, a warrior of the Spirit."

Mercy walked toward the golden crib and placed Eliana inside. The baby cried, and Mercy stood over the crib, watching her. She did not lift Eliana, did not comfort her, for the baby would have to learn that the world is cruel, would have to learn to be strong.

Sudden pain swelled inside Mercy, cold, filling her belly. She winced. Memories of that day returned to her, that day more horrible than any other.

Mercy grimaced.

She hugged her belly and doubled over. Cold sweat washed over her, and she couldn't breathe. Again she felt his fists drive into her belly. Again she bled. Again she wailed, mourned, a young priestess, hurt, her daughter—

No.

She clenched her fists.

No, she would not summon that memory now. It had happened to another woman—to a married priestess, not a widowed paladin devoted to her god. She had thrust her blade, slaying him, slaying that memory. It had happened to another woman. Not to her. Not to Lady Mercy, a warrior of the Spirit.

She turned away from the crib, walked across her chamber of gold and jewels, and approached the window. The city of Nova Vita spread outside the Cured Temple, rolling for miles, only a few scattered lanterns lighting its streets. The stars shone above. The Draco constellation glowed ahead of Mercy, ever taunting her, ever a reminder of the cruelty in the world.

"I pray to you, Spirit, for the Falling," Mercy said softly, and a cold breeze played with her hair. "I pray for a night when the Draco constellation goes dark. When King's Column cracks and falls. When all the evil of weredragons is gone. When the world is safe for the babe I saved, for the daughter I adopted."

As Mercy thought of Eliana, her memories strayed further back, reaching toward another lost child, and fresh pain clutched her chest.

It had been years ago; Mercy herself had been barely older than a babe herself. She had only vague memories of that night. She remembered her father crying out, snatching his son, fleeing into the night. She remembered her mother screaming, mounting a firedrake, flying out to reclaim her stolen boy.

Mercy placed her hands on the windowsill and lowered her head.

"I had a brother once," she said softly, perhaps speaking to Eliana, perhaps to herself. "Not a useless brother like Gemini, but a precious babe. Father stole him away." Her jaw clenched. "Mother burned him for that. She burned and buried him." Her eyes dampened, and she turned back toward the crib. "But I'll never lose you, my child."

Eliana's crying faded. Perhaps the child was sleeping. Some said that her father had served the Horde; others claimed that he had served the weredragons. Mercy swore that she would ravage cities, would slay millions, all to save this new babe who had come into her life. She had lost two babes already. For Eliana, she would burn the world.

A knock sounded on her door. Mercy narrowed her eyes. Who dared knock at such a late hour?

She rubbed her eyes; they were still damp. When she looked into her mirror, Mercy no longer saw the proud paladin; she wore her cotton night tunic, not her white armor. Her hair, normally flowing across her right shoulder, was bound in a ribbon. She looked like a damn commoner.

"A moment!" she barked.

She spent that moment unbinding and smoothing her hair, clasping a belt around her waist, and hanging her sword there. If she had no time to don her armor, at least she would still appear the warrior.

"Enter!"

The door opened to reveal a young servant. Mercy recognized the little red-headed girl Gemini had hired.

Domi, her name is, Mercy remembered.

The girl knelt and bowed her head. "My lady, the High Priestess requests your presence in the Holy of Holies. She says the matter is urgent."

Mercy stared down at the girl, eyes narrowed. "Look at me, girl."

Domi raised her eyes—large, green eyes full of fear but also a hint of resistance. They reminded Mercy of the eyes of her old firedrake, that beast called Pyre she had ordered put down. The firedrake too would stare with such green eyes that hinted at recalcitrance.

Mercy frowned. "I thought my brother hired you to serve him alone."

Domi lowered her eyes. "He has, though Her Holiness the High Priestess has begun to give me work as well. She says I must prove myself more useful than just wiping Gemini's arse. Pardon, my lady, but those were her words."

Mercy tilted her head. She wondered. Beatrix rarely bothered giving commands to lowly servants. There was something about this Domi—about how her brother had shown up with her one day, about how Beatrix seemed to be keeping an eye on her, even about the hint of amusement she saw in Domi's eyes as she repeated Beatrix's words. Mercy stared into those green eyes, judging, scrutinizing.

Who are you, Domi? You're no simple servant.

"Remain here and watch over my daughter," Mercy said. "When I return, you and I will speak more. I look forward to learning all about you, Domi. I like to learn where all our servants come from."

Domi bowed her head. "Yes, my lady."

With that, Mercy brushed past the servant and entered the corridor. She walked through the lavish halls and stairways. Lanterns hung on the walls, glowing softly, and only a few servants scuttled about, pausing to kneel as Mercy walked by.

Finally Mercy entered the Holy of Holies—the vast, white chamber, forbidden to all but her family, where rose King's Column.

Her mother, High Priestess Beatrix, knelt here in prayer. Mercy came to kneel beside her, facing the column.

"I pray for the Falling," Beatrix whispered.

Mercy nodded. "I pray for the Falling."

The High Priestess turned her head toward her daughter. Her shrewd eyes, pale blue and piercing, shone with a strange light. "Mercy, you have failed me again."

Iciness spread through Mercy, and her jaw tightened. "I told you, Mother. I will find the missing weredragons. I will crush them, I will—"

"Do you know what Requiem is, child?" the High Priestess asked.

Mercy sucked in breath. Her eyes widened. "That is a forbidden word, Mother!"

Beatrix huffed. "Forbidden to the masses, yes. We do not want the commoners to speak of such rubbish, to remember the weakness of our fallen kingdom, a kingdom infested with disease. But you and I, here, in the Holy of Holies . . . we have no secrets from each other, nor from the Spirit who watches this place, waiting for the column to fall." Beatrix rose to her feet. "Yet now commoners too speak of Requiem. Books have appeared across the Commonwealth, the word 'Requiem' emblazoned on their covers."

Mercy rose to her feet too. She gripped the hilt of her sword. "What books?"

Beatrix stared at her, eyes like blue pools of demon fire. "Books challenging the Commonwealth. Books depicting Requiem as a noble kingdom, weredragons as blessed beings, not monsters. The book urges commoners to hide their babes, to leave them with the disease of weredragons. These books call for open rebellion."

"Weredragons printed them!" Mercy drew her sword, and her chest heaved. "I will hunt down these books. I will burn them all! I will burn those who printed them. I will burn all those who read them. I will burn down the world if I must!"

"Sheathe your sword in the Holy of Holies!" Beatrix demanded, eyes flashing. "You've become a wild, errant beast, no more mindful than a firedrake. A brute can swing a sword. It was your incompetence, Mercy, that allowed the weredragons to escape. It is those very weredragons who likely printed these books, spreading their filth across the Commonwealth."

"I slew weredragons!" Mercy retorted. "Two above the islands."

"Two whose bodies you never found," said Beatrix. "Reports speak of weredragons among the Horde now, perhaps the same ones you let escape. Sometimes I think your brother more competent than you."

"My brother?" Mercy scoffed. "Gemini has been spending all his time with that little whore he dragged into the palace."

"And you spend all your time with that babe of yours." Beatrix shook her head in disgust. "Your brother is pureborn; he can never marry. I found you one husband, Mercy, and you stuck a sword in his gut. I tried to find you a new husband, to see you bear me an heir, and instead you drag a common babe into my temple. I should have the little wretch tossed into the fire."

Mercy hissed. These were forbidden words! These were memories that should never rise again!

"Then you might as well burn me too," Mercy said. "I would protect that child with my life. Husband? I have no time for such foolishness. I am busy hunting weredragons."

"And failing at it." Beatrix turned her back toward her. "Find these books, Mercy. Find them and burn them, and find the weredragons who printed them. If you cannot, your babe will be the one to burn. Now leave this place."

Mercy stormed out of the chamber, chest shaking, eyes stinging. She shouted as she moved through the hall, calling for soldiers, for paladins, for steel and fire.

Dragons Lost

In the darkness, twenty firedrakes rose from the underground and soared into the night sky. It was time to go hunting.

CADE

The two robed, hooded figures walked down the cobbled street of Lynport, heading toward the piers.

This city was old, among the oldest in Requiem. As Cade walked, stooped over, he felt the ancient ghosts all around him, whispers and memories in every stone. Many of the buildings were under a hundred years old, built of clay, humble and domed—constructions of the Cured Temple. But unlike in the capital, some of Requiem's original buildings still stood here in the outskirts of the empire. Their foundations were built of wood, white clay filling the spaces between the timbers, and true glass filled their windows. Down the cobbled road, still distant, Cade could see the southern ocean and the masts of ships at the docks.

As they walked, Fidelity turned her head toward Cade. He could just make out her face within the shadows of her hood. Her eyes were bright, and a smile spread across her face.

"We're actually in Lynport! The legendary city! It's—" She swallowed her words as an old woman hobbled by, leaning on a cane, then spoke again. "It's named after Queen Lyana Aeternum, a legendary heroine of Requiem who fought the phoenixes and rebuilt Requiem from ruin. Her story's in the book. I'm surprised the Cured Temple never renamed the city, though once it *was* renamed. It used to be called Cadport, named after General Cad—"

"No history lessons!" Cade whispered. "Hush now. No talk of Req—I mean, of you-know-what until we leave this city." He glanced toward the elderly woman who was hobbling away in the distance. "There are ears everywhere. And we know that Mercy's after these books."

He pointed at a poster glued to a wall. They had seen such posters in every town they had visited so far. With large red letters, the parchment proclaimed:

"Heretical books have infiltrated the Commonwealth! Turn your eyes aside from the Demon King who infests the pages of lurid tomes! Storing heretical texts is punishable by stoning. Turn in forbidden books to your local paladin to earn a silver coin."

Fidelity nodded, examining the poster. "If nothing else, we're costing the Temple some money."

Cade grumbled. "They have more silver coins than we'll ever have books. So keep quiet and let's keep going. We've got to hide these books better. I don't want a repeat of last time."

He shuddered to remember how at their last town—Balefair in the north—the paladins had found the heavy *Book of Requiem* before Cade and Fidelity had even left the city. The paladins had burned that book in the town square, shouting that they'd find and burn whoever had printed it too. Cade winced to remember that night he'd spent with Fidelity huddled in an alleyway, finally sneaking out the southern gates before dawn.

They kept walking through Lynport. The huts rose around them, pale in the afternoon light. A priest walked by, swinging a bowl of incense, chanting to the Spirit. A couple of stray cats chased each other down an alleyway. The steeples of a monastery rose ahead, pale and thin like finger bones. Cade tried to imagine this city back in the days of Requiem—the Requiem of the awe and magic that had filled Domi's voice, the Requiem of the stories from the book. Dragons would be flying above, thousands of them in every color, their scales gleaming in the dawn. Temples to the Draco constellation would rise here, their columns carved of marble.

When he looked at Fidelity, he saw that she was smiling wistfully, a huge, trembling smile, and he knew that she was imagining the same thing. Their eyes met, and their hands clasped together. They did not need to speak. As they walked here, staring at these old cobblestones and bricks—stones carved in the days of Requiem—Cade and Fidelity shared something more powerful than words. They shared the bond of their magic, the memory of Requiem, the dream of seeing Requiem reborn, and it seemed to Cade that his thoughts in the forest—his love or lust for Fidelity as a woman—seemed insignificant beside this bond, as trivial as a torch by a great pyre.

Requiem, he thought. Requiem of Domi holding him, whispering into his ear. Requiem of the stars of the dragons flying above. Requiem of his sister, free from pain, back in his arms. Requiem—the anchor of his soul, the beacon of his heart.

They reached the boardwalk. The Tiran Sea spread ahead, calm and pale blue and gray. Several merchant ships docked between the breakwaters, wide carracks with many sails. Beyond the port, warships patrolled the sea, their hulls lined with cannons. Many other cannons lined the boardwalk, and soldiers moved among them, clad in chainmail and white robes embroidered with tillvine blossoms. No other city in the Commonwealth lay so close to the Horde; the continent of Terra, home to that ragtag army from many nations, lay beyond this southern sea.

"There it is," Fidelity whispered, pointing. "The Old Wheel."

Cade followed her gaze and saw the tavern. It rose two stories tall, built of wattle and daub. Three chimneys pumped out smoke, and stained glass filled its windows. One sailor sat slumped outside the tavern, perhaps thrown out the night before. As he saw Cade and Fidelity approach, the man groaned and crawled into an alleyway, perhaps thinking them priests. A stray cat hissed on the roof.

The tavern wasn't much to look at, perhaps, but Cade knew its significance. Here, within these very walls, the famous Releser Aeternum had hidden from the cruel General Cadigus. Here was the center of a great war that had liberated Requiem from darkness three hundred years ago. Perhaps here Cade could now plant the seed of a new rebirth.

"The Old Wheel," Fidelity repeated. "To us, it's a place of history, of dragons. To most people, it's a place where sailors share tall tales, where wine and beer flows, where women can doff their stifling robes, and where priests do not enter." She grinned. "A perfect place to leave a book. From here, news will spread across the Commonwealth."

Cade bit his lip. "Assuming any of these sailors and loose women know how to read."

"Not all will know," Fidelity said, "but perhaps some old storyteller, long of beard and grainy of voice, will sit by the fireplace, reading from *The Book of Requiem* to merchants, sailors, and travelers from distant lands, and those stories will spread. The mythos of Requiem, told from mouth to ear, father to son. Sometimes such stories can spread faster than any printing press can work." She hefted the pack across her back; a copy of the book lay within. "Come."

They entered the tavern, wrapped in their cloaks. It was a dusty place, and Cade imagined that it had changed little in the past three hundred years. The wooden floor was scarred, and a wagon wheel chandelier hung from the ceiling. Casks of ale rose behind the bar, and an aproned man stood there, polishing a mug. A few patrons were nursing mugs of ale; they raised their drinks in salute as Cade and Fidelity walked in. An old man sat in the corner, playing a lute.

"This doesn't even feel like the Commonwealth," Cade whispered to Fidelity. "It's an old building from before the Temple, and . . . it feels like we're back in time."

She nodded and a mischievous light filled her eyes. "We should stay for a while. Order a drink. It'll make us look less suspicious."

Cade wasn't sure about that. He didn't like staying in any one place for too long, not as a wanted man. But before he could object, the barkeep raised his voice.

"Oi, friends! What'll be?"

Fidelity walked toward the bar, motioning for Cade to follow. As part of her disguise, she did not wear her spectacles, and she nearly tripped over a stool. Cade had to help her approach the bar. They sat on stools, and Fidelity banged her hand on the bar; she would have hit a bowl of walnuts had Cade not quickly tugged it aside.

"Two spirits, good sir!" Fidelity said. "Strong rye." She glanced at Cade. "You can handle spirits, can't you?"

"You're damn right I can," he said, never having drunk any.

At least the sort people drink, he thought, *not those they worship.*

The bartender placed two glasses on the bar, and they drank. The spirits burned down Cade's throat, so strong his eyes bugged out and he nearly choked. Fidelity seemed unaffected, and she punched his arm.

"Good for you." She winked.

He turned back toward the bar and raised his chin. The world seemed a little blurry. "Another round."

They drank again.

After his third drink, it seemed to Cade that his eyesight was blurry too, just as bad as Fidelity's. In the haze, she seemed to him prettier than ever—which was saying something, since he had always thought her beautiful. More people were pouring into the tavern for their evening dinners, and more drinks flowed, and the flutist in the corner began to play a jaunty tune.

Fidelity grabbed Cade's hand. "Let's dance."

He blinked at her. "Are you crazy?" He tilted his head. "Or drunk?"

She bit her lip. "Drunk. Now let's dance."

She tried to drag him off his stool, but he wouldn't budge. "I don't dance."

"Just because you've never danced doesn't mean that you don't." She tugged him mightily; he slid off his stool and nearly fell. "Dance. Now. That's an order, young man."

With a few drinks under his belt, Cade didn't feel able to object. They left their pack, the book inside it, at the bar, and they headed to a space between tables in the common room. Fidelity grabbed him and began to sway to the music.

"Fi, there are people watching!" Cade whispered, face red.

"So you better put on a good show." She grabbed his hands and placed them on her waist.

Cade was thankful when a couple of young women leaped forward to dance too, then an old man and his wife. The jaunty tune soon morphed into a sad old song, and Fidelity leaned her head against Cade's shoulder, swaying with him. Her golden hair brushed against his nose, and when he tried to push the strands back, he found himself stroking that hair, again and again, feeling incredibly awkward and incredibly stupid but unable to stop.

Fidelity pulled her head back and looked at him, eyes huge and blue, eyes he thought he could drown in. Cade looked away, his cheeks flushing, and it was not from the booze this time.

She held his hand. "Come with me. There's another place I want to visit."

They left the inn.

They left the book behind—for one of those young dancers, for the barkeep, perhaps for a sailor or a singer of songs.

They walked along the boardwalk and on the beach, and they kept walking, leaving the town behind them. The sun began to set, and soon the sounds of Lynport faded behind. All was sand and sea.

"Where did you want to go?" Cade asked.

She pointed ahead and her wistful smile returned. "Here. Ralora Cliffs."

The cliffs rose ahead from the sand, overlooking the sea. Cade knew them from the books. Here in Ralora, the great King Elethor and Queen Lyana had fought a battle against the cruel Queen Solina from the south. Here in Ralora, the lovers Rune and Tilla would walk along the sand, their light shining over all Requiem. It was a place of legends forgotten, of legends they would resurrect.

When they reached the cliffs, Cade and Fidelity found old ruins in the sand: a fallen porphyry column, a statue of a king half-buried in the sand, and old pots of clay and bronze.

"Relics of Requiem," Fidelity said. She lifted half an old urn. Dragons were painted onto the clay. "Do you see? The red dragon painted here is Agnus Dei, and the golden one is Queen Gloriae. They were twin heroines who fought the griffins." She smiled. "I always wanted to be like them, to—"

Cade kissed her. He was surprised at himself. He had not meant to do it. Yet one moment she was speaking, eyes bright, and the next moment he held her in his arms, his lips against hers.

And for just a moment, she kissed him back.

Then she pulled away. She blinked a few times. Her voice was soft. "I especially wanted to be like Agnus Dei. I used to draw her in my notebooks, and . . ." She looked back at him, then down at her feet. "I'm sorry, Cade."

A lump filled his throat. He refused to look away from her. "Do you love him? Roen?"

Fidelity sighed. "I don't know. Sometimes I think I do. Oh, Cade." She placed a hand on his cheek, and she smiled—and this smile was warm and good, no trace of hesitation or awkwardness to it. "Are you crazy? Or just drunk?"

He couldn't help but grin. "Drunk."

She laughed and lay down in the sand, and he lay down beside her. Night was falling, and Cade pulled out bread, cheese, and apples from his pack, and they shared the meal, listening to the waves, watching the stars. They talked about Requiem, sharing the old stories of heroes and villains, monsters and dragons, castles and halls of marble. Finally they slept, lying entwined in the sand, and they dreamed of dragons.

KORVIN

He knelt in darkness, head lowered, the weight of the world upon his shoulders.

All is darkness. All hope is lost.

Korvin knelt in the bowels of the Gosharian mountains, this realm across the desert south of the sea. He could barely remember the soldiers of the Horde dragging him down tunnels, plunging deep under the mountains, beating him, shoving him into this cell. He felt like the weight of the entire mountains lay on his shoulders, creaking above him, ready to crumble and bury him.

A chain ran from his ankle to the wall. The floor was rough against his knees, stained with old blood, some of it his, some the blood of previous prisoners. Craggy brick walls rose around him. Mad scribblings were etched into the stone. Some marks were letters, the names of men and women trapped here, while others were simply raw scratches, fingernails drawn again and again across the stone until they cracked. A stone door rose ahead, and dim light seeped around it, the only illumination.

So here I end. In darkness. Chained. Broken. Half the world away from my daughters.

"Bloody sacks of horse shite!" Amity was screaming, banging against the door. "Let us out, you puke-guzzling, hairy griffin bollocks!"

Her shoulder was bruised from her many attempts to break the door. Chains clattered around her ankles too, keeping her in human form. Sweat dampened her short blond hair and clothes, and she panted.

"I need to break these chains." Amity growled and slammed her fist against the metal links again and again. "Damn it, I can't shift with these chains on me!" With a roar, she tossed back her head and tried to shift again—she had been trying all day—only for the chains to tighten around her growing legs, shoving her back into human form. She fell to her knees, breathing raggedly.

"It's no use, Amity," Korvin said.

She growled at him. "Help me, damn you! Stop moping there like a flea-bitten pup and help me break the door, or break these chains, or break the walls." She bellowed in rage. "I'm going to kill them all! I'm going to kill every last pig-shagging man in this maggoty Horde!" She rushed back toward the cell door and kept banging against it.

Korvin looked away. It hurt too much to look at Amity, to see her caged, hurt, waiting for death.

As Amity screamed in rage, again Korvin heard it, the sound that had been echoing through his nightmares for fifteen years: his wife screaming, crying out his name . . . then falling silent.

Korvin clenched his fists and closed his stinging eyes. Every time he had loved a woman, tragedy had followed.

I loved you, Beatrix, the light of my youth, he thought. He remembered himself as a young soldier returned from the war, scarred, hurt, haunted. He remembered a young, beautiful woman, a priestess of the Cured Temple, healing his wounds, praying above him, kissing him, soothing him. Beatrix had nursed him during his long recovery, healing his wounds and soul, and she had loved him, lain with him, wanted to marry him. And Korvin had loved her too—his healer, his savior. He had loved Beatrix with every breath until that day—that day she had caught the Vir Requis child, the day she had slaughtered the boy, crying out in ecstasy as the blood stained her hands. The day she had screamed, vowing to hurt him, vowing to crush his life because he had left her, spurned her, saw the madness inside her.

And I loved you, Mishal, my wife, he thought. He remembered the day he had met her, a young milkmaid in a village, how she had sheltered him on his wanderings, watched the stars with him, laughed with him. He remembered how he had told her about Requiem, about his secret magic, how she had vowed to never purify her children. And he remembered her giving birth to their children, to beautiful Fidelity and wild Domi, how they had traveled from town to town, fleeing the paladins, keeping the girls' magic secret.

I miss you, my daughters. The pain clutched at him, forever lurking behind his ribs. *Are you safe? Do you hide, waiting for me to find you?*

And he remembered the day Beatrix had found them. The day the High Priestess had laughed as she thrust her blade into Mishal's heart. The day he had fled, holding his daughters, his own heart shattered.

Kneeling in the cell, Korvin looked up at Amity. She was still screaming, pounding her fists against the door, crying out that she'd slay every man outside.

And I dared to love another, Korvin thought, looking at Amity. *I dared to love again, and I will see another woman lost.*

Amity was only thirty-one years old, a whole fifteen years younger than him. Amity was wild, loud, and headstrong while he was gruff, laconic, and stubborn. But he knew how he felt, knew how she felt, knew what could have happened between them . . . yet again darkness had fallen.

"Amity," he said, voice hoarse. "Amity, come here."

She groaned, fists bloodied. Her eyes were red. She turned toward him and whispered, "I have to break free."

Yet she trudged toward him, shoulders slumped, body bruised, chains rattling. She sat down beside him.

"The abina said he'd feed us to . . . a beast," Korvin said. "What did he mean? Can we fight this beast?"

Amity looked at the stone walls around her. "We'd have an easier time fighting these stone walls."

"What is this beast?" He stared at her. "You've spent years with the Horde. Tell me everything you know."

"I don't know much about it." She gulped. "I've heard tales of Behemoth, the beast of the south. The Horde executes its prisoners by feeding them to the creature. They say it feeds upon disobedient griffins, mighty salvanae who dare fly free, and even firedrakes caught patrolling the coast. They say it makes those creatures seem no larger than mites."

He raised an eyebrow. "I've never known you to be scared, Amity."

"I'm not! I'll face this beast in battle. None have ever defeated Behemoth, not in hundreds of years." Amity growled. "But I will."

Korvin sat beside her and leaned back on his elbows. He stared up at the ceiling. "Do you know what *The Book of Requiem* says of the afterlife?"

She snorted. "Can't read. Don't care."

"I can and do. It says that great, celestial halls, woven of light, rise above the Draco stars, a heavenly twin to the fallen halls of Requiem below. They say that the souls of Vir Requis rise to those stars, that our fallen sing and drink wine there for eternity among our ancient heroes."

"Then soon I'll be singing myself hoarse and drinking so much I piss my pants." She sighed and looked around her. "Unless they bring us a chamber pot soon, that might even happen in this life."

Korvin couldn't help but smile—a thin smile that creased his craggy skin. "Who are you, Amity? How did you end up here?"

"By saving your hairy backside, remember?"

"I mean in the Horde. This life."

Amity rolled her eyes. "Trying to get to know me better before we're both beast food?"

He nodded. "I'd like to."

She groaned. "Parents fought for Requiem. Parents died. That's all you need to know. After they were gone, I figured their life—hiding in the Commonwealth, spreading the word of Requiem—was not for me. So I flew overseas. I joined the Horde and vowed to fight against that piss stain Beatrix." She grumbled. "Thought I'd fight with the Horde, not die in their pit." She began to work at unlacing her tunic and tugging off her breeches. "Help me with these, will you? Stars, be useful for once. Grab my pants legs and tug."

He frowned at her. "What are you doing?"

"Getting naked, what do you think? Go on, tug my pants off!"

He raised an eyebrow. "Did you piss them already?"

"Stars!" She groaned. "You said you wanted to know me better before we died. To the Abyss with that shite. I'm not dying talking about Requiem or old stories of some fancy-arse heroes. You're going to get to know me the proper way, and don't pretend you haven't wanted this! I've seen how you look at me. If I'm going to die, I'm going to know you first."

Finally she had removed her clothes and stood naked before him, all but for the chain that still ran from her ankle to a post in the floor. Her body was long-limbed, muscular, covered with small scars and bruises, the body of a warrior. Before he could say anything, she grinned and leaped onto him, and she began working at his own clothes, tugging them off.

"Come on, old soldier," she whispered into his ear and bit down on his lobe. "You got one more battle in you."

He closed his eyes as her hands worked at his belt, and soon he found himself naked as well. His body was leathery, hard, covered with old scars, and she straddled him and grabbed his shoulders. When he tried to speak, she grabbed his hair and kissed him, and he closed his eyes, and all he knew was the heat of her body, their sweat mingling together, and old fire. In her lovemaking, she was as wild as in battle, digging her fingernails down his back, biting his shoulder hard to stifle her screams, so hard he bled. Korvin had not made love to a woman in what felt like eras, and he had almost forgotten the passion of it, and now he surrendered to that heat. One last time to love. One last time to feel young.

For a long time afterward, they lay side by side, drenched in sweat. He panted while she grinned, trailing her fingers across his chest, and she nibbled his ear again.

They were pulling their clothes back on when keys rattled, many voices chanted outside, and the door creaked open.

Firelight flooded the chamber, blinding. The roar of a crowd gushed in. The silhouette of a soldier stood at the doorway, holding a spear.

"Move!" the man shouted. "Move, weredragons! The beast is hungry. The beast will feed."

Korvin blinked in the light, nearly blinded. Thousands of voices chanted outside, and above them rose a single cry, deep and deafening, louder than the roar of dragons.

CADE

They had printed forty-seven books when they ran out of paper.

"Fidelity." Cade waved his hand and cleared his throat. "Another sheet?"

"All out." She pushed her spectacles up her nose and tugged her braid. "No more."

He frowned and tilted his head. "What do you mean no more? You said we had enough paper to print a hundred books. We haven't even printed fifty."

She placed her hands on her hips. "Well, somebody keeps making mistakes, spilling ink, spilling out letters, and ruining sheet after sheet. So now we're out, and you better find more."

Cade rolled his eyes. "Well, somebody has been spending most of her time climbing trees to watch for firedrakes, as I've been working away here. If you had helped, maybe we'd have—"

"Cade!" She took a step toward him. "Hush. Let's return to the paper mill." She opened her pouch. "We have enough money . . . I think. If we haggle. And if I tug my tunic low enough." She sighed. "You might have to show some leg yourself, Cade."

"Yes, and then we can steal the paper as they flee in horror." He tugged up his belt. "Let's go."

They walked through the forest, daring not fly as dragons, not with the sun still in the sky, not with firedrakes still patrolling. Even now as they walked, they saw two of the beasts glide above. Cade and Fidelity had to crouch, hide in a bush, and wait for the enemy to fly off before walking again.

It took all morning before they emerged from the forest. In the distance, across grassy plains, rose the city of Oldnale. Its walls were pale, and behind them rose the domes of many huts. Several monasteries sent up their spires, and from them fluttered the banners of the Cured Temple. A river crossed the city, flowing out through an archway. Outside the city walls, along the riverbank, rose the paper mill.

It was a large building, constructed of wood, its roofs tiled. Its many chimneys belched out smoke, and even from the distance, Cade heard the clank of machinery and smelled fire, oil, and metal. It was the only building noisy and smelly enough to be banished outside the city, which suited Cade fine; within the city walls lurked priests and paladins, and he preferred some clanging machinery and foul smoke any day.

Cade and Fidelity walked across the fields, heading toward the mill. An old man and his wife, both nearly deaf, owned the place, employing twenty workers. Most of their business was supplying paper to print holy books, flyers for the Temple's announcements, and sometimes sheets for the nobles to write or draw on. Cade and Fidelity paid double the usual price—for the paper and for no questions asked.

When they reached the mill, they saw Old Hilda outside in the yard. Cade waved toward the grandmother, the owner of the workshop.

"Oi, Hilda!" he said.

The plump woman stared at him, nodded curtly, and retreated into the mill.

Cade bit his lip. "She's in a mood." He hurried his step. "Let's grab the paper and get back. I—"

"Cade, wait." Fidelity held his arm, stopping him.

He froze and frowned. "What is it?"

"I don't know." Fidelity tugged her braid. "It's . . . Hilda was a bit odd."

"She's always a bit odd. I saw her kissing her pet frog once. Mental, that one."

"Odd but usually happy. Something's wrong."

Cade's heart gave a twist. "Paladins in the paper mill?"

Fidelity rocked on the balls of her feet. "They know we're printing books. They've been trying to find us. They'd go wait in every paper mill in the empire, knowing we'd have to show up and buy more." She looked at him. "We should turn back."

"Turn back? Fi, we already bought a printing press. We're not buying a whole damn paper mill to hide away in the forest. How are we going to print our books now—on very big leaves?"

"I don't know," she said. "Maybe printing these books has become too dangerous. Maybe we need to spread our word differently—with songs for poets to sing in every tavern in the Commonwealth, or maybe with spoken stories told at hearths and bedsides." She glanced at the paper mill again and sighed. "At least let's find a peasant. We'll pay him to buy paper for us."

"And if the paladins are in there, who's to say they won't follow our paper mule? The fewer people who know about our operation, the safer we are. I'll go check the mill." He hefted up his belt. "Wait for me here. I'll be back soon. And if I'm not, don't follow me!" He looked at her, suddenly somber. "If something happens to me there, I want you to run. To hide. To keep going. All right?"

"You're scaring me, Cade."

He forced himself to smile, though he himself was scared. It felt like he had dodged capture too many times, and his innards shook. He patted her hand. "I'll see you soon, Fidelity."

He left her standing in the grass. He walked onward toward the mill. When he turned back, he saw her standing in place. The wind rustled the grass around her, and she watched him, not turning away, still as a statue. This was the first time in months, Cade realized, that he would be apart from her.

He walked onward toward the paper mill. A great wooden wheel spun in the stream, tall as a man, turning gears hidden inside the factory. Cade could hear those gears clanking as machines of wood, rope, and metal pounded wood pulp into paper. Chimneys blasted out smoke, and the smell filled Cade's nostrils.

He knocked on the door. "Hilda, you in there?"

When he peered through the window, he saw the mill operating as usual inside: gears churned, wheels turned, and beams of wood moved up and down like birds dipping to drink. Soggy wood pulp filled stone troughs. Workers were busy handling the machinery, pounding out sheets of paper and hanging them to dry.

He saw no paladins. No soldiers.

With a deep breath, Cade opened the door and stepped into the mill.

"Hilda!" He spotted the old woman standing by a towering wooden wheel at the back. "Are you all right? I'm here to buy some paper for our local monastery. We're looking to write more prayer scrolls." It was an old excuse he knew nobody believed.

Hilda looked up at him, and a tear trailed down her cheek. "I'm sorry," she whispered.

Cade froze.

He sucked in breath and took a step back toward the door.

The door slammed shut behind him, and Cade spun around to see two soldiers standing there, armed with crossbows.

When he spun back toward Hilda, he saw Lady Mercy emerge from behind the wheel. She wore her white plate armor, and she too held a loaded crossbow.

"Don't shift." The paladin smiled thinly. "Don't resist. This doesn't have to hurt."

Cade snarled and summoned his magic.

He began to shift. Scales clattered across him. His wings burst out from his back, slamming against the machinery. Claws sprouted from his fingers and toes, digging into the floor, and he sucked in air, prepared to blow dragonfire.

Mercy fired her crossbow.

The bolt slammed into Cade's chest, cracking through his thickening scales, and he bellowed. Two jabs of searing, impossible pain slammed into his back—quarrels from the crossbows behind him—and Cade pitched forward. The pain drove through him, twisting, tugging at his muscles, squeezing his ribs.

The bolts are covered in ilbane, he realized.

Desperately clinging to his magic, he tried to reach toward Mercy, to lash his claws while he still had them.

Smiling thinly, Mercy loaded and fired her crossbow again. The bolt slammed into Cade's neck.

White, burning, all-consuming pain filled him, driving down his throat, into his belly, through his skull.

He was barely aware of losing his magic. He slammed onto the floor, a boy again, his muscles too stiff to move.

"Chain him!" said Mercy.

More soldiers emerged from behind the machinery, bearing chains. As they tugged Cade's limbs, he cried out in pain; his muscles felt like splintering wood. He couldn't move, could barely breathe. The poison coursed through him. The soldiers slammed the manacles around his wrists and ankles, then slung chains around his torso.

Smiling thinly, Mercy stepped toward him.

"It hurts, doesn't it, sweet boy?" She knelt and stroked his sweaty brow. "The poison burns. The pure ilbane that burns all weredragons. You thought you could escape me, didn't you? I'm taking you to see your sister now, Cade. I've adopted Eliana as my daughter. She will watch as I hang you from the tallest spire of the Temple and the crows eat your flesh."

Cade managed to stare at her, and through a clenched jaw, he hissed, "And you will burn when Requiem rises."

Mercy straightened and drove her fist forward.

Pain exploded across Cade's head.

He saw no more.

FIDELITY

Two firedrakes burst into flight from behind the paper mill. Ten more rose from the city walls a hundred yards farther north, blasting streams of fire.

Fidelity stood in the field, staring with wide eyes.

"Cade," she whispered.

Her fingers trembled. Her breath quickened. Her heart beat against her ribs as if trying to escape her body. The firedrakes rose higher, screeching, blasting out flame. Paladins rode on their backs, angelic figures all in white. Mercy herself rode one—a beefy copper beast—her banner streaming in the wind. And in the copper firedrake's claws Fidelity saw him: Cade, chained, beaten, bleeding, unconscious if not dead.

"Cade . . ."

Fidelity summoned her magic and began to shift.

No! a voice cried in her head. *No, Fidelity, you cannot!*

She released her magic and stood panting. The dozen firedrakes rose higher, then turned to fly west—toward the capital—taking Cade with them.

Fidelity's knees shook. She wanted to scream. She wanted to chase them. Yet she had promised him! She had promised to stay behind if he fell, to keep printing the books, to keep fighting for Requiem. If she chased him, she too would be captured or killed. Yet how could she just stand here, just let them take him?

She was panting now. Cold sweat drenched her, and her eyes stung. She could barely breathe. She had to calm herself. She had to think. Think!

She sucked in breath.

The firedrakes were flying farther away, Cade in their grip. *Think, Fidelity.*

If she charged recklessly into battle now, a single dragon against a dozen firedrakes and riders, she would die. She knew that. She could only become a small dragon, smaller than these firedrakes; she could hope to perhaps best one of the beasts in battle, maybe two, not a full dozen.

Yet if she simply remained here, doing nothing, Cade would die. Perhaps he was dead already; that would be a blessing, she knew. If Cade still lived, Fidelity knew what his fate would be. She had been fighting for Requiem long enough to know. A couple of years ago, the Cured Temple had captured another Vir Requis, a man Fidelity had never even met. But she had heard the tales of his fate. The Cured Temple had the man whipped in the Square of the Spirit before a crowd of thousands, then proceeded to cut off his manhood, and finally had him drawn and quartered, letting mules rip off his limbs. The remains were hung upon the walls of Nova Vita, a piece at each gate, a warning to any who chose not to purify their babes.

I can't just stay here as that happens to Cade, Fidelity thought, tears in her eyes. *Yet if I chase him, if they catch me, the same will happen to me.*

As she hesitated, the firedrakes were moving farther away, becoming but specks on the horizon. Fidelity fell to her knees, struggling for each breath.

"I will not abandon you, Cade," she whispered. She raised her chin and squared her jaw. "I will not abandon you to torture and death. I promise you. I promise."

She knew what to do. She would seek Julian and Roen. She would have to convince them to finally leave Old Hollow, to finally join her fight.

"And then we will come for you, Cade," she said, staring as the firedrakes vanished across the horizon. "We will come to the city of Nova Vita, and we will stand before the Cured Temple as they bring you out to death." Fidelity clenched her fists. "And then the Temple will see three dragons of Requiem, blowing fire and flying in all their glory."

She turned around. She shifted. She rose as a blue dragon and flew south—to the forest, to Old Hollow, to the only two who could help her.

DOMI

She stood at the window, wrapped in a sheet, as the firedrakes flew into the city with Cade in their claws.

Domi knew it was him. Even standing here, far from them, she knew. Cold sweat trickled down her back, and her knees trembled. A dozen firedrakes were flying outside above the city, crying to the sky, and upon them rode paladins in splendor, their white armor filigreed and jeweled. Mercy herself rode there, and her firedrake clutched him. Cade was bruised, chained, his face bloody, but even from this distance Domi recognized him.

"Cade," she whispered, her breath quickening. "Oh stars, Cade."

A voice rose behind her, slurred with sleep. "Domi . . . Domi, sweetness, close the curtains. Come back to bed."

The firedrakes glided down outside, moving away from her view. They would be heading to their dungeon, leaving Cade to the mercy of the torturers. Domi's eyes stung.

Oh stars, it has to be him. He didn't listen to me. He tried to fight and they caught him. She trembled. *What do I do?*

"Domi?"

She spun around, her breath shaky. Gemini lay in his bed—*their* bed now—eyes opened to slits. He reached an arm out toward her, but it thumped down a second later, and he closed his eyes.

"Come to bed, Domi," he mumbled. "Let's cuddle."

She spun back toward the window. The firedrakes were gone.

"I have to save him," she whispered. Her eyes stung. She remembered the day she had met Cade, how he had stood over the graves of his parents, how she had embraced him, whispered "Requiem" into his ear. She could not let him die here. Could not let one of the last Vir Requis perish before a crowd screaming for blood.

Domi forced herself to take a deep, shuddering breath and walked toward the bed. She leaned over Gemini and kissed his lips.

"Sleep, my sweetness," she whispered. She grabbed a pillow and placed it within his arms; he embraced it as if holding her. "Sleep well."

His breathing deepened. Domi raised her chin, swallowed the lump in her throat, and grabbed her white livery. She slipped on the garment, then sneaked out of the bedchamber.

She tiptoed through the Temple. It was still early morning, but already hundreds of people were bustling about. Two paladins raced down a hall, their armor clanking. Priests knelt in a chamber, praying to a marble statue of Druid Auberon, the ancient founder of the Cured. Servants rushed from here to there, some bearing plates of breakfast for their lords, others hurrying back and forth with laundry, dishes, and chamber pots to wash. Five soldiers in chainmail—Domi had never seen lowborn soldiers inside the Temple—ran by her. All across the Temple, she heard more footsteps, muffled conversations, and prayer. Whenever she passed by a window, Domi saw more signs of activity: hundreds of firedrakes perched upon roofs or patrolled the skies, and thousands of soldiers gathered along the streets and in the Square of the Spirit.

Soon the bells of victory will clang, Domi thought as she rushed down a staircase. *Soon the news will spread across Nova Vita that Cade Baker, a weredragon, is here.*

She shuddered. Two years ago, Domi had lived here in this city, a wild firedrake, when the last Vir Requis had been captured. She had stood outside the Temple, gazing over the square with her dragon eyes, as the priests had tortured the man. The sight of blood and gore, the screams, the stench of death, and the cheering of the crowd still filled Domi's nightmares.

I cannot let this happen to Cade. Her eyes stung. The guilt of watching one Vir Requis die still hung across her shoulders; she would not add to it.

"I'm going to save you, Cade," she whispered.

Where would they take him?

Of course, she thought.

To the Temple dungeon! She had heard Gemini speak of it during his nightmares, pleading in his sleep, desperate to escape. The paladins would take Cade there first, she surmised. They wouldn't execute him right away, not until they spread the word, until they gathered a crowd.

I have time. I must simply find the dungeon. I can still save him.

A soldier raced down the corridor, clanking in his chainmail. Domi came to stand before him, blocking his passage.

"Wait!" she said.

The man halted, cursing, and wiped sweat off his brow. "Out of my way, girl."

Domi allowed her lip to quiver, and she breathed deeply, chest heaving. "I . . . I was told to hasten to the dungeon! I . . . I'm new here, and I don't know where that is, and I'm scared." She let a tear trail down her cheek; with everything happening, it wasn't difficult to conjure.

The soldier grunted. "Bloody Abyss! Walk down the hall, take two lefts, and down the stairs—four stories down, and keep to the south wing. And get out of people's way! There's something up." He leaned closer to her. "A weredragon's captured, I hear. Maybe several. Every soldier in the city is summoned to duty."

He ran on, leaving her in the corridor. Domi squared her shoulders and hurried on her way, following his instructions. She got lost twice, had to backtrack, but eventually found herself moving under ground level. There were no windows here, and lanterns hung on the walls, lighting her way. Here too activity bustled. Guards raced back and forth. A paladin marched down a corridor, barking orders to several men-at-arms. A priest hurried forth, and a healer rushed by Domi, carrying bloody rags.

Cade's blood, Domi thought, belly twisting. It chilled her, but she hoped it was a good sign. Perhaps fresh blood meant that Cade was still alive, that they were bandaging his wounds, healing him so he could be tortured to death later. Domi just had to make sure she rescued him before "later."

She sucked in air and squared her jaw. There was only one way she could save Cade now.

I'll have to become the dragon. I'll have to blow my fire. I'll have to burn every last guard, grab the damn boy, and fly.

She stepped down another staircase, entering a dingy corridor. The floor here was not tiled, and the roofs were but craggy stone. The burrow seemed to have been carved into the living rock. Screams echoed ahead, and Domi smelled blood and human waste. Another priest rushed by her, holding a bloodstained book wrapped in leather. Domi had a chance to read the spine: "The Book of Requiem"

She shuddered but kept walking. Soon she reached a stone archway, its heavy doors open. In the bustle of priests and guards, she stepped through and entered the dungeon.

A hallway stretched ahead, roughly hewn from the subterranean rock, and many cells lined it. Screams echoed and the smell of blood, sweat, and urine flared so powerfully Domi nearly gagged. Many soldiers stood here, rushing back and forth, talking and cursing. A priest stood at the back, chanting and praying to the Spirit.

There's room to shift here, Domi thought. *Room to become a dragon. To kill them all.*

But not yet. If she shifted here, if she filled the hall with dragonfire, the flames might enter the cells, might roast Cade and the other prisoners. She had to get closer, to make sure she stood with her back to Cade, protecting him from her fire.

She raised her chin and entered the corridor. As she walked, she glanced into every cell, looking for Cade. She grimaced. Inside the first cell she passed, a whipped man hung from chains, blood dripping from his lacerated chest. In a second cell, a guard was laughing as he stretched a woman on the rack; the prisoner screamed and wept as her arms popped from her sockets. Domi trembled and felt close to fainting, but she forced herself to keep walking. In a third cell, a mere boy lay curled up in the corner, not even reacting as rats fed on his legs.

The holiness and glory of the Cured Temple, here in all its sanctity, Domi thought and clenched her fists. On the surface, the High Priestess and her champions spoke of godly light, of righteousness. Here Domi saw the true rotted soul of the Cured Temple.

I must save them all, she realized, tears in her eyes. Along with her fear, loathing filled her, deep and hot—loathing for herself. She had been living here for months, a servant of this evil. She had slept in the bed of Lord Gemini himself, second born of the High Priestess, letting him invade her body, while here in the darkness lurked these terrors.

Some of this blood is on my hands, Domi thought, tears in her eyes. She raised her chin. *I will fight this. I will redeem myself. For Cade. For Requiem. For all who scream here in pain, and for all who cry across the Commonwealth.*

She passed by a few more cells, a few more pits of anguish and torture, until she reached a crowd of guards too thick to walk through. Two guards were laughing; another spat into a cell. Domi could not see past their shoulders, could not see inside that cell, but she heard a soft moaning.

Cade. Her chest shook and her heart seemed to shudder. *He's alive. He's hurt.*

She had to see him. She had to move closer, place herself between him and the guards, to protect him.

And then I'll shift. She dug her fingernails into her palms. *Then I'll fill this whole damn dungeon full of fire.* Perhaps she would burn the tortured prisoners inside the other cells. Perhaps that would be a mercy.

She inched closer. "Excuse me! I'm here to collect the rags. Excuse me!"

Domi began to worm her way between the soldiers when a hand clutched her shoulder.

"Domi."

Her heart sank. Fear leaped through her. Domi spun around and saw her there.

Mercy.

The paladin still wore her fine armor, and Domi saw blood on it. More blood speckled her boot and fists. Mercy's long, white hair fell neatly down her right side, revealing the shaved left side of her head. Her lips smiled, but her blue eyes were colder than the heart of winter, crueler than daggers of ice.

"My lady," Domi said and began to kneel.

Quick as a striking asp, the paladin grabbed Domi's neck and tugged her up.

"What are you doing here?" Mercy hissed. She leaned close and bared her teeth.

Domi wanted to mumble an excuse, wanted to shed a tear, to tremble, to play the part of a frightened servant, so confused in this great big temple full of lords and ladies.

Instead, Domi found herself staring firmly into Mercy's eyes, found herself hissing with the same rage. "Let me go."

Mercy growled and tightened her grip on Domi's neck, constricting her.

"You little whore." The paladin leaned closer, so close their noses almost touched. "Who are you?"

Domi would wait no longer.

She summoned her magic and, fast as she could, shifted into a dragon.

Her growing body shoved Mercy back. Her wings banged against the ceiling. Her claws dug into the floor, and her scaly flanks slammed into the cells at her sides. She filled the corridor, too large to move.

But not too large to blow fire.

And Domi blasted out that fire.

Her dragonfire shrieked forward, white hot, casting out red tongues of flame. Through the inferno, she glimpsed Mercy rolling aside and scuttling forward. Soldiers ran and fell, blazing. Prisoners screamed.

Domi glanced down, pausing for air. Instead of fleeing, Mercy had rolled forward, passing under the fire. The paladin now leaped up, shouting, and drove her sword into Domi's shoulder.

Domi screamed, whipped her head aside, and grabbed the paladin between her jaws.

"Die now," Domi said, driving her teeth into Mercy's white armor, bending the steel, seeking the flesh, ready to taste the blood and—

Pain drove into Domi's back.

She opened her mouth to scream, and Mercy fell from her jaws.

The pain drove into her again—swords behind her cutting her scales—and she lost her magic. She fell to the floor, a woman again.

"Weredragon in the dungeon!" men cried. "Loose weredragon!"

Soldiers charged toward her from all sides. Men screamed. Domi tried to shift again, and scales grew across her, and a crossbow fired. Men leaped forward with ilbane, and the poison pressed against her, and Domi couldn't even scream. All her magic faded.

"Open a cell!" Mercy shouted.

The paladin grabbed Domi's hair and dragged her across the floor. Domi struggled to breathe. She saw stars. She could barely see anything but shadows and floating lights. Before the darkness covered all, she saw Mercy leaning above her, smiling thinly.

"Two weredragons with one stone," the paladin said.

Then her fist drove forward, and Domi plunged into a land of blood, shadows, and endless screams.

CADE

"Domi." His voice rattled, barely more than a scratch in his throat. "Domi . . ."

The soldiers grabbed him. They tugged him to his feet and pulled him out of his cell. His feet dragged across the floor. He was too weak, too hurt to walk on his own.

"Domi!"

As they dragged him across the corridor, Cade looked aside and saw her in a cell. Domi lay on the floor, unconscious, maybe dead, bleeding from several cuts. Cade's eyes stung. There she lay—the woman he had dreamed of so often, the woman who had told him about Requiem. Her red hair spread around her head like another puddle of blood, and her eyes were closed.

Cade tried to break free. He tried to rush toward Domi's cell, to break through. He was too weak. Too many chains covered him; he could not break free, could not become a dragon. They dragged him onward. He moaned.

Mercy was walking ahead, leading the way. She looked over her shoulder at him. "Be silent, boy. My mother wants to see you. Save your breath for her. She has many questions for you, I'm sure. And save your strength too." She smiled thinly. "You will need it."

The soldiers manhandled him onward, and Cade struggled to walk, to place one foot in front of the other, not to let them drag him. They left the dungeon, rose up a flight of stairs, and walked through the Cured Temple.

It was a lavish building. The Temple preached humility and poverty, forcing commoners to live in huts and wear burlap, but here within the Temple itself, Cade saw splendor. Precious metals, gems, and marble coated the halls. Murals sprawled across the ceiling, and statues rose everywhere, depicting ancient druids in flowing robes. Cade took some satisfaction that his blood dripped behind him, staining the priceless mosaic floors.

He forced himself to look away from the wealth, to stare at Mercy who walked ahead of him. He let everything around him disappear until only the paladin filled his vision, let all his pain fade until only rage simmered inside him.

I'm going to kill you, Mercy, he thought, and a resolution rose in him. Before they killed him, he would shift. He would become a dragon. The chains were not a part of him like his clothes; they would not be absorbed into his dragon form. When he grew into a dragon, the manacles would likely squeeze and squeeze until they ripped off his hands and feet. He would let it happen, let the manacles mutilate him. With his dying breath, he would become a dragon and blow his fire, taking Mercy with him to the pits of afterlife.

And he would do it in front of the crowd. He would roar his fire for the Commonwealth to see, and before he died, he would roar one word: *Requiem.*

After what seemed like miles, they reached a doorway, and the guards released him. Cade stood on his own, wavering, still bound in chains.

Mercy placed a hand on his shoulder. "Come, Cade."

She opened the door and guided him through.

Cade found himself in a vast chamber, wide as a village square, with a plain floor of marble tiles. Round walls soared hundreds of feet high; this chamber rose like a shaft, probably spanning the entire height of the Cured Temple.

In the center rose a marble column, pale and smooth. Seeing it, Cade lost his breath.

"King's Column," he whispered.

Tears filled his eyes. Throughout *The Book of Requiem*, this column appeared like a silver strand, connecting all generations of Requiem from its founders to him here today. King Aeternum himself had carved this column thousands of years ago, and the legendary Queen Laira—Mother of Requiem—had prayed before it. Blessed with the magic of the Draco constellation, this column had withstood Requiem's fall to the army of griffins, the fire of Queen Solina's phoenixes, and even the cruelty of General Cadigus the tyrant.

A middle-aged woman knelt before the column, seeming deep in prayer. Slowly, she rose and turned around. She wore simple white cotton, though the robes were richly woven and hemmed with silver. Her hair was white, flowing down the right side of her head; the left side was shaved. Her smile did not touch her blue eyes. Cade did not need to be told her name; she looked just like her daughter. Here before him stood High Priestess Beatrix, ruler of the Cured Temple and the lands of the Commonwealth.

"Hello, Cade," Beatrix said softly. She looked back toward the column. "Magnificent, isn't it? Over four thousand years old, and not a scratch on it. No matter how many hammers we swing. No matter how many men try. The column stands." She looked back at him. "It will stand so long as the dragon curse exists in the world. Until you and your kind all perish. Until the Falling." She clasped her hands together. "That day, the column will shatter, and the Spirit himself will descend to the world."

Cade grunted. "Yes, I've read *The Book of the Cured*."

Beatrix smiled thinly. She stepped closer to him and reached out a pale hand to touch his bruised cheek. She looked over his shoulder at Mercy.

"Daughter, I told you not to harm him."

Mercy shifted her weight, armor creaking, and sneered. "He resisted. So he bled."

"Again, you act like a butcher when I want a surgeon." Beatrix sighed and returned her eyes to Cade. She brushed the hair back from his brow. "Do you know why the dragon magic is a curse, Cade? As an impure child, you probably think it magical, a thing of wonder. You probably grew up flying at night, in secret, the wind beneath your wings, fire in your maw, feeling so free, so powerful. When Domi told you about Requiem—oh yes, I know all about Domi—you probably imagined that you could be like those old heroes. Like Kyrie Eleison who fought the griffins. Like Rune Aeternum who fought in the great civil war. I can imagine how, for a boy in a village, a dragon might seem enchanting, magical."

Cade stared into the High Priestess's eyes. "I'm guessing you're going to explain why I was wrong."

Beatrix laughed—a short, trill sound with no mirth or joy. "Because those old heroes, Cade . . . they all suffered. The hero Kyrie Eleison fought in a world of death, when griffins hunted our babes, when all but seven of us died. Because Rune Aeternum knew war and hunger and pain, a Requiem torn asunder. Because even King Aeternum himself, founder of Requiem, was a man full of grief, his wife and daughter slain because of their magic. To you, Requiem is a world of myth and wonder, but to those who lived in it, Cade . . . theirs was a kingdom of endless war, endless agony." Beatrix caressed his cheek. "We had to abolish that kingdom. We had to root out that magic. We had to become . . . normal. Only this way can we live in peace. Only this way can the Spirit come and bless us. We must all be cured."

Cade stared into her eyes, and he spoke hoarsely. "You didn't bring me here to debate theology. You brought me here for death. So do it. Kill me and get it over with."

But before I die, he added silently, *I'll be taking both you and your daughter with me.*

Beatrix raised her eyebrow. "Death, my boy? Oh no. I did not bring you here to kill you."

Mercy gasped. "What? Mother!" The paladin stormed forward and drew her sword. "We will flay him before the crowd! We will draw and quarter him! We will—"

"—do no such thing," Beatrix finished for her. "Sheathe your sword."

"I will not!" Mercy said. "I will slay him here myself, here in the Holy of Holies!"

"Sheathe your sword!" Beatrix demanded. "I will not allow you to slay your brother."

Mercy froze.

Cade blinked.

Beatrix smiled. She turned back toward Cade. "Yes, Cade." She touched his cheek, and those cold, heartless blue eyes suddenly dampened. "For years I sought you. For years after your father stole you away, I scoured the Commonwealth for you. You've returned to me at last. My lost son."

Cade stared at the High Priestess, then laughed.

All his pain, fear, and rage melted away into the laughter. His chest shook, and he fell to his knees, consumed with the laughter, with the madness.

Mercy seemed less amused. She stared at the High Priestess, pale, fists clenched. She managed to whisper only one word: "What?"

Ignoring her daughter, Beatrix knelt before Cade and caressed his hair. She stared into his eyes. "We're going to cure you, son. We're going to burn out your dragon magic and make you a paladin. And then, my son . . . you will hunt for me. You will hunt weredragons until this column falls."

Cade fell and lay on his side, too weak to laugh anymore, too weak to cry, too dazed for thought. King's Column soared above him, stretching toward the sky, a pillar of memory, of legend, and of dying magic.

The story continues in . . .

DRAGONS REBORN

REQUIEM FOR DRAGONS, BOOK 2

NOVELS BY DANIEL ARENSON

Dawn of Dragons:
Requiem's Song
Requiem's Hope
Requiem's Prayer

Song of Dragons:
Blood of Requiem
Tears of Requiem
Light of Requiem

Dragonlore:
A Dawn of Dragonfire
A Day of Dragon Blood
A Night of Dragon Wings

The Dragon War:
A Legacy of Light
A Birthright of Blood
A Memory of Fire

Requiem for Dragons:
Dragons Lost
Dragons Reborn
Dragons Rising

The Moth Saga:
Moth
Empires of Moth
Secrets of Moth
Daughter of Moth
Shadows of Moth
Legacy of Moth

Alien Hunters:
Alien Hunters
Alien Sky
Alien Shadows

KEEP IN TOUCH

www.DanielArenson.com
Daniel@DanielArenson.com
Facebook.com/DanielArenson
Twitter.com/DanielArenson

Printed in Great Britain
by Amazon